STUCK WITH YOU

AIMEE BROWN

Boldwood

First published in Great Britain in 2023 by Boldwood Books Ltd.

Copyright © Aimee Brown, 2023

Cover Design by Alice Moore Design

Cover Photography: Shutterstock

A CIP catalogue record for this book is available from the British Library.

Paperback ISBN 978-1-80426-821-6

Large Print ISBN 978-1-80426-822-3

Hardback ISBN 978-1-80426-823-0

Ebook ISBN 978-1-80426-820-9

Kindle ISBN 978-1-80426-819-3

Audio CD ISBN 978-1-80426-828-5

MP3 CD ISBN 978-1-80426-827-8

Digital audio download ISBN 978-1-80426-826-1

Boldwood Books Ltd
23 Bowerdean Street
London SW6 3TN
www.boldwoodbooks.com

This book's for you. That's right, YOU — the reader of this book. Without you, it's just me sitting in front of my screen, laughing at my own jokes.

1

JADE MONROE

Today is my twenty-sixth birthday. Picture it: we're at Chuck E. Cheese (yes, because I'm still ten years old deep down), with its video games, ball pits, lights, sirens, prizes, a human hamster cage I stay well away from as a kid always pukes in it, and a life-size dancing rat. It's the best knock-off Disneyland I've ever been to. I've had every birthday party I can remember at this place, so I wasn't about to stop as an adult. My dad even booked the party room, and Chuck himself is due to make an appearance at any moment. Are we getting some 'you're weird' glances from the parents in the joint, considering we brought no children at all? Yes. Do I care? Nope. This place makes me smile and brings back many memories I never want to forget.

For the first time ever, a man is sitting next to me who *wants* to be here – not just the boy in whatever school class my mom invited – but the man of my dreams. God, that's a big statement. Conner, the guy to my left, pursued me hesitantly, but sweetly. Would I have preferred a guy to knock the wind out of me or stop my heart mid-beat like romantic comedies on the big screen are always suggesting? Uh, yeah. But in my ten years of dating history, no one has done that, and thus far, Conner has marked all my 'man of my dreams' boxes.

I glance over at him, sitting nervously, picking the label off his beer, attempting to remove it in one piece while avoiding my father's stare from across the table. I'd probably be nervous, too, knowing exactly two people in the room.

He looks up, catching my gaze and flashing that dashing smile I've fallen for. He's so freaking adorable with his perfectly manicured dark hair swept to one side, dazzling hazel eyes, and astonishingly straight teeth only an orthodontist could be responsible for. I could stare at the man all day long.

Patients will be so lucky to have him as their doctor one day. Not because of his looks (I mean, who doesn't love a Dr McDreamy type?), but because he's intelligent, caring, a great listener, and just all the things you want the person in charge of your health to be.

He successfully lays the beer label on the table in front of him, then taps the neck of the bottle with his spoon, earning my family's attention. Once everyone has stopped chattering, Conner stands and turns my way.

'Jade, today is your birthday—'

'Yesterday,' I remind him softly. Dad wanted the party on the weekend so more people could come.

Conner shakes his head, now flustered. 'That's right; *yesterday* was your birthday.'

I don't know how he forgot, considering he showed up at my apartment at midnight to give me my 'gift'. *Himself*, which he had topped with a bow on the tip of his—

'Until now...' He interrupts my trip down memory lane.

The man is making a speech, Jade. Perhaps you should focus on more than his tip.

'I wasn't sure when the best day of my life would be, but after two months of you, I'm pretty sure it was the day you were born,' he says, nodding his head my way, his adorably crooked smile a little more hesitant than when we're alone.

Awe. That's sweet. 'Thank y—'

'I think you're my person, Jade. My "one".' He cuts me off.

My dad mumbles something to Laney through a disbelieving chuckle. He doesn't love Conner. In true overly-protective-father style, he hasn't loved any of my boyfriends. He says that's what dads do, scrutinize boys after their daughters and break them before they break their little girls. He's good at it, too. Laney had a boyfriend that once dumped her as he pulled out of the driveway after meeting Dad. Who could blame the guy when a scary-looking biker-dude tells him as casually as he can that he owns a shotgun, a shovel, and isn't afraid of prison, so don't even *think* about hurting his daughter. Really, Dad doesn't love how Conner and I have moved so fast. 'I was once a twenty-something-year-old dude; *trust* me, you're a summer fling to the guy, Jade. Don't fall so quickly. Make him work for it,' he'd said when Laney let it slip a couple of weeks ago that he was spending nights with me.

'I know this is fast, but when it's right, it's right.' Conner continues to talk, turning my attention back to him.

When it's right, it's right? What does that mean? Did I miss something he said while I was shooting my father a shut-up stare? I glance around. All eyes are on me. Yep, I missed something. The room is eerily silent, besides the delightful squeal of children in a ball pit outside the party room, as we wait for this man I've known for two months to finish telling us what's so right.

Yes, cat's out of the bag, we've been 'dating' for *two* months. Eight weeks. Fourteen days. Or eighty-six thousand and four hundred minutes, approximately, if it really matters.

Conner and I met online in the comments section of a mutual friend's Facebook post. That 'friend' is my younger by two years sister, Laney. The two of them went to high school together. She had posted a tribute to our mother just after her death from breast cancer, and Conner sent me a private message. *If you need to talk, I'm a great listener.* It was that simple. And he was right. I did need someone to talk to. An outside source to help me sort through all the 'why mes' and 'what ifs' going through my head so I didn't have to lay it on my family who were going through the exact same thing.

Children bury their parents. I know this. But it's not supposed to happen before your adult milestones do. Yet it did, and because of that, Conner got an earful. Somehow he knew all the right words to say precisely when I needed to hear them. After that, we exchanged numbers, and he would greet me every morning with a 'hello, beautiful' text message and send me to sleep with a 'goodnight, gorgeous'. The man charmed me into meeting him face to face, and after only a few weeks of 'knowing' him online, he became a staple in my life. We did everything together. I couldn't have swooned harder.

Suddenly Conner drops to one knee beside me.

'Shut the hell up,' Laney says flatly as the family gasps around her. Her 'say it, don't think about it' personality breaks some of the tension, but family members attempt to shush her so they don't miss the show.

I glance at Conner, who's looking up at me with his hazel eyes, thoughts I can't make out flashing through them.

What *is* he doing? And why is he down on one knee? Is this some new birthday toast tradition I'm not aware of? He grabs my left hand, pressing his lips against my ring finger.

Oh.

My.

Holy.

Heavens.

Is he...? Suddenly, I get Laney's earlier word vomit.

'Jade Nicole Monroe—'

'Noelle,' my father mumbles through the fist over his mouth, hiding what he truly thinks about this, but his eyes scream it at me silently.

'Right.' Conner points his way apologetically. 'Noelle, I'm so sorry.'

I lift a single shoulder. What am I supposed to do? Correct him *now*?

He closes his eyes momentarily, possibly summoning the courage to continue now that he's made mistakes twice in only a handful of sentences. His eyes snap open, and I can see someone confident, at least momentarily. 'Jade *Noelle* Monroe, will you marry me?'

Right then, I choke on nothing but confusion. A coughing fit has him flustered but finally I mumble out the words flashing through my head. 'Marry you?'

Conner's face goes from bliss to 'shit' in milliseconds. Oops, that came out way more honestly than intended. I did not expect this. We haven't even talked marriage. But I can't turn him down like this, publicly. Truthfully, I don't know if I want to turn him down at all. I love Conner. We've both said it. Isn't this where love goes? To marriage? I mean, why not? Surely he knows we have some details to iron out later, though?

'What's your answer?' Uncle Paul calls from the back of the room.

Paul's my father's doppelganger, only three years younger and more 'angel' on your shoulder than Dad's 'devil'. They like to call each other once a month and send the other on some well-thought-out ridiculous 'mission' to pick up something one bought for the other. Once, my dad rode across the city on his Harley only to discover he was picking up a six-foot unicorn stuffie that he then strapped to his waist and rode back into the city with. People honked, and he was spotted on Instagram a few days later looking like he was promoting the upcoming gay pride parade. Now he wants to do a 'ride' in the parade in support. Which is the side of my dad that *I* know. He may look a little *Duck Dynasty* meets Hells Angels rough, but deep down, he *is* a six-foot softie.

'Earth to Jade,' Laney barks. 'There are only two answers to that question, big sister.'

Right. My gaze moves to Conner. Sweet Conner, innocently kneeling in front of me after having asked the biggest question of his life, as I stall with confusion while he shits his drawers.

'Yes!' I say, with a little jump of enthusiasm. Is there a part of me questioning this? A very tiny whisper that I'm going to smother until later. I just said yes to marrying Conner! Oh my stars. I can't wait to see the ring! I pull my hand from his, waggling my fingers his way.

He frowns. 'This was sort of last minute; I went with my gut. So, I don't have a ring—'

'Probably because it's been a day,' Dad grumbles.

Like my sister, Dad's never been one to keep his thoughts to himself. His personality in list form (most to least important) goes a little like this:

1. Family
2. Archibald – his Motorcycle (yep, he named it)
3. Devil's Beard (his motorcycle gang)
4. Motorcycle rallies
5. Motorcycle TV shows and movies
6. Tattoos
7. *Duck Dynasty*-style facial hair
8. Frito (the cat he never wanted yet is now having a rabid love affair with) and Starbux (an enthusiastic chocolate and

caramel-colored Yorkie my mom so loved
– he has a helmet and rides in my dad's
jacket sometimes)

That's it. There is no chit-chat or other interests with Dad. He says what he needs to say and softens when tears arrive. (He is a man with two daughters; tears sometimes do make an appearance.) He may not always say the exact right thing at first, but he comes around. He's soft like that and would do anything to see his girls smile.

Since Mom died, he's been alarmingly quiet. I've resorted to asking question after question to pry words out of him. I know what he's watching on Netflix (*In the Dark*), that he's become surprisingly good at crock-potting his own roast, and that he's watching through all of his old favorite movies. Considering I saw a stack of DVDs pulled from the movie shelf and sitting near the front door–all of mom's favorite eighties comedy and romcom – I'd say he's skipping a few. But stubbornly the moment I mention my mom, he shuts down, putting on his usual 'don't fuck with me' mask. 'We don't need to relive the past,' he always says.

Laney and I see right through it. You can't pretend like your wife of decades didn't just die. Eventually he'll have to deal with it, and oh how I dread that day. I've been so worried that I call him every night before I go to bed to ensure he's not slurring his words or over contemplating life. If I'd lost my spouse, that might be where I'd go, so I understand; I just don't want to chance it. Each night he answers with the same words. 'Stop worrying, Jadeybug. People die. I know this. I'm fine.' But I know he's not fine. He lost his best friend and the love of his life; he's heartbroken.

'Even better,' I say to Conner. 'You not buying a ring yet means we can shop together.'

'Y-yeah,' he stutters. 'We'll shop for a ring before I leave.' He stands, wrapping his arms around me, lifting me off the floor. Sirens and horns congratulating young patrons with wins and the clicking delivery of 'tickets' to 'buy' a prize at the end of the night echo through the pizza place in a peculiar childhood proposal fantasy way. I don't think flashing red lights and sirens were ever in those dreams. Those daydreams rarely come to fruition I've learned.

We sit back down, and he scoots his chair closer to mine, leans against me, resting his hand on my shoulder. As usual, I sink into him as he whispers sweet nothings into my ear.

'We'll have a long engagement and get married after my residency.'

The bubble of excitement I just felt bursts... that's not a sweet nothing. '*After* your residency?' I ask meekly. Now, I realize that I was just shocked at his unexpected proposal, but now he wants to get engaged, without a ring, then leave for medical school and do this long distance for years before finally tying the knot? That's three to five years, depending on what he specializes in. And that currently feels like a lifetime. I can imagine my future conversations.

'You're engaged? Let's see the ring.'

'Oh, I don't have one, yet.'

'When's the big day?'

'No date set, right now we live on opposite sides of the country until he's done with his medical residency when I'm *thirty*.'

Right now, he wants to be a general surgeon, specifically an emergency room general surgeon. He's been staying in Portland with his parents while on break between terms but leaves this weekend to start said residence in Boston. He's returning to his real life – a place where I don't exist. I've been desperately trying not to think about it. But deep down, I've wondered if maybe my dad is right; I'm a fling for Conner – something to 'do' while on summer break. But he just *legit* proposed. I don't feel like that's something guys do unless they mean it. I've got to be more than a fling.

'We're engaged!' Conner announces excitedly, lifting his beer at his success in bagging a fiancée then kissing my cheek.

The whole room falls silent – momentarily, while it sinks in – then my family erupts into semi-enthusiastic chatter. Most of them don't even remember his name, and one, in particular, doesn't look enthused.

There he sits, silently beside Laney, stroking his graying beard – his go-to move when considering something troubling him. A mood I'm not thrilled to see today because I have bigger issues. *I'm engaged!* This is a big deal. Surely, Dad gets that! I'll smooth things over with him later. For now, I tap my drink to Conner's and answer the battery of questions surrounding me. I'm getting married?!

2

RIVER MATTHEWS

'Jade,' Mercy says as we approach the Black Tide Tiki room bar counter.

I stumbled into this bar a few months ago – a tropical paradise in the center of rainy Portland. It's like walking into a temporary vacation. It's full of island-y things, including hula bartenders, of which Jade is one.

Three walls are covered with giant beach photo scenes – floor to ceiling as if you're in a bar on the beach. A white noise machine plays soft ocean wave sounds, setting the tropical mood. Net and sea floats hang from the ceiling, and a colossal swordfish I was told the owner, Jameson, caught himself, is stuffed and hanging from the rafters over the entrance. I wouldn't want to swim into one of those in the ocean. In the center of the room is an atrium full of tropical plants and colorful chattering birds. Six-foot-tall tiki statues are sporadically placed around the room and wearing dozens of leis that patrons leave. The drinks are on brand, too, with vintage tiki glasses complemented with tiny umbrellas, tropical fruit as garnish, and, more often than not, fire. Once you've had a few, you'd never know you were in Portland. Plus, it's not far from my apartment, so I can have a drink, or three, then safely walk home.

They occasionally hire musicians to play tropical tunes to set the mood, and tonight it's Mercy on the ukulele – a gig I landed for her – and since this place has become my fave local bar, I come with, so I'm not sitting at home alone watching *UFO Hunters* again.

'Hey you two!' Jade greets us with a grin on her pretty face.

You know those bartenders who click with everyone, remember your name, and people pour their hearts out to? She's one of those. Only, she's also a talker, so she doesn't just listen, she talks. I'll admit that I first spoke to Jade because she's beyond gorgeous. Perfect curves, five six-ish, long caramel brown hair, big brown eyes, and looks good, like *really* good, in her hula girl uniform. I now overlook that she's wearing a bikini top and grass skirt in front of me because this is not a strip club (something I've heard the girls tell men during previous visits).

Before she approaches us at the bar, she grabs a bottle of our favorite tequila and three shot glasses. As she pours the shots, she looks me over suspiciously, as if something is wrong. Tequila spills onto the bar between glasses as her jaw drops.

'You cut your hair!'

I shake my head. 'Just an undercut. I'm still sporting the man-bun you all make fun of.' I turn to display it as she nods with approval.

She leans towards me, the bar separating us. In a soft voice, she says, 'I *like* the man-bun. Never get rid of it.' There's a sparkle in her eyes from the lights above. The way she smiles says she truly means it.

'Yeah, it's very Portland hipster, bud.' An elbow in my ribs earns a groan and a familiar chuckle invades my head.

Ugh. Conner – Jade's boyfriend. I didn't even notice the guy; that's how 'normal' he is. You know the kind of guy I'm talking about. The ones you can find in any bar, dressed business casual, acting like trust-fund frat boys, exaggerating whatever story they're telling to impress their equally loser-y friends. He blends into the background while I wear bright red skinny jeans and my father's old leather jacket over my favorite vintage Duran Duran T-shirt. Not that 'normal' is bad, it's just a little boring and Jade is far from boring. The woman is prancing around the place delivering drinks with a smile, in a freaking hula skirt and bright pink bikini top – every night she wears a different top, not that I've noticed. (Shut. Up.) – a lei around her neck and a flower behind her ear. She is absolutely out of Conner's league.

'Was that supposed to be a compliment?' Mercy snaps at Conner, pulling her ukulele from the case and handing Jade her things. I can always count on Mercy to both tease and attempt to protect me. It's what she does for her chosen family.

'He's kidding,' Jade answers for him, resting her hand on his, flashing a 'be nice' look in his direction. 'Guess what?' she asks me as Mercy downs the shot poured for her.

A guessing game? I'll play. Perhaps Conner's decided to follow in his father's footsteps and overcharge people for homes. I suppose it's no secret that I don't love the guy. Jade talks about him a lot. *Conner is so great. Conner is so smart. Conner is so sweet. Conner. Conner. Conner.* Thing is, she never looks truly happy while she talks about him. It's almost like she's trying to convince herself. One night he walked in while we were talking and maybe she thinks I didn't notice, but I saw her face drop when she saw him.

'Has Conner selflessly joined Doctors without Borders and is headed for Guatemala to help save lives?' I say hopefully, making Jade laugh.

Conner doesn't. Instead, he leans in, speaking directly into my ear in a tone just above a whisper. 'Why would I leave the country to help someone else when there's plenty of money – er, *people* to be helped here?'

'Damn,' I say as I lean away from him, sipping my drink, hoping he gets the hint that I translated his brand of asshole. Truthfully, I'm a little shocked he'd say that out loud. Thus far, besides the fact that I just truly think Jade could do better, there's been absolutely no reason for me to dislike Conner but the way he just said that is a red flag even for me.

Then there's the fact that he seems so uninterested in her romantically, like she's a trophy or a business deal. He's got the vibe of being an obnoxious pre-nup, twice a week blowjobs, home-cooked dinners will be on the table at seven on the dot and you must weigh in every morning kind of guy and nothing more. I've never even seen them kiss besides a peck like they're family. There's a kiss that says I love you and there's a kiss that says I tolerate you, and theirs leans to the latter. If I'm kissing a woman I love, she won't wonder if I've had garlic for lunch, she'll know. I chuckle at my own thoughts.

'No,' Jade says with a playful roll of her eyes as if she understands whatever I'm laughing at. She might, I make this girl laugh many times a week. I'd bet she could guess my reaction to most things at this point. 'We're engaged!'

My phone, that was once in my hand, falls to the bar and slides over to her side. She grabs it, handing it back to me, a single eyebrow lifted in confusion as she does so. She said she'd marry that guy?! *Why?*

'*What?*' Mercy half squeals, grabbing her left hand. We both inspect the pretty hand now in front of us, bright blue fingernails recently done and no ring. Usually, Jade's a multiple-ring kind of girl. Now she's cleared the field, and he hasn't provided.

'Where's the ring?' I ask, downing my shot of tequila.

Before Jade answers, she takes the third shot, swallows it like she needs it to say the words about to leave her lips. Something's wrong.

'We haven't bought one yet, but soon.'

I look at Conner, not even needing to tell him what I'm thinking because he immediately speaks.

'The proposal was kind of a last-minute decision,' Conner says. 'You know how it is; when you feel it, you feel it.'

Shockingly, I do know how it is. But I find it hard to believe that these two felt that. They don't seem very 'in love'.

'You two felt it, huh?'

Conner nods proudly as though he doesn't just mean feelings – more than I needed to know.

'Like in your bones?' Mercy asks, her face scrunched as we exchange glances.

'I'm sure one bone felt it,' I say to her under my breath, making her snicker.

When Adam, one of Jade's co-workers, introduces tonight's musician, Mercy backs away from us, heading for the small performance area.

'Congratulations,' I say, my eyes on Jade, who smiles shyly. 'When's the big day?'

'Oh, a long ways away.' Conner answers the question I was asking her. 'We're waiting until I'm done with my residency.'

Her face falls when he waves the wedding off with 'long ways away'. Not sure she was on board with that part.

'Conner leaves for Boston tomorrow, so we still have some things to discuss. Nothing's been set in stone just yet,' Jade says, refilling the two shot glasses before me. I may not know this woman as well as Conner thinks he does, but I know his words just stung, hence her second shot of the night with me.

'Besides the fact that she said yes,' Conner throws in, winking.

'Jade's an awesome girl, so congrats on that win, I guess.'

'What's with you, sport? Are you ever going to settle down, or is the bar scene your future?'

'Well, *tiger*, not that you need to know, but I've got some lady fish on some hooks.'

I don't. What I do have is the offer of my mother managing my dating profile and picking women I usually wouldn't. She can't possibly do any worse than I have. And with her busy attempting to find me a wife, I can focus on editing the documentary about her life as a teen/pop star without her needing to approve of every decision I make. It's a win-win.

'Awesome,' Conner says, lifting the beer he's peeling the label off of unsuccessfully. 'I hope these dates feel the same way Jade does about your hair.'

I glance at Jade, who grimaces, lifting her shoulders as she overhears his words while pouring someone else's drink.

'And *I* hope you don't fail out of medical school,' I say, with an equally douchey tone.

As guys, we know this is where the conversation ends. We are not friends. I'm friends with Jade. Usually, he doesn't come in, and she goes on and on about him with her words.

I shouldn't even be involved in this relationship. What I know about the situation is that he swept her off her feet with romantic talking sessions and deep-feeling dives. He's one of those smooth talkers who somehow makes women feel comfortable enough to open up to them, but in their head they're replaying the last X-rated movie they watched. Not my style, and I don't understand how in the hell he sold it to her.

When the joint gets busier, I decide to feel Conner out. What could a little conversation hurt? He already thinks I like him. I turn on my stool, now facing him. 'So, you worried about leaving her ringless alone in a city full of hipsters looking for love?'

He turns my way, doing that Justin Beiber head flip to fix his hair without hands –yet *I'm* the hipster. 'Perfect lead-in; it's like you read my mind. I wanted to ask you something. You two are friendly; maybe you could keep an eye on her for me while I'm gone?'

I stare at him, confusion probably all over my face. Did he seriously just ask me that? A guy he's met a handful of times, who mostly comes to this place to chat with his new fiancée? You don't ask another dude to look out for your woman unless she's family. It's like, cardinal bro code.

'You're asking *me* to watch your fiancée?'

'I'd ask her family, but they don't love me. I have a feeling they'll be pushing her to dump me while I'm gone.'

Really? Guy fucked up, did he? I want to ask why, but I think I know. He's just a douche. How doesn't she see it?

'Jade doesn't need babysitting. She's a grown woman,' I remind him.

He drops his head with frustration. 'This I know, *man-bun*.' The way he says this as a slam makes me want to knock him off his stool. I won't, but let it be noted I want to. 'She likes talking to you for whatever reason, and you don't seem like you've got much going on being a barfly and all.' He reaches inside his jacket, pulls out a business card, and hands it to me. 'With residency taking up all my time, I may often be out of reach. Text me if she's got any real issues. Deal?'

Any *real* issues? What's that mean? I stare at his card. Conrad Francis Walsh III. Jesus, this guy is as lame as they come. He just called me a barfly with nothing going on, yet he wants me to 'watch his lady' when he's too busy to care. It seems like something an absolute moron would do, but alright. Jade's the coolest girl I know, not one part of me wants to say no to this – besides that part that knows if I say yes, she'll somehow find out and shit will blow up. I'm a movie guy, I know exactly what kind of situation that would present. Thing is, I'm not telling Conner this. He doesn't get a yes or a no. Just his word against mine.

'Also, could you *not* tell her any of this? I don't want it to seem like I don't trust her. You know?'

I nod. Jesus, this guy is making it easy. I wish I was recording this conversation. 'Obviously,' I say as if I'm on board, slipping his card into my back pocket. 'Consider her in safe hands.'

He laughs, nodding as if we have something in common – we both like Jade.

* * *

The city is dark when Mercy and I leave the bar. Lights from buildings around us sparkle like stars, and not many folks are on the streets like they are during the day. Summer is coming to a close; it's jacket weather, as the evenings are starting to get cold in the pacific northwest.

'He asked you to babysit her?' Mercy balks, clearly offended for Jade, as we walk back to our apartments directly across the street from one another.

I've known Mercy since I was a kid. She's a bonus sister I never wanted. Hollyn, my actual sister, and she have been BFFs since they were in grade school. After Hols and my best friend, Dax, got engaged and took over my apartment, Mercy and I decided to be roomies. It worked well until Brooks swept the girl off her feet, and now she's playing house in his apartment across the street.

'That's weird to ask a guy you don't know. Is he aware you're attracted to her?'

'Pretty sure everyone who goes to Black Tide is attracted to her.'

She laughs.

'How would you feel if Brooks asked Dylan to watch you while he was unavailable and only contact him with the *real* issues?'

Her jaw drops as she stops mid-step. 'He *said* that? Offense on the field, sir.'

I nod.

'Pffttt, what a cock-monger. I knew something seemed off about him. Did you see her face when we asked to see her ring? Who proposes without a ring?'

'Conrad Francis Walsh, the third.'

Mercy giggles. 'That's his full name? Jesus, what were his parents thinking? To answer your earlier question, though, Brooks would never be that stupid. He knows I can take care of myself, plus he'd never be so unavailable that if something was wrong, I couldn't get a hold of him.'

'That's how you know he truly loves you,' I say.

'Exactly,' she says with a bit of a bashful grin. She's still getting used to this whole 'love' thing. 'Poor Jade. She's such a sweet girl. What are you going to do?'

'Well.' I shove my hands into the pockets of my jeans as we walk the city sidewalks illuminated by the moon and the streetlights. 'I guess I'm gonna keep an eye on her, and when I spot the red flags coming from across the country, I'll tell her.'

'Gently, Riv,' Mercy suggests. 'Jade seems softer than the rest of us, and I know how you are – brutally honest.'

'At times, though, I do have manners too.'

'Sure ya do...' she jokes.

This could be a complete disaster, but I feel the need to do this. For *her* sake, *not* his. I see her all the time anyway; the least I can do is check in on her and listen like she often does for me.

3

JADE

'Hi, I need two Venti Americano coffees with room for cream and sugar. Four of the blackberry scones. Two of the banana bread slices and these.' I drop the cheese and fruit trays onto the Starbucks counter, expecting to spend fifty bucks from my tips last night on a breakfast I didn't make but am going to lay out as if I did. Typically, I would have, but last night I was preoccupied with mine and Conner's last night together for a while, so I snuck out before he woke up and drove like a madwoman to the nearest coffee shop.

The woman at the counter rings me up, bags my items, then hands me a drink tray with the two coffees. For safekeeping, I seatbelt the tray into the front passenger seat, setting the food bag onto the floor-boards before racing home. With the bag over my arm and coffee tray in my hand, I unlock the front door and head in, hoping Conner is still asleep. I hear the shower running, so perfect timing.

'Hai, pretty lady!' Spike squawks, making kissing noises as though I've been gone for a week and not twenty minutes.

'Does he know I left?' I ask as if he's human. With as many things as he says, it sometimes seems like he is.

Spike is my roommate, my talking Congo African gray parrot I inherited from my grandfather. He's twenty-two years old, knows too many words, refuses to learn the silent game, and hates his cage. He's been calling me 'pretty lady' since I was three. If a stranger walks by my apartment door or windows, he yells, 'Intruders will be shot!' It's as good as having a guard dog.

'Lemme out!' he screams.

'Nope, not while Conner is here. He can't afford to lose a finger before he leaves this afternoon. He needs all those fingers to help repair broken bodies.'

'Conner. Conner. Conner,' he repeatedly says, bumping his body up and down as he walks around the elaborate cage setup.

My place is nothing special. There's a kitchen to the left of the large living/bedroom you walk into. At the far end is an enormous bathroom. It's practically as big as the kitchen. Almost everything in here was passed down to me from my grandparents' home after they passed. Or I've utilized one of my favorite pastimes and thrifted it.

'Spike, no like.'

'No like what?' I ask as I spread the Starbucks contents across my kitchen island, quickly pouring the coffee into two mugs.

'Spike needs out. Hurry! Fuck!' he commands.

Yep, Grandpa taught him all the swear words. Along with catcalling when I ask how I look, speaking about himself in the third person, knock-knock jokes, dirty jokes, games, and songs that he now annoys me with on a minute-by-minute basis. It's kind of nice, though. You could say I'm never lonely, and it's like a piece of my grandpa still exists through smart-ass comments and unexpected conversations. He still makes me smile even though he lives in an urn on my dresser.

'Not until Conner leaves, buddy. I'm sorry, you can be a tad mean.'

He stares at me wordlessly, as though he understands and is deeply offended. After a moment, he turns his back on me and stares out the window. Finally, the silent treatment. It's rare, but it does happen. How a bird with a brain the size of a peanut responds more intelligently than some humans I know is beyond me. I'm not sure he even realizes he's a bird.

When Conner exits the bathroom, his hair is still wet and he's shirtless as I get the evidence that this is store-bought into the garbage. I can hardly keep my eyes on what I'm doing.

'Good morning! I made breakfast.'

He glances over at me with a smirk. 'Sure you did. That's why you were gone when I woke up?'

Damn it. 'Note to self: do not apply to be a spy...'

Conner chuckles as he pulls on a T-shirt. 'I don't have much time; my flight got moved up. Can you help me pack? I need to leave, like an hour ago.'

'Your flight got moved up? *How?*' I ask the first thing that comes to mind allowing the words to snap out sort of angrily. We haven't done anything he promised we'd do. No wedding date is set. He only told his parents yesterday. And I've looked at exactly zero rings.

'Because I requested it.'

'You requested it? But *why*? I thought we were

going to spend the day together, shop for rings, and discuss the wedding.'

He's tossing the clothes he's left here over the last couple of months into a suitcase on my bed that I swear wasn't here when I got up. Did he bring it over from his parents' place? 'No time, babe. I promised Blake we'd meet up later, and considering I haven't seen him in months, I can't cancel.'

My heart sinks through my chest. He's leaving, just like that, without a second thought about how *I* feel right now. I meander around my apartment, looking for his things and tossing them onto the bed. Who in the hell is Blake, and why is he taking precedence over my ring shopping?

'At least have some breakfast or coffee?' I suggest.

He glances at the island, now all set with breakfast for two. 'I'll take some to go. It smells fantastic, by the way. Can you get it ready for me?'

'Bark! Bark! Bark!' Spike yells, scaring the crap out of both of us. Spike's gaze is glued to Conner.

'You see a dog, bud?' Conner asks, glancing out the window Spike's cage sits near. When he doesn't see anything, he looks at me with worry. 'Can birds lose their minds? Because I see no dogs.'

'Spike, see dog,' Spike says, his line of sight never leaving Conner.

Insults. I forgot to add that one. Spike loves insults, and he's good at them. He's reading my mood and putting in his two cents like my grandfather would have.

As I pull the Starbucks packaging from the garbage to make Conner's 'doggy' bag, I'm fighting away the part of me that wants to call him a dog too.

'Scone?' I ask.

Conner shakes his head as he zips his suitcase closed. He sits on the bed to tie his Adidas tennis shoes. 'I'm off sugar. Have to keep this machine moving while I save lives.' He pats his stomach, where I assume he thinks a six pack lives? If so, it's just beneath the surface. 'Just fruit and coffee for me.'

He's off sugar? Last night he drank a Mai Tai and ate my remaining chocolate-covered coffee beans. That's not exactly sugar-free. I glance down at the protein cheese trays I bought and shove them into the bag. I'm not off sugar, so I'm keeping the scones and banana bread. My lunch and dinner are set.

There's a knock on my door, but it's drowned out by Spike screaming about shooting intruders. When the door opens, I realize it's my next-door neighbor, Thomas. He's a sweet, seventy-seven-year-old man who likes to bring over nearly spoiled fruit to feed Spike.

I've known him since I was a kid, as Thomas is part of Dad's biker club. The age range of Devil's Beard (that's their 'gang' name, and yes, they're all ZZ-top-style hairy) is twenty-one to eight-five. This 'gang' has regulations listed on their framed 'Devil's Beard Written Law' that the original founding members created back in the fifties, and it graces the entry wall of a 'secret' dive bar they've creatively named DB. (Does it stand for Devil's Beard or dive bar? No one knows.) I've never been to this place, nor do I want to. I've heard rumors, and I have a feeling it's where the younger guys keep gonorrhea alive. Gross.

As a kid, I thought all my dad's friends were badass. I'd threaten boys at school that my father would request his buddies to come 'take care of them' – like I was the daughter of a mafia lord. That was a tad deceiving, as most of them were pretty docile, but some were downright scary. Mostly, they're rough-edged guys obsessing over their motorbikes, enjoying the biker gang stereotype and the freeing feeling riding gives them. Look out, world! Docile or not, they carry brass knuckles, mace spray, weapons, and God knows what else on their persons. The elderly crowd, like Thomas, mostly ride to the beach and back nowadays, and they stay in luxury hotels because sleeping on the sand like they did when they were young would get them drowned when the high tide came in before they could get up again.

Thomas is how I got this apartment. He looks out for me for my father, and I look out for him for God. He's recently had some health issues so I've got an open-door policy, and he has my spare key. I want to make sure this sweet old man lives the life he deserves, so we spend a lot of time together. We even binge watch shows together.

Once, when I got home, Biggie Smalls was blasting through my apartment. Leave it to Laney to teach the bird to use Alexa. Thomas was inside, keeping the beat much like Spike was, with mostly his upper half. He said he came to turn it down, but it was catchy, and Spike told him to dance, so he danced. A vision I will never forget, especially since I danced with them when I realized a dance party was needed for the day I'd had.

'Jade sweetheart, do you, by chance, have enough coffee for the crazy old man who forgot to buy some at the store last night? I went for *one* thing and, of course, came home without it.' Thomas glances at Conner as he stands from the bed. 'Oh my,' he says. 'Am I interrupting?'

'Nope, I'm just heading out,' Conner informs him.

This morning isn't going as I had planned. 'Here, Thomas.' I hand him the steaming mug of coffee on my island that I was going to drink.

'Thank you, darlin'. Time for you to head back already, eh?' he asks Conner.

'Yep,' he says with a smile I've never witnessed – like he's going on the trip of a lifetime – as he yanks up the handle of his suitcase and pulls it towards the front door.

I follow him over, ushering Thomas out first. 'Can you give us a few, Thom?'

'Of course. I'll be right next door, honey.'

After he exits, I close the door behind him and stand between Conner and the only way out of my apartment.

'Here,' I say, handing him the bag free of sugar and the coffee he's drinking black whether he likes it or not.

'Thanks, babe.' He pecks a kiss on my lips as he reaches for the doorknob, but I step in front of it. 'What are you doing?' he questions. 'My flight leaves in an hour and a half. If I don't leave now, I'll never get through traffic.'

'Why'd you change your flight without telling me?' I ask, the disappointment I'm trying to hold back surfacing with my words.

He sighs but doesn't look remorseful. 'I'm excited to get back. All my friends are in Boston.'

'But your fiancée is here.' I wave my ringless hand in his face again.

'That's right,' he says with a guilty grin, sliding his hands around my waist and pulling me close. 'I know exactly where to find you, and as soon as I have some free time, I'll be just as excited to get back here to see you, and when I do, I'll be able to afford the ring you deserve.'

'Really?' I ask, unsure if he's blowing smoke or not.

'Jade. Do you think I'd ask you to marry me and not be serious?'

Honestly, I'm starting to wonder, but I won't say that out loud.

'I love you,' he reassures me.

'More than Blake?' I ask with a snap.

He laughs. 'Different kinds of love, babe.'

'If this Blake gets a ring first, Conner, I will be pissed.'

'Don't worry, babe. Soon you'll wear a rock so big your hand will tire.' He kisses my lips again and then goes for the doorknob. 'I'll call you when I land, alright? Shoot...' He's staring at the phone in his hand as it buzzes. 'I better tell my mom I won't be home for dinner too.'

He didn't even tell his mother he'd moved up his flight? She'd planned a going away/last minute engagement dinner with his family. It would've been the first time I met them and now he's going to blow her off like this? He pulls his suitcase into the hallway with him as he texts with one hand. Standing up his mother via text message is just wrong.

I linger at my door, lost for words considering I would do anything to talk to my mom again, but he's preoccupied by his phone so he doesn't even look back at me.

'I guess I'll talk to you later...' I call after him, irritation filling my tone, but he doesn't notice. He lifts a single hand, before the front door of the building slams shut behind him, stopping my heart in a way that's painful.

Well, this feels just great. But what can I do? I don't want to be that stage five clinger fiancée no one loves. He's excited to get back to his friends. That's normal. I just didn't realize how excited he'd be to leave me behind – so much so that he requested to change his flight out of here.

After I go back into my apartment, I walk to

Spike's cage, letting him out before he starts swearing at me again. He flies to the top of his enclosure, looking out the window with me. We watch as Conner pulls his suitcase through the front locked security gate towards his car, never once looking back.

'Spike, see dog. Bark. Bark. Bark,' he chirps, bouncing around.

Sigh. 'God, I hope you're not right.'

4

RIVER

Well, I did it. I bravely showed up for a blind date with a woman my mom chose, and I've been waiting on her for an hour. I thought no one could do worse at picking women than me, but at this point, I doubt she's showing.

'River.' My best friend, Dax, answers his phone the same way he always does when I call while he's working – with the 'hurry up, I'm busy' tone.

'You ever been stood up?' I ask, moving from the table I was at to the line in front of the window of one of my favorite Portland food joints, the Dawg House. Gourmet hot dogs to die for. The place sits on the corner of a busy SE Portland road in a small A-frame building with a bright orange roof, no indoor seating but picnic tables for diners. It's not precisely a primo first-date venue, taking a woman out for wieners, but I figured if she hates this, she's not going to love me, and it's best to know that early.

'Nope. I've never been stood up,' Dax says proudly.

I groan into the phone. 'Read my mood, pretty boy. I need ya right now.'

He goes silent for a beat before speaking again. 'Oh, then yeah, girls stand me up all the time. Fuckin' women, am I right?'

There's the best friend my sister stole from me.

'Girls, what?' Hollyn's muffled voice echoes in the background.

The phone shuffles as Dax probably pulls it away from his mouth and to his chest. He's doing his best to stay neutral in this relationship as my bestie and his fiancée being my sister. 'It's Riv. He needs – emotional support?' he says, his voice muffled.

'Oh, how the tables have turned,' she laughs.

'Can you tell my sister that if I wanted her stupid opinion, I'd have called her?' I'm joking and they both know it. I adore Hollyn. She's my favorite sister. He-he, another joke she hates considering she's my only sister. We pick on one another out of love, I swear.

'Never saying that,' Dax says. 'Did you really get stood up?'

'Yep.'

'You think maybe she showed, saw you, and fled?' he asks, laughing into the phone.

I sigh heavily. 'That's something Hollyn would say. Congratulations, you two have officially morphed into one person. I knew you'd betray me at some point.'

'Betray is a bit of a heavy word,' Dax huffs. 'You're not possibly emotional over some Tinder girl standing you up?'

'I'm not *emotional*; I just think standing someone up is pathetic and was hoping my best friend could remind me I'm not some loser no woman wants.'

Dax chuckles into the phone, which I expected, but he could have stifled it better than he did. 'Don't worry, Riv. You're a beautiful man with hair to die for. Your lady is out there somewhere. Perhaps you're meant to be one of those old rich guys with a twenty-two-year-old trophy wife. If that's the case, relax, she's not been born yet.'

Funny. Not. 'You annoy me, Hartley.'

'Back at ya.' Dax has been my best friend since I was four. We're like brothers really, so our teasing is also out of love. Mostly.

'What can I getcha?' the woman working the order window asks as the man before me steps away.

'I gotta go. Thanks for the pick-me-up; you're terrible at it.'

'Get me this girl's number, and I'll have Hollyn call and pretend to be your pissed-off girlfriend. No woman treats my best friend this way! She will rue the day she crossed our paths!' he bellows angrily, putting on a real show.

I laugh, disgust intertwined. 'Hollyn as my girlfriend – ew – bite your tongue, Daxy-boy. I'll lose my appetite with that kind of talk. Now seriously, I gotta go. I've got a last-minute solo date with a hot dog I will whisper sweet nothings to since no one else is interested. Later.' With that, I hang up, shove my phone into my pocket and glance back at the menu. 'One overloaded foot-long dog, please.'

I'm getting ready to devour this hot dog, when someone clears their throat as they approach. I glance up, seeing Brooks, along with his work partner, Andrews, an old guy who only ever thinks about food from what I'm told, and currently is standing in line to order, clutching his wallet to his chest like a kid with five bucks at an ice-cream truck.

Brooks is an inch taller than my six-one, built to the hilt, loaded with tattoos, always wears a different

ball cap, works for the Portland Police drug and organized crime unit, and is infatuated with Mercy – in a
good way. They're madly in love. Since they started
dating, he's fallen in as a member of our friend group
as though he's been here the entire time.

'I saw your car, and Andrews was starving, as
usual, so I thought I'd join you. I kind of expected to
see Dax with you.'

'He's working,' I say, wiping my mouth. 'I was
supposed to be joined by a gorgeous woman named
Marissa, but it seems she couldn't make it.'

'Did she forget to call?'

I roll my eyes. 'I hate that you read between the
lines in every conversation.'

'I'm a detective, Riv. Reading between the lines is
my job. You seem annoyed by this woman not showing. Why? I thought you were over dating and now
waiting for miss right to find you.'

I glare as I chew, never letting my gaze leave his.

He plays along but finally cracks. 'It's just pillow
talk,' he says guiltily.

'Also known as hearsay, *detective*. What else did
she tell you?'

I knew Mercy would blab anything I told her.
That seems to be the couple rule. My once treasured
bro code no longer exists, and couple code has taken

over. It's annoying as fuck. Apparently, they're allowed to tell one another everything, even if they've been instructed not to. Couple code trumps bro code. Sigh. I didn't exactly ask her to keep her mouth shut, but considering we're all so close, and we're up in one another's business at all times, I'm not surprised he knows.

'She said you're supposed to be keeping an eye on some other guy's fiancée? Which, I'm not going to lie, is a weird request. But you said yes? Wouldn't dating distract you from that?'

'Jade is a grown woman. When I see her next, I'll make sure she's alright. Until then, I'm not about to start following her around. Stalker laws and all that.'

'It's *Jade*? From Black Tide?'

I nod, taking another bite from my hot dog. We all know this woman; that's how often we visit Black Tide.

'Since when is she engaged?'

'It's recent.'

Brooks fidgets with his hat. 'Wild.'

'Why's that wild?'

He sits across from me, shrugging his shoulders. 'Honestly, with how you two flirt, I thought she was single and interested.'

'Interested in what exactly?'

Brooks chuckles as if I'm pathetic. '*You.*'

I shake my head. 'Dude, she's a cocktail waitress. Flirting is her job. There's nothing there.'

'So you're not attracted to her at all?'

Damn it, Mercy.

'I can't deny that she's beautiful. But she's taken.'

'That's too bad. I had a good feeling about you two.'

'You're suddenly so in love with love that you're taking a page from Norah's book?'

Norah is his mind-reading ex-wife who predicted Mercy was his one. When it turned out she was, everyone wanted me to pay Norah a visit to find mine. No thank you.

Andrews sits down next to Brooks, two foot-long dogs and a giant soda on his tray.

'Thanks,' Brooks says, reaching for one, but the older man swats his hand away.

'Neither of these is for you, kid. You want lunch; you buy your own.'

Brooks glowers. 'You're going to eat *two* feet of hot dog loaded with sauerkraut, then go back to work?' he asks, clearly not on board with this plan.

Andrews fills his mouth, now talking between chews. 'I'd suggest cracking a window,' he says, his gaze moving to me. 'Nice ponytail,' he says with a smirk.

'Impressive crumb catcher of a stache, my man. I thought those thick broom-style lip warmers died out with seventies porn.' I return the 'compliment' to the silver-haired man and watch him wipe a napkin over it.

'Thank you,' he says proudly.

'*Anyway*,' I say, looking back to Brooks. 'Jade's not interested like that. We're just bar friends. I don't know why Conner would ask me to watch her. 'Cause he's an idiot?'

'Perhaps. *Or*... maybe it's a sign.'

'If you pull out a crystal ball, I'm out of here.'

He chuckles. 'I don't believe in all this sign shit,' Brooks defends himself. 'At least not *completely*. But that's the vibe I got when I saw you two chatting at the bar one night. I thought you were charming her, and she was eating it up.'

Why don't I remember this?

'Was I drunk?'

In all reality, I can't pretend it might not have happened because I'm rather flirty under the influence.

'You may have been a tad inebriated.' Brooks

grins. 'I can't believe you don't remember. You moon-walked for her.'

I did *what*? Now he's got my full attention. I feel that whatever this story is, it won't be as flattering as I hope. 'Tell me about it,' I say, returning to my hot dog.

'It was three months ago. Jade was upset over something, and you found her crying back by the bathrooms during her break.'

I nod. 'Her mom had just been moved into hospice.' I remember this part. I was drinking water between shots, my attempt to cancel out the booze (sometimes I've got great ideas, but this was not one of them), so I had to pee a lot. During one of these many bathroom trips, I spotted her in a dark corner, her forehead pressed where the two walls came together by the back door, across from the bathrooms. Her sniffling stopped me in my tracks. She was crying. I'm not great at crying women, but when I touched her back and asked if she was okay, she turned and wrapped her arms around my neck, crying into my shoulder as she told the story of what was going on in her life. The only words that left my lips were, 'I'm so sorry.' After that, I held her until she let go.

'That was nothing.' I wave a hand. 'I simply

hugged the girl. Her mother received a death sentence; I feel like that's hug-worthy.'

'Agreed.' Brooks nods. 'But that's not the part I'm talking about. It was a while after that, just before closing.'

With everything I have, I cannot remember leaving the bar that night. That's not promising whatever I did was charming, cute, or even forgivable.

'Keep talking...'

'It was just the three of us.'

I shoot him a glare. 'You'll need to be more specific; currently, my role in life is the third wheel, remember?'

Brooks rolls his eyes. 'You, me, and Mercy. You walked out behind us, dancing I might add, and Jade ran out, calling your name. Something about it sounded flirty, so Mercy wanted to eavesdrop.'

I scrunch my face. Of course she did.

'You know you picked the weirdest woman on the planet?'

He beams. 'Isn't she awesome?'

'Back to me.' I snap in front of his face as he dreams of a girl who's like family to me. No thanks to witnessing that. 'So, I danced. That's not terrible considering I'm pretty damn good. But, uh, what did I say?' I ask, setting the hot dog in front of me, a little worried about the story I'm about to hear. Andrews seems into it, sitting with his elbows on the table, double-fisting his second dog, his full attention on Brooks. Lunch and a show at my ego's expense.

Suddenly the scene he's referring to flashes through my head. Shit. *How* did I forget this, and why has she never brought it up? First, I was *very* drunk – which happens about fifteen minutes before horny drunk, then leads to emotional drunk. When she burst out the bar door calling my name, I greeted her with an overly confident 'Hey, pretty lady.' I stepped closer to her. 'You know what I was thinking earlier? We're like nachos with jalapeños, you and I.'

'Why?' she asked, a coy smile on her face.

'Because I'm super cheesy and you're incredibly hot. Obviously, we belong together.' I slung an arm over her shoulder as she laughed at my proving how cheesy I am. It wasn't only that, though, I'm pretty sure I was wearing a T-shirt that said *I'm a Barbie Girl* that night. I've never been as aware of my obnoxious taste, passed down by my mother, as I am right now.

'You are pretty cheesy,' she said. 'I just wanted to say thanks for earlier,' she'd continued. 'I guess sometimes a girl just needs a hug.' She laughed shyly. 'For the record, I like your brand of cheese.'

I remember going in to kiss her because I got the

vibe that's what she wanted. Hell, I was sure as fuck feeling it, but something stopped me. Ah, that's right, Brooks and Mercy were dragging me away. 'Come on, we don't drunk kiss sober girls...' they'd said in unison.

After that, I yelled my phone number into the dark streets, not giving a flying fuck who else got it, and to this day, I don't know if she kept it. I'd guess not, as she's never called me. Cheesy wasn't even the right word. Jesus. Why does no one ever remind me that tequila is not my friend?

'Is it all rushing back?' Brooks asks suddenly, waking me from my day-mare.

I drop my head into my hands. *How* did I forget all this? 'Yeah, yeah, no need to spell it out. At least verify she *wanted* me to kiss her, right?'

Brooks nods. 'You don't want your first kiss to be a drunk kiss, that's what I know.'

Andrews slurps his now nearly empty soda. 'As interesting as that was, story time is over. We got creeps to spy on.' He stands from the table, heading to the garbage can, then to the unmarked police SUV they drive.

Brooks stands, shoving his hands into his pockets as he gets in line to buy his lunch. 'My dad says I have to go back to work now. But I'm glad I could remind you that you're an idiot when you drink.'

'Thank you. Can ya make sure you spell my name right on my trophy?'

I can't believe this. Why did I block this out? Was that my shot? Her giving me a chance that drunk me fumbled? That happened before her mom died. *Before* she met Conner. Crap, had I been sober, that night could have changed things between us, but Conner slid into her DMs first because I chose to get too drunk the night she hinted that she liked me.

5

JADE

'Where have you been?' Kai, my best friend, asks when I finally show up to work thirty minutes late. 'You're never late; I was about to call your dad and ensure you hadn't boarded the plane with Conner.'

Not sure he'd have allowed that considering he practically ran out of my apartment this morning. I thought about calling in sick tonight because lovesickness should count as a genuine illness. But I convinced myself to head to my happy place and shockingly, my job *is* my temporary happy place. As I fall asleep at night, I don't count sheep. I pretend I'm lying on a white sandy beach, with the waves lapping at my freshly painted toenails, palms blowing in the gentle warm breeze, flamingos meandering in the surf, and a private bartender named Wells, who laughs at my jokes and reminds me of my worth. (Thank you, *Bachelor in Paradise*, for bringing us him.)

The first time I walked into this place, I felt like I was nine years old and revisiting Disneyland's Enchanted Tiki Room, which I sat in with my grandfather for an hour. I was officially in love with all things tropical. I even have a photo of him and me from that day on my fridge. My smile couldn't have been bigger.

As a kid, I wondered if I was mistakenly born in the wrong part of the world, the rainy pacific northwest. I'm the type of girl that, with a hint of cold, I dress as if I'm headed into sub-zero temps, and currently, fall is upon us in the Rose City. I'm freezing and it's only September. Fog, rain, cool temps, and falling leaves have me pulling out my vintage fur jacket, fingerless gloves, and scarf, which I've left in my locker in the back employee room.

'I had a long night, an irritating morning, and then I fell asleep.' I stash my phone under the bar top where we employees keep them because, inconveniently, grass skirts have no pockets.

'You slept through Conner's family dinner? I thought you'd walk in here on cloud nine after spending time with your new fiancé.'

I heave a sigh. 'Conner canceled dinner. He canceled ring shopping. He even walked out on breakfast.'

Both Kai and Adam, our manager, turn my way, their eyes wide.

'Did he also cancel the wedding?' Adam asks.

'You broke up?' Kai's question intertwines with Adam's as he speaks over her.

I shake my head, but as I open my mouth to explain, Adam interrupts.

'Wait!' he commands. 'First things first...' He grabs three shot glasses, pouring a shot of Stolichnaya's Elit Vodka – his favorite – for each of us. 'Jade obviously needs to drown her salty heart, so she gets a double.'

He's a mind-reader. This is our nightly routine – well, not the double shot. Usually, a single shot helps me get through my shift and gives me the courage to do our bar top hula dance. Even Adam wears the uniform, minus a bikini top (except that one night when he wore the souvenir coconut bra hanging from one of the walls as decor – he made bank in tips that night).

'My heart is not salty.'

'Sure it's not,' Adam says, lifting his glass for a toast. 'To a good night.'

Kai lifts hers, tapping it to his. 'One where Jade doesn't mace some unsuspecting asshole guy because she's in a mood,' she adds with a smirk.

'It was *one* time,' I say defensively, knocking my glass against theirs before downing my shots. Yum. This vodka is velvety smooth, a bit sweet, and doesn't go down like you just drank a cup of firewater. 'He deserved it.'

Kai laughs. 'The best part about that guy was when he asked if we were going to sixty-nine him.'

'Then he fought with us when we told him it was eighty-six, which isn't sexual, just a lifetime ban and your photo on the office wall,' Adam says.

Finally, I crack a smile at the ridiculousness of that entire night. 'I'm glad my presence can provide you two with such fun memories,' I joke, grabbing a bottle of water to help wash down the vodka because, while it might be tolerably better than other booze, the aftertaste isn't great.

'The fact that he posed for his photo like it was going to be his new Facebook profile pic was the cringiest part. One day we'll see that guy's mugshot on the news.'

'And he'll be *smiling*.' Adam grimaces as he finishes her sentence.

Those two are a lot alike; it's why we've bonded so

much since working here. We work well together and read each other easily. I explain the Conner thing vaguely to avoid making him look too bad, as I'm hoping this is just a hiccup in our relationship. We did move quickly, so the details of things haven't been ironed out. That takes time; and apparently, Conner didn't have any this morning.

'That's a big ol' red flag, Jade. Don't let those stack up, or you'll end up miserable,' Kai says.

'Thank you for the advice, but I'm not calling any flags on the field yet. It's *one* mess up.'

'Besides the time he got your name wrong while publicly proposing in front of everyone you know,' she reminds me.

I blow a long breath out. 'I'm pretending that didn't happen. He was nervous; really, it's kind of a cute story. Now let's get to work, can we? I'm not really in a chatty mood.'

Kai and Adam don't push the conversation, and we part ways to get the place ready to open. There's never a night we're not busy, so keeping on task is vital to not getting overwhelmed and quitting on the spot. (It's only happened a couple of times in two years.) I'm so glad these two have a way of lightening any mood. I couldn't ask for better friends or co-workers.

Kai is twenty-six, like me, and is originally from Maui, not like me. She has long black hair, naturally tanned skin, and is as gorgeous as women come. She calls the garbage 'rubbish' and the refrigerator an 'ice box'. Little details I've come to love. She's an inch taller than my five-five, slender, with hips that don't lie.

Her family moved to Oregon when she was thirteen after her parents divorced. We met on the first day of eighth grade. When I got to my locker, I discovered I'd been partnered with the new girl. I'd requested to be locker mates with Josh Jericho, our class's most desirable thirteen-year-old boy. Now that he's married to a lovely man named Stefan, it makes sense that he denied my request all those years ago. I may not have realized it then, but partnering with Kai was the best thing to ever happen to me. We instantly became best friends.

Adam is thirty-one and he's originally from Haiti. A local family adopted him when he was two. He's got dark brown skin, short shaved black hair, and more abs than are natural. Let's just say beer goggles aren't necessary when admiring Adam; he's always gorgeous. The women who come in don't miss that little detail either.

The three of us bonded almost immediately, and

we now work the same shifts every week, along with our bouncer, a giant of a man named Roman. He ensures those unruly asshole men Kai mentioned keep their shenanigans to a minimum.

I am the sole white hula girl on our shift. I'm thin but not perfectly smooth in the places society thinks I should be (damn thighs). My boobs could be bigger, and my belly button is an outie, so no shots off me. Kai is the body-shot girl, and let me tell you, men will pay decent money for anything if a woman in a bikini top is doing it, no matter how stupid.

If anything, I'm overly average and good with it. What's there to hate? I'm a human with flaws, but I also have *really* good hair. It's my best feature by far. It's thick, lustrous, long, caramel-y brown with golden highlights that I wear in big beachy waves and get compliments on daily. 'What hair products do you use?' is often asked of me. *It's all-natural, sweets, just like my itty-bitty titties* (thank you, Laney for calling me that all through my teen years – she was wearing a training bra at nine – a gift not passed down to me). I don't even buy expensive shampoos; I just got good hair. Laney has to work at the hair thing. YouTube videos, an entire cabinet of hair gadgets, extensions, and a countertop of products that precariously line the edge of her bathroom sink. One wrong move and you send them over the edge like a hair product bottlefall.

Spray tans keep me at a consistent level-two glow, so it always looks like I've just come home from a weekend vacation in the sun, even though I never have. Anytime someone asks if I went somewhere fun to achieve my bronzy glow, I make something up and keep going until they smile.

I was on a tropical cruise where I had the love affair of a lifetime.

I spent the weekend in sunny Las Vegas, and you know what they say about Vegas – what happens there, stays there.

I had a bikini photo shoot in southern Cali and will soon grace the pages of some Instagram swimsuit designer.

None of it's real, but who cares if I made it up? It's not like I'm ever going to see that stranger again. As my grandfather once said, 'The smile you put on someone else's face might be the only one they have all day.' Granddad was wise, so now I attempt to make people smile just because that's what he always did.

I'm also the only bartender enrolled in a bi-weekly hula class. Jameson, the owner, insisted (and he covers the cost) because those hip movements didn't come naturally to me. Shakira, I am not. The fact that all my classmates are teen girls isn't at all embarrassing (sarcasm), but the recitals they requested I take part in were, so I skip those. You'll never find me participating in the Miss Aloha Hula like Kai's mother once did, but I can sell the fact that I *can* do the hula for tips once a shift.

Just after ten, and long after Conner's plane has landed, my phone finally rings. I race to the back room to hear through the chaos of the bar.

'Hi!' I say enthusiastically, even though I'm mad at him for bailing like he did. 'You made it?'

'I did. I've only got a few minutes, though. Blake got us on the list for a club that's impossible to get into as a welcome back. The place is lit, Jade. No Portland bar could compare.'

'Look at *that* rack,' I hear in the background, from someone close enough it sounds like he's on the phone too.

'Can you shut—' Suddenly, there's a jostling sound, as if Conner is shoving the phone into his clothing.

'I don't know why you're wasting time with that wannabe diamond when this sparkling masterpiece is right here.' The same voice complimenting someone's rack a moment earlier comes through clearly.

'Who is that?' I ask, hoping it's just some douche in the same line as him.

'Blake, ignore him. He's kind of—'

The phone jostles again. 'Is this Condor's PDX lady?' This time the voice is on the line and speaking directly to me.

'Condor?'

'He-he. Is your name really Jade?'

He told his friend about me. That's a good sign. The bad sign is that he's slurring his words and just called me Conner's PDX lady. How many other cities does he have ladies in is all that makes me wonder.

'Yep, my name is really Jade.'

'Huh. Why not Diamond?' he says. 'Parents afraid you wouldn't live up and went semi-precious instead?'

Irritation bubbles in my gut like lava. How rude is he? 'You must be Masterblake? Conner told me nothing about you, but now I understand why,' I snap, my father's quick wit surfacing without me even trying.

His smarmy laugh pisses me off. 'Darlin', occasionally I may take care of business myself, sure, but when you look like Conner and me, women volunteer more often than not.'

Gross. 'Can I talk to Conner?'

'Hey,' Conner says again, a little more sheepishly than before.

'*That's* the guy you ran back to?'

'He's a little rough around the edges at times, but he's also got a couple of drinks in him.'

He doesn't apologize, just excuses his behavior.

'The rock is making you less fun,' Blake says. 'Hang up; we're headed in.'

'Conner, *that's* your best friend? He's a douche.'

'Dude, we're in, lose her. Here – psshht, sssshhh-hcccchhhh.' Someone attempts to disguise what I've already heard by pretending the line is static-y like I'll buy it. 'Connection's not great. Sssscht.'

'You do realize it's no longer 1999, right? Cell phones rarely sscchht anymore.'

'Don't worry, Jade.' Conner is back on the phone. 'Blake can be a tad obnoxious, but you know I'm all in with you. Don't be insecure already, or this will be a miserable engagement. I'm just out experiencing life like you are. Men ogle you all night at your job. You flirt for tips. Should I be jealous?'

'Maybe,' I retort. At least jealousy would make me feel like he cares, because nothing he's done today has succeeded at that. I feel as if he just wants to escape me.

'Hello?' Kai's voice echoes through the small

kitchen when she walks in. She spots me in the walk-in. The door is open, but even so, it isn't making me warmer. 'Are you trying to freeze or transport to Boston via the walk-in? We need you out front.'

I sigh. I feel no better talking to Conner tonight, so what's the point of continuing? We'll fight, and we can't fight the first day he's gone. That has to be a bad omen of things to come.

'I gotta go,' I say. 'Call me tomorrow morning?'

'Yep. Talk later,' Conner says.

'Love y—' As the words leave my lips, I realize he's already hung up. Nice. It's been one day, and this is already going disastrously.

'Was that your boy toy?' Kai teases. 'Is he all settled in and studying his nights away?'

'Yeah,' I say, leaving the walk-in fridge and closing the door behind me. 'He's up to his ears in medical terms.' Yes, I'm lying to my best friend. But only because everyone I know warned me about this, and I'm not ready to say they're right. It's been *one* day, and he's excited to be back. I'm sure he'll settle down the longer he's there.

6

JADE

On the walk to my car after work, I called Conner three times. No answer. If it's three in the morning here, it's six there. He should be home and perhaps asleep but ultimately available to answer for his fiancée – but nothing. Three phone calls are my limit, as I'm not about to beg someone to talk to me. Disappointment floods through me like a tidal wave.

Suddenly my phone buzzes in my hand, and I rush to answer, only to realize it's a text – from Conner. Finally! I tap the notification box and stare at his message. Thumbs up. Clock. Zzz smiley. Purple heart.

Emojis? Are you fucking kidding me? He won't answer, but he'll send emojis? What are we, twelve? I frustratedly shove my phone into the pocket of my fur coat. Is this how he'll act when we get married?

Don't overthink it, Jade. Maybe he's just tired? Or... what if he's not the guy you thought he was? No. He couldn't fake it for two months and he definitely wouldn't have proposed if he wasn't truly interested. Would he?

As I reach Riverfront Park, I decide to drown my worries in the rain. Because of the weather, few people are hanging about other than several homeless folks sleeping under trees, but I'm keeping my distance. I walk this path nightly, and never has anyone even so much as spoken to me. Could it be because I announce I'm armed (with mace) if anyone gets close? Possibly, but it works.

I glance up at the dark sky, raindrops hitting my face softly. The moon shines behind the clouds in clear spots, and although it's the middle of the night, it's lovely out here, rain and all. It's not like a monsoon or anything, just a steady drizzle, so I lie down on the ground, wholly bundled up tight, so only my face and fingers are hit by raindrops as they fall. This same sky used to hold the answers to help me clear my head, so why not try now when most of the city peacefully sleeps in their beds and cannot witness me crying in the middle of a public park?

When Laney and I were kids, we'd sit at the computer or in front of the TV for hours. Eventually, Mom would kick us out of the house and force us to play outside 'like she did when she was a kid'. Laney would take off across the street to her best friend's house, and I'd wander around the property for a bit, looking for anything to do. But every single time, rain, shine, or snow, I'd end up lying in the middle of our backyard, staring at the sky.

I don't know what Conner is thinking. Do I text him back? And if so, what the hell do I say? Words or emojis? Ugh. If I replied now, while I'm mad about it, those emojis would undoubtedly make this situation way worse. Why are relationships so complicated? You go into them thinking it's all bliss and rainbows, then the tiniest pebble in the path trips you up, and you fall right off the cliff. Will you break something? Might you die? Who knows – you only find out *after* you've taken the risk.

'Hey. You alive?' Someone kicks my foot.

Please don't let it be someone with ill intentions. I'm afraid to look, so I spew my usual threat instead.

'At the present moment, yes, I'm alive. But be warned, I've got *no* money. I *have* mace and am not afraid to use it. If you're here to rob me, you should know that my purse has old receipts, hair ties, tampons, and ChapStick – no cash. So, if you could just go away and leave me be, I'm trying to drown; thank you very much.'

The male voice chuckles. 'You're trying to drown by way of raindrop? Why take an entire season when the river is right there?'

How dare he! I snap my eyes open at this stranger suggesting I jump into the river. He's smiling wide, his shoulder-length blond hair pulled into his usual bun at the back of his head, headphone wires hanging from his ears. River. This is the first time I've ever encountered him outside the bar.

Propping myself up on my elbows, I glance at my Apple watch. 'It's three thirty in the morning. Why are you stalking the city at such hours?'

He yanks the headphones from his ears. 'I got a bat signal earlier so I was out fighting crime.'

I laugh.

'If I can't sleep, I run,' he says honestly.

'You couldn't sleep?'

River nods, his hands on his hips as he talks through a heavy breath. 'I've got one of those minds that sometimes don't stop. Running tires it out. I was just headed home when I saw what I momentarily thought was a body wrapped in a fur rug and that I'd stumbled onto a crime scene.'

'You thought I was a body that someone dumped yards from the river?'

He lifts his shoulders. 'This isn't exactly the safest place to be at this hour. Did you fall?'

'No,' I answer, lying back down.

'If I help you up, you won't mace me, will you?'

I forgot I told him that story. 'Just let me drown in peace,' I moan. Obviously, I'm kidding, but do you know what he doesn't do? Leave. Instead, he gets down onto the wet ground next to me and lies on his back, allowing the rain to fall onto him the same way it is me. I look over at him, lying there with his hands on his chest, staring at the sky.

'This is the opposite of letting me drown in peace.'

'I just ran seven miles and could use a rest and a cool down. Plus, there are a lot of weirdos downtown at this time of night. I wouldn't feel right leaving you here alone. If ya made the news in a bad way later, I'd have to live with that shit forever. Can't have that on my conscience.'

'You are such a gentleman.'

'I have my moments,' he says, glancing over at me with a wink. 'Wanna tell me what could be so bad you want to drown the hard way?'

'Oh, it's nothing much, just that men suck.'

He laughs. 'All men, or just one in particular?'

I roll my head his way. 'Conner rushed out this morning and hardly even said goodbye, and now he's out partying with his douchey friend who totally insulted me earlier without ever having even met me. It's been less than twenty-four hours since he left, and things are going downhill quickly.'

'How'd he insult you if you've never met?'

'Via telephone. He was such an ass, and now I'm a little worried Conner was on his best behavior while here, and his Boston bestie, Masterblake, is a true view into his real personality.'

'Masterblake?' River repeats with a chuckle. 'That's something I would say.' He holds a hand my way to celebrate my dirty nickname, and because I'm proud of it, I high five him. 'Let me get this straight; Conner couldn't wait to get back to Boston to his friend Blake and that made you feel like the third wheel?'

'Pretty much.'

'I don't know if you know this, but I'm the king of third-wheeling things. Everyone I know is coupled up.'

'But Conner is partnered with me, and he didn't even say he loved me before he hung up tonight, then after calling him multiple times, he sent back a text with emojis.'

The streetlight above us is illuminating River, and I'm only just noticing the hint of freckles that dot the bridge of his nose. He's not hard to look at, that's for sure. Very male model-ish with bright blue eyes, the color of the tropical oceans I dream of, a strong jaw, and eyelashes women pay money to achieve.

'Emojis huh? I suppose that'll buy him some time.'

'What do you mean?'

'I mean, if I'm sending someone emojis, I don't want to talk. A smiling pile of shit will shut people up pretty quickly. Am I in a shit mood? Or am I sitting on the throne in misery? No one wants to ask.'

'That's an image,' I say, trying not to picture it but laughing at his thought process.

'Truth be told, you don't really know Conner that well, do you? What's it been, three weeks?'

I sigh. 'Two months.'

'Shit, you've known *me* longer. Maybe *we* should get married?' River jokes then looks somewhat frazzled by his own statement.

He's right, though. I have known him longer. He and Mercy started coming in about six months ago. His question flashes through my head like a news headline in all caps. *Breaking News. Does Jade really know the man she's engaged to? She's agreed to spending eternity with him so, she probably should.*

'I'm kidding,' he says, obviously concerned about my silence. 'In all seriousness, why did you say yes after only two months?'

'I love him,' I say meekly.

River raises a single eyebrow as if my answer doesn't convince him. 'So, you're super serious about a guy who proposed *without* a ring, hasn't made that a priority, your family hates him, and he's currently texting in emojis? I'd say even without words, he's saying a lot.'

'How do you know my family hates him?' I ask suddenly, not remembering telling anyone that part because it's humiliating that my family isn't on board with my recent engagement.

He blinks, looking back up at the sky. 'I, uh, I'm pretty sure you mentioned it once.'

Did I? I guess it's possible. Sometimes I talk more than even I remember.

'What would you do?' I ask.

'I'd dump him.'

'Really?'

'Hell yeah. If your relationship is troubling you

this much so early on, it's not right. Never settle, is what I say.'

'Is that why you're single?'

He clears his throat. 'Sure, that's why.'

'So men *and* women suck.'

River shakes his head. 'Boys suck. Men don't get all douchebauchery about a woman they love enough to propose to.'

'Douchebauchery?'

'Definition: excessive indulgence in being a douche. I may have struggled with this trait in my younger years, but I'm growing out of it.'

I reach over, patting his hand at his side. 'Some guys take a long time to hit puberty, but don't worry, it'll happen,' I joke.

His gaze meets mine. 'You're a funny lady, Jade. Your taste in coats is a bit questionable. But I can promise you, I'm well past puberty,' he says proudly. 'Maybe Conner's being weird because he's secretly married with a family, and you're the side chick across the country?'

I groan, not wanting to even think about that. 'No way...' But now the scenario is playing through my head and making my doubt worse.

River gets to his feet as the rain picks up, extending a hand to help me. 'How about you stop trying to un-alive yourself via raindrop over some idiot dude and allow me to walk you home before we both get pneumonia?'

Taking his hand, I let him to pull me up. 'I'm parked in the garage across the street.' I motion in that direction.

'Then let me walk you to your car after your rough day.'

I agree, walking next to him through the park. 'Will you answer something honestly? No matter how much you think it might hurt my feelings?'

We stop on the sidewalk, looking for traffic that's sparse at this time. 'That's kind of my life's motto.' He steps into the street first, me following at his side.

'It's also one of the reasons I like you. Do you think Conner is telling people he has a fiancée?'

He shakes his head. 'Nope,' he says without hesitation.

'What makes you say *that* so confidently?'

'He let his friend insult you. If I were in love with a woman, I'd never let my friends diss her. Not to mention he's sending you emojis. That's a total cop-out. Grow a pair and talk to your lady.'

I bite my lip to hide the smile growing on my face. 'You're sweet, Riv. I've never ended a conversation with you without feeling better. That's talent. Thank you.'

'The pleasure is all mine. For the record, and keeping myself honest, I think you're dating a boy, Jade. Maybe you should ask yourself what you truly want in a man and decide if Conner has any of those qualities. It's not too late to say no to his proposal.'

How do I figure that out while he's hardly speaking to me *and* across the country?

River stops with me in front of my bright blue Mazda.

'This is me,' I say, avoiding letting those last words he's just said sink in. I click the unlock button on my keys, and River opens my driver's side door for me.

'Your chariot awaits, madam.' Before he closes me into my car, he leans down to look me in the eye. 'If you ever need to talk, I'm always available. I'm a fun guy too; hang out with me and I'll lead you astray, far from all your worries.'

He says it with a wink, a hint of flirtatiousness in his voice. My heart may have also done a little dance with the playful way he approaches life. This is why I like River, he seems fun. That's dangerous considering the situation I'm in. But we could totally be friends while I figure my relationship out. 'Platonically,' I suggest, partially to remind us both that I'm an engaged woman.

'Right,' he says, lifting his hands as though he wouldn't dare make it anything more. 'Platonic is my specialty. How else do you explain nearly thirty and single? Let me distract you from your current boy problems – in a completely non-romantic way.'

I grin. 'It's a plan, *and* I even have your number already,' I tease.

He shouted his number to me as he left the bar one night after he'd said all the right words when I was having a rough go of things. We've never talked about that night, and I assumed it was because he was so intoxicated he didn't remember. But based on the look on his face right now, I'd say he may remember more than I thought he did. Life got so busy and traumatizing that I never brought it up, and neither did he.

His eyebrows shoot up his forehead, a hint of humiliation on his face. I'd think he was blushing if it wasn't so dark in here.

'You need a ride home?' I ask.

He shakes his head. 'I'm only a couple blocks that way. Lock your doors, and do *not* call him again. Make him call you. He needs to work for it to prove he's really into you, 'cause, as of now, I'm not convinced, and I think you deserve better. Trust me, I've fucked up enough with women to learn all the lessons.'

'I find that hard to believe, but there you go with the sweet words again. Thank you.'

The way he bows as though he's proud of himself is cute. He backs away from my car as I pull out, shoving his headphones back into his ears and doing a little dance, swaying his hips and waving his arms in front of my car, making me laugh, before running out of the garage towards the street. He is a good distraction.

7

RIVER

I am again at Mr. Tux for wedding suit fashion show number three. It's getting a little old. They're suits; how many options could there be? I don't see the difference in any of them, and I'm not allowed to bring my style into this because Hollyn thinks my attraction to all things colorful is ridiculous. I say she's just dull.

I'll never know how I snuck this velvety blue masterpiece in without her demanding I put it back, but I did, and now that I've got it on, I'm in love with it. I've paired it with the black slacks of the previous suit, and I have to say, it looks as good on me as it did on that Chris Evans fella. I pull my hair into a ponytail to look more put together, glancing at myself in the mirror from all angles. Damn. This blue brings out my eyes so much, even I can see it, and that's a good pitch point. If I want to wear the suit jacket Hollyn's banned, I'm gonna have to sell it.

The fitting rooms here are three separate curtained-off rooms within one large room, with a sitting area in the middle so parties have a little privacy from rando shoppers. I'm in one fitting room, Dax is in another, and Jake is in the third. Jake is a good friend of Dax's who will be playing the part of groomsman alongside me as the best man. Hollyn sits outside our rooms, impatiently waiting for us to impress her.

'This one is *nice*,' Jake says confidently from his dressing room.

'You've said that about all of them,' Dax mumbles.

'Well? It *is* nice,' Jake defends himself. 'What do you think, Riv?'

'I think I fucking love it,' I say, straightening my tie before exiting the room to answer questions. To get Hollyn's approval, I gotta look perfect.

'You *love* it?' Hols asks, sounding relieved. 'These are the ones; I just know it,' she says without seeing what I'm wearing.

She uses that 'these are the ones' line each time

she coaxes us out of the dressing rooms. They've yet to be the ones, but I feel like I'm about to change that. The three of us guys exit our dressing rooms simultaneously, and immediately both Jake's and Dax's heads snap my way.

'What the hell?' Jake's gaze lands on my suit jacket. 'I thought we weren't allowed colors? If that's changed, I want that plum jacket we saw when we walked in.'

Hollyn stands, looking me over. 'How did you get this past me?'

'As your little brother, I get a lot of shit past you,' I say, admiring my reflection as I adjust the jacket. 'I love this one.'

Hols runs her fingertips over the fabric at my bicep, then glances at Dax, a clenched-tooth grin on her face. 'Jeesh, first he picks my wedding dress, now this? Have you ever considered being a wedding planner?'

'Not once.'

'I like it,' she says to Dax, her tone perplexed as if I'm not good at picking out anything, as she lifts her shoulders.

'I know you're not supposed to steal the show from the groom, but dayum, I look hot as hell.' I do a spin, catching Dax rolling his eyes.

'Ew,' Hols says. 'You're my brother, so hot as hell isn't in my vocab when it comes to you. However, I do like the blue. It pops.'

'Perfect, 'cause I'm buying it, and I plan on wearing it to the wedding whether you like it or not.'

Hollyn bites her bottom lip, glancing at Dax, who lifts his shoulders. They have a lot of silent conversations these days.

'You decide,' he says.

'We're deciding this *now*? If so, wait!' Jake says, suddenly fleeing towards the front of the building. When he returns, he's wearing the plum-colored jacket (it looks fantastic), and he carries an obnoxiously floral print that screams Dax's name. 'I feel like we should stick with your floral essence, considering how you two got together.'

'I don't know...' Hols says.

Jake holds a hand her way. 'Let us try them on before you reject them, woman.'

She rolls her eyes, crossing her arms over her chest as Dax shakes off his jacket, trying on the floral one.

'What if this is too much? I mean, we're florists, so it makes sense for the flowers to be our color. I don't know, try them on, I guess, but I'm pretty sure my answer will be n—'

Before she can finish her sentence, Dax has on the jacket. Her face lights up even more than usual around him.

'You practically said the same words when I picked the wedding dress you loved. The one you *bought*,' I remind her proudly. 'So, suck on that while we model these fly-as-fuck suits.'

Hols laughs to herself but goes straight-faced once we're all in the jackets. As the three of us act as though we're walking a runway, one by one, she carefully looks us each over, her gaze lingering on Dax.

'What do you think, babe? Do I look hot enough to marry?'

'You did before we got here,' she reminds him, stepping back to admire him. 'I can't believe I'm about to say this, but... I think I love them. *This* is the look! But only colored jackets; otherwise, it'll be obnoxious.'

Dax grins. He's a man who enjoys a floral suit jacket. Weirdo. He glances at Jake and me as he turns to the mirror, pulling his lapels. 'We look—'

'Bomb as fuck.' I finish his sentence. 'Just like I knew we would. Now, if you'll excuse me, Mom is awaiting my arrival. I'm editing today, and you know how she wants a say in every damn decision. Never again will I do work for family.'

'Riv,' Hols moans. 'You promised you'd set up cameras to film the wedding.'

'*That's* the exception,' I say, returning to the changing room. I put my original clothes back on but wear the jacket to the counter to pay. I have to break this thing in because wedding receptions equal dance parties, and if I can't bust a move in it, it won't work. 'I'll see you dorks later,' I call as I exit the shop.

* * *

'Front door opened,' echoes from multiple speakers that are a part of the security system at my parents' place.

I drop my bag onto the bench in the foyer and head straight for the fridge – my usual arrival path. I yank the door open and smile. My two favorite things are always stocked at my parents' place just for me. Chocolate milk and string cheese. The same snack I had every day after school for twelve years. I'm a creature of habit, I suppose. I grab the milk carton and a handful of cheese sticks, then head to the glass cabinet.

'River?' Mom calls on her way down the stairs.

I don't live with my parents anymore, but I'm at the ass end of a documentary about my once-famous pop star mother, also known as Penny Candy, so I spend far too much time here. Today I'm editing, and she likes to help with that because God forbid I air an image of her that isn't from her best side. Her left. Seriously, she's that fucking nuts. I tried to distract her with the online dating thing, but she failed at that. I'll give her that good news later.

'I'm in the kitchen,' I yell, already halfway into a cheese stick while pouring my chocolate milk.

She stops in her tracks as she walks in, a goofy smile on her face as she looks me over. 'You look handsome! New suit jacket?'

'Meet my new wedding jacket,' I say, arms out as I turn for her to see every inch.

'Wedding jacket?' Mom asks, her eyes wide. 'You're wearing it *now*? Hollyn is going to kill you. Not only for wearing it ahead of time while drinking chocolate milk, but she said no colors. The flowers are her color, remember?' Her voice is deadly serious as if she's worried about me, but the smile on her face says she approves.

'How could I forget? She beat it into our heads, but I'm not a compliant kind of guy regarding fashion. You know this.'

'River,' she says sternly as I pick up my milk cup. 'Put the milk down.'

'Nothing's gonna happen,' I insist, not putting the milk glass down. 'Plus, it's Hols approved. One impromptu fashion show, and the guys and I convinced her to have a change of heart,' I say, putting the milk carton back into the fridge. 'Now we're all wearing colors.'

She gasps excitedly, her hands in front of her chest like her prayers have been answered. 'I no longer have to wear black like I'm headed to a funeral?'

'You're welcome,' I confirm.

'Oh, Riv! I've got a closet full of colorful gowns. Come upstairs and help me pick.'

I shake my head. 'That sounds like a Dad job.'

She's the reason this documentary is taking me so long to finish. There's always something else she's planned for me when I'm here, not to mention I've got to make money, so I'm still shooting commercials and music videos while working on this in the background.

Mom rolls her eyes, following me into the foyer, where I grab my bag and head to the family room to work.

'Come on, Riv. When you were little, you loved helping me choose my dresses. Even at five, I knew you had style. Please help. You can veto just like you used to until you think Hollyn would approve.'

'At five, that was fun. Now your sense of fashion is way dated. What if I veto everything?'

'Then we'll pack it up, you'll take a day off editing, and we will head to Nordstrom.'

Mom's a personality. Five foot two, barely a hundred pounds, currently has a chunk of purple in her shoulder-length blonde curly hair and doesn't look a day over thirty-five thanks to Botox. She's overly involved in our lives and says what she wants, even when it makes the rest of us cringe.

Reluctantly – because I know she won't drop it until I say yes – I agree to help with the dress thing, and three cheese sticks later, I'm sitting on her bed, my laptop still downstairs and my phone next to me, so I don't miss anything. When she finally walks out of her closet, she nearly blinds me. I lift a hand over my eyes to block the glare.

'*Vee-tow*.' I exaggerate each syllable as the neon pink shines back at me so brightly I momentarily fear a pink glow is now just a part of my vision.

'Riv!' she says with a stomp of her foot. 'You have to actually look.'

'I can't,' I say. 'Not when the color burns my retinas. How about we make you one rule?'

She groans exactly like Hollyn does when frustrated. 'What?'

'*No neon.* It's no longer the 1900s, and despite what you think, you're not twenty-two anymore. You can't go upstaging the bride with obnoxious revealing dresses worn on music videos of your past.'

'I only wore this once, during a show... that may or may not have been recorded.' She says that last part quietly, as though the dress affected my hearing and not my vision.

'I don't care where you wore it. Veto.'

She marches back into her closet, yanking something from the far back before displaying it to me over her arm. 'What about this one? It's never graced anyone's TV screen.'

'That's the same dress,' I say, the electric blue version of what she's wearing now assaulting my vision.

'This one is blue. *We* could wear blue! It'll be so adorable. You're walking me down the aisle; it's perfect. I'll even do blue highlights to match. Want me to make you an appointment with my hair girl?'

'I never want you to do that.' I shake my head repeatedly. 'Mom, this isn't prom. You're not my date. You're not going as Penny Candy. You're the *mother of the bride*. Find that dress. I'm sure it has more fabric, less spandex and won't destroy anyone's vision.

These are just – no – double vetoes. Try again. Thank you, next.' I wave her back to the closet as I scroll through my emails, mostly junk, then peel open another string cheese.

'You're not going to be able to poop for a week if you eat an entire bag of cheese,' Mom warns as she closes herself into her closet once again.

'You worrying about my poop stopped the day I graduated from diapers. Boundaries, Mom. Jesus.'

Yes, she treats me like I'm her 'miracle baby'. Mostly because I am. The story I've heard a gazillion times and that Hollyn hates goes like this.

When Mom was sixteen weeks pregnant with me, her doctor couldn't find a heartbeat after hearing one every visit before. They booked her a second ultrasound at the hospital for the next day to be double sure. That night, she was feeling bubbly little motions from within. At first, she thought it was the tacos she and Dad had for dinner. But eventually, she realized the doctor may have been correct, and her worst fear was happening: she was having a miscarriage. Dad claims she was distraught, lying in bed for hours, rubbing her swollen belly. He says he spent the night trying to calm her, hoping maybe the doctor had been wrong the day before, but nothing helped.

At her ultrasound the next day, she got what she still says was the best news of her life. Lo and behold, I'd risen from the dead and kicked around like I was fighting my way out early. It wasn't the tacos she was feeling. It was me. For some reason, the doctor wasn't getting a good look the day before and mistakenly put her through the torment of thinking her baby had died.

Because of all this, Hollyn decided decades ago I was the favorite child. Mom isn't exactly quiet about that, either. If someone were to ask if she had a fave kid, my name would leave her lips without hesitation. It can be embarrassing as fuck. I'm nearly thirty; cut the cord already, right? I don't dare say that out loud, though. It'd crush her. Her clinginess may stem from believing she'd lost me before birth *and* Hollyn leaving for college and rarely contacting Mom and Dad for nearly a decade. Mom was afraid to lose another kid, so she now hovers.

She's even got a tracker in my phone to ensure I don't go missing. I know it's there, so I like to check in at random places she won't approve of because why not? It's a fun little party trick. 'My phone will ring in thirty seconds, and it will be my mother; bet ya twenty bucks.' Every time it happens, and each time she greets me flatly with, 'River, you're not *really* at

Chubbies, are you?' It's the easiest twenty bucks I could make.

Chubbies is the dirtiest strip club in town. Their parking lot is the place to go if you're looking to die accidentally by unintentionally getting in the middle of a gang war. I've never really been there, mostly because I'd rather not die, but also because when the outside of a building looks like an STD, you don't chance going in.

Despite me messing with the woman constantly, Mom and I are close. We spend a lot of time together because of the documentary, and I've discovered she's not as insane as child me once thought. She is batty, don't get me wrong, but I'm very much like her. She's got a lot going on in her head, and hyperactivity is her middle name. Hollyn and I each inherited it in different ways. Hols struggles at night with insomnia, and I have that; *plus*, I get distracted easily by things like bagel shops, food trucks, women, shiny objects, and puppies (amongst other things). Because of that, my projects often don't move as quickly as I'd like.

I run a company called Wilde River Films. I went to art college, which is fantastic if you know what you want to use it for, but at the time, I didn't. When I enrolled, all I knew was that I didn't want to work nine to five for some asshole whose comfort was more important than mine.

The Penny Candy documentary I've been working on is my back-burner job. I've got VH1 interested, but my timeline has been open since Mom isn't precisely the singing sensation she once was. In the eighties, she was a mall performer. Once she was discovered and hit it big, she powered through the early nineties touring the world until my dad finally convinced her to settle down and reproduce. Settling wasn't always in her cards, but she finally calmed down for most of mine and Hols' childhood. She's been in the slow lane for a long time and now wants to jump back onto the freeway. That's what we're attempting with this documentary, and she's taking *forever* to record an entire album to release simultaneously.

My dad is a workaholic who spends a lot of time with other women. Patients, as he's an obstetrician/gynecologist, not Hugh Hefner. Mom hates being alone, so when he's gone, I end up helping her with things. Things that are not the documentary. Filming TikToks, helping her with her social media, cleaning the pool, fixing the laptop she broke, reorganizing closets, hanging photos, picking dresses – it's always something.

She again walks out of her closet, this time in something black-and-white striped with only one shoulder strap.

'Veto,' I say instantly.

'You barely looked!'

I lift my head, glancing her over, my honest thoughts probably all over my face. 'Are you about to referee a fancy schmancy soccer game?'

'No.'

'Are you becoming a zebra?'

She laughs. 'Nooo.'

'Prison fashion show organizer?'

A sigh leaves her lips. She's tired of this game.

'Then, once again, veto. Onto the next.'

As she reluctantly disappears inside her closet, my phone buzzes next to me with a text.

You busy tonight?

Hmm. A text from a random unknown number. Interesting.

Depends on who this is.

I stare at the phone, watching the bubble of someone typing pop up.

Only your fav bartender who could use an unromantic distraction and possibly some advice from a guy. Can you bring one with you? ;)

Jade. Can I bring a guy with me? Ha-ha. I laugh to myself, typing a response. I can't believe she kept my number and is finally using it.

'What are you grinning at?' Mom asks as my fingers tap the keyboard on my phone frantically.

No way am I telling my mother who I'm talking to. She'll have advice, and I don't need advice right now. If Jade needs a distraction, I'm happy to oblige.

I do know a guy. Perhaps I'll bring him in for a drink. ;)

'River! Is that her?'

'Who's her?' I ask, my eyes on my phone.

'Marissa! The woman I set you up with. Did things go well?'

I almost forgot about Marissa. I haven't thought much about her since she stood me up. Time to tell Mom she's fired from my dating life.

'I would stick with being a singer, Ma, because matchmaking isn't your gift. Marissa never showed.'

'She didn't show?' she snaps, then she focuses on one thing and shoots me a glare. 'Do *not* call me, *Ma*,

Riv. We're not the Ingalls family. I can't believe she didn't show. I'm going to email the woman right now,' she says, marching to her laptop.

'No you're not,' I say, stopping her in her tracks. 'You're officially fired from my dating life. Now back to showing me every ugly dress you've ever owned.'

'Fired? That's ridiculous. And my dresses are gorgeous, you've just lost your taste...'

I ignore her words as a new text from Jade buzzes through.

Don't come in. I'm not working tonight.
Meet me at Red Robin on 185th at seven.
I have a two-for-one coupon!

She wants to meet at the Red Robin in NW? That's a drive. *And* she has a coupon? Why does that make me laugh? Oh, right, because I can be cheap as fuck at times. It's a running joke amongst my group of friends. I can respect the frugal, I suppose. Plus, the place has the best bottomless fries ever. How could I possibly say no?

OK. At seven, I will unromance you like you've never been unromanced.

Yikes. I stare at the text. Did that seem flirty? It doesn't matter, I can't take it back, not to mention we sent winky faces earlier. Can we just not help it? Was Brooks right? Ugh. She specifically said un-romantic, so I best be the best un-romantic man alive. *Don't overthink it, River.* You two are friends, and friends hang out. Though I don't usually have this 'I can't wait' feeling when I hang out with Dax. Huh. I might need to figure that out.

8

JADE

'You're going to dinner with a man who is *not* your fiancé?' Dad asks, confusion on his face but a hint of interest in his tone.

'He's just a friend,' I say, stirring the pot of macaroni and cheese he doesn't want to make himself because my mom 'always made it better'. His words. He won't say her name, just 'your mom' as if trying to distance himself.

I come over once a week to spend time with him, and tonight, he requested I stay for dinner. But I already made plans with River, so instead, I'm making mac and cheese like Mom used to.

'Any word from the man who's lost his tongue?' he asks.

I snap my head his way. '*How* do you know about that?'

He only smirks for a moment. 'Your little sister likes to gossip.'

Damn it, Laney.

'Tell me, what does Conner think of you going to dinner with another man?'

It's been a week since Conner left, and we've hardly spoken. He claims he's busy, so our conversations are, 'Hey, I'm still alive; call you later,' and then later, he sends emojis I don't understand.

'He's got no opinion either way because only people capable of having an actual conversation get to tell me their thoughts. He's sending me strings of emojis, so his point of view is null.'

Dad laughs. 'What do you send back?'

I grab my phone from the counter and scroll to mine and Conner's text thread, which usually I wouldn't even consider showing my father, but in this case, there's nothing to see but a bunch of tiny cartoons that mean absolutely nothing and he's talking voluntarily so I'm not about to interrupt that.

Dad pulls his reading glasses from the neck of his shirt where he keeps them and inspects my texts. 'Man, dinner plate, firework.' He looks at me with concern. 'This is implying you're going on a date.'

'Oops,' I say, not even a little bit sorry.

'It's not like you to intentionally antagonize a guy. You're my sweet daughter.'

I smile proudly. 'I'm not *sweet*, I'm polite. It's called manners. And since Laney doesn't have any, she thought maybe he'd have something to say to those particular emojis.'

He looks at my phone again, attempting to scroll to Conner's response. 'Making him jealous enough to call you was Laney's idea?'

'Yep.' I scoop macaroni and cheese – with the spiral noodles 'cause those are his fave – into a bowl and carry it across the kitchen to the island he's now using as a dining table. He refuses to sit at the actual table because 'too many memories'. I set the bowl in front of him, grabbing the salt and pepper from the lazy Susan in the middle of the bartop because I know that's his next step before he even tastes it.

'What'd he say?' he asks setting my phone on the counter before scooping a few noodles out of his bowl and setting them on the counter in front of Frito, his cat, who gobbles them up and patiently waits for a second helping.

'Nothing,' I grumble, sitting at an empty chair next to him. 'He said absolutely zero and I sent it two hours ago.'

Dad shakes his head, securing his glasses back onto the neckline of his shirt before he seasons his dinner with enough salt that I'm sure he'll one day die of a heart attack.

'Sweetheart,' he says before tasting his meal and nodding with approval as if I'd whipped it up from scratch and didn't just boil water and stir. 'Conner's not calling for a reason. If I had to guess, I'd say that reason is that he has nothing to say because his newly discovered freedom has him rethinking the bad decisions he made while here, and ignoring it – er, *you*– is easier.'

My heart slows. I'd already had this thought, but hearing it come from my dad hurts a little. '*I'm* a bad decision?' I ask, woefully.

'Not to me,' Dad reassures me, patting my hand. 'But I have a sneaking suspicion he regretted his little proposal the moment the words left his lips.'

'Why do you think that?'

'I was there, remember. You nearly gave him a heart attack while you figured out what was happening and what you should say. Also, because I glanced through the gifts people brought and his name wasn't on one of them. He got you nothing and last minute he needed to do *something* for you so, he proposed.'

That hadn't even crossed my mind. Not that I care about gifts, but he's right. Besides Conner showing up at my door to 'gift' me his penis, he didn't bring me anything for my birthday. No flowers, no dinner reservations, no nothing but a late-night surprise booty call.

'A last-minute proposal to make up for not buying a gift seems a tad extreme,' I suggest, hoping he's not right. Is a booty call romantic? Not really. But he stayed the night and we even ordered in breakfast the next morning.

'Don't forget he got your name wrong, *and* had no ring,' he says, shoveling mac and cheese into his mouth as though he's starving.

I sigh. 'Spike barked at him as he left my building. Said he saw a dog. There was no dog.'

Dad laughs. 'Oh, there was a dog. Spike is a smart bird; I'd take his advice.'

'You won't even be in the same room as him unless he's caged; now you want me to take his advice?'

'Damn bird bit off a chunk of my ear, Jade.' Dad turns his head, displaying the perfect V snipped from the top of his ear when Spike once thought he was an intruder and attacked. 'Usually Spike can't be trusted, but in this case, I agree with him. I saw a dog when Conner was around too.'

Great. Not only did everyone warn me about the two of us moving too fast, but now Dad is in agreement with my parrot who knows more insults than compliments. This whole thing is starting to feel very nightmarish.

There's a honk outside Dad's house and, to be honest, I'm a little relieved. I'd like to stop reliving every red flag I never saw. 'That's my ride.'

Immediately, Dad stands from the table. 'Do I get to meet this man?'

I laugh as I grab my purse, my favorite one, shaped like red lips. Weird purses and fur coats are kind of my thing. Why be trendy when buying what you actually like is so much more fun?

'You can meet him if you want to, but he's only an Uber driver so...'

'This mystery man isn't picking you up?'

'I'm going for dinner with a friend, not on a date, remember?'

'Back in my day, dinner with a "friend" usually was a date.'

'Well, thankfully we're no longer living in the 1900s, Dad. In my world, men and women can be friends and nothing more.'

He smirks. 'Good luck with that, Jadeybug.'

* * *

'I have to ask about the fur coat,' River says as he walks to the table near the front door. He's dressed in black skinny jeans, bright green Converses, and a gray and black Nike hoodie. He's usually got on something that surprises me, but tonight he seems pretty low key. 'What kind of fur is this?' he asks, petting my arm before sitting across from me. 'Squirrel?'

'No,' I say with a laugh as I pull the coat off, setting it on the booth bench next to me. 'I think it's mink?'

He scrunches his face. 'Did you shoot it yourself, calamity Jade?'

I've been here two minutes and he's made me laugh twice. He's right. He's the perfect distraction.

'Do I seem like a gun-toting, mink-hunting damsel?'

He grins. 'Not even a little bit. I gotta know the story behind it though.'

I glance down at the vintage fur coat I so love, and wear the second the temp dips below fifty-five, giving it a pet as a 'sorry you had to die' gesture, feeling the tiniest bit bad about how this coat came to be. One day, a gang of PETA folks will rightfully cover me in paint, and I'll lose the memory that makes me happy every time I put this coat on.

'This coat was my grandfather's.'

'Well, wasn't he fancy,' he says. 'Did he get invited to a lot of Jay Gatsby-style parties?'

'He wore it ironically, mostly to irritate my grand-mother while they dated. She hated it.'

River's got a menu in his hands, but he glances over it with a grin. 'Don't stop there, I feel like I have to know the rest of this story or I won't be able to sleep tonight.'

'I can't have you losing sleep over my family dra-ma,' I chuckle. 'Get ready for a story you'll never for-get,' I say, jokingly. 'My grandpa found the coat in a thrift store when he was nineteen and had to have it the moment he tried it on. The sales associate talked him up, so suddenly taken by him that she asked him for coffee afterward. He'd found his lucky charm with the ladies – he even used it to reel in my grandmother.'

'So, it's got superpowers. Interesting. I may need to borrow it, the next time I've got a hot date.'

'Oh really?' I need to hear about his dating life as he's never really mentioned it. Not once have I heard River talk about a girlfriend. 'Well, my grandpa was a very slight man, and... not that I've noticed or anything, but you're not. I'm not sure it'd fit you.'

A smile grows on his face, and his cheeks go pink. I'm just going to keep talking and pretend I didn't just tell him I've noticed his body.

'Really, it's pretty cool for the age it is. Great condition, mostly because it lived in the back of Grandpa's closet except for special occasions like first dates, parties, and anything considered a celebration. His lifelong joke was that he knew my grandmother was the one because he felt the same way about her as he did the coat – she was another perfect fit.'

River bursts out the same laugh everyone did when Grandpa would tell that story – a little bit of shock, part confusion, then the realization that this sweet little old man possibly just made a cute story into a dirty joke, without shame.

'I like Grandpa already.'

'He was amazing,' I say with a sigh. 'Any time I had a bad day, he knew what to say or do to turn things around. He didn't take life too seriously. His mission was more to make those around him smile. I loved that about him the most.'

'Did he pass?' River asks softly, concern in his voice.

I nod. 'Three years ago. My grandma was so

crushed she died a year later. Mom said she died of heartbreak. Can you imagine that? Then my mom went. Now I'm just trying to keep my dad's head above soil so I'm not completely parent-less.'

He frowns at my string of family deaths. I must sound like a girl in mourning who should be wearing a black veil like they used to.

'Do you believe in that? Dying of heartbreak?' he asks.

I shrug. 'No idea considering I've never had the kind of love those two had.'

River cocks his head, setting the menu on the table. 'Shouldn't you feel that way about the man you're engaged to?'

Painful words have never been more true yet I haven't even considered it until now. 'Probably.'

'I have one spiked freckled lemonade and a Sand in Your Shorts.' I've never been so thankful for a waiter. I preordered drinks before River even got here and now they're sitting in front of us. 'And one slice of mudd pie, two forks.' He sets the pie in the middle of the table. 'Anything else?'

River inspects the table, then looks at me questioningly. 'We're having pie and drinks for dinner?'

After my conversation with my father, I was worried maybe despite our clear 'unromantic' rules, that dinner and drinks might be a little bit date-like. So... I came up with a plan on my ride over.

'This is an anti-date so I figured to make it that we needed to do things differently. Dessert first, dinner later?'

He laughs. 'How about no dinner, and we stick with dessert, drinks, and appetizers? Add an endless basket of fries, my friend,' River requests.

'And a tower of onion rings!' I throw in. 'Appetizers and dessert definitely aren't romantic.'

'Totally not,' he agrees, with a smirk.

'I'll be right back,' the waiter says with a flash of a smile. He's earning his tip with his happy aura alone.

'Have you ever eaten one of these by yourself?' River asks, not waiting a moment to scoop the first taste.

'Only when I've ordered it for delivery as comfort food. Crying over a massive heap of ice cream pie isn't a great look in public places. You know?'

'Shit. Are you a crier? I should warn you now that crying women aren't my thing.'

I can't say I'm surprised by that. Not many men I know enjoy a crying woman. 'Do tell. What part of crying women scares you?'

He cocks his head, a pinched lip smile on his face. 'I didn't say I was scared. I just never know what to say, and that's usually when the worst possible words leave my lips.'

'You didn't say the worst possible thing when I cried to you once. In fact I walked away from that feeling a bit better, honestly.'

'I can't wait to experience that, but you can rest easy because I don't cry in front of people unless it's serious. You know, like the one day I cried in front of you.'

He cracks a shy smile. 'I guess that's something.'

'It's totally something. By the way, sorry I put you in that position. It was one of those cries I couldn't control and you helped, so thank you.'

'You're welcome,' he says like he did it on purpose. Maybe he doesn't realize he's better with teary-eyed women than he thinks.

'Typically I'd rather escape a tearful situation by running into a dark, scary forest. I'd rather live a horror film than cry in public.'

'Why?'

I shrug. 'I'm not really sure. As kids when we'd get hurt, my dad would throw his hands into the air and excitedly congratulate us for living through it. He made it this big performance to take our attention off our skinned knees or broken hearts, and we giggled along with him as he fixed up what he'd call our boo-

boos. I think the technique scared away any impending tears because we were busy celebrating. Now, my body questions whether a situation is worthy of the time and emotional energy it takes to cry. Usually, it's not.'

River waves his fork my way. 'That's genius. I'm gonna need to write that down for when I have kids one day.'

'You want to bring children into this hellfire world?' I ask before shoving an embarrassingly huge chonk of chocolate into my pie hole. Somehow being around River feels comfortable. Like I can be myself without worry.

'Isn't that the American dream?' he asks between bites. 'Graduate, find your dream job, a romantic partner, buy a house, then pop out a few new personalities onto the earth and hope they don't become serial killers or Kanye West.'

The laugh that leaves my lips earns our waiter's attention as he delivers our appetizers.

'One fry, one ring. Shall we encourage this laughter and get you two fresh drinks?'

'How'd you get here?' River asks.

'Uber. You?'

'Also an Uber. In that case, yes, good sir, keep the drinks coming!'

The drink I ordered is so sweet I practically pucker after each sip. But considering it's full of vodka, the taste bud surprise also lessens with each sip. River is drinking a tropical drink filled with vodka, schnapps, and triple sec. It's a berry-flavored sweet and sour thing that he knocked back pretty quickly before our appetizers were even served.

'To answer your question before: I don't know for sure if I want kids,' River backtracks. 'At one point I was on board with it. I mean, it'd be cool to have a mini-me, but truthfully, they seem like a lot of work.'

'As someone who babysat often as a teen, I think parents should be paid by the hour for having kids, that's how much work they are. Instead you just dish money out constantly and hope they stay alive.'

The front door not far from us dings open with hungry customers.

Our waiter drops our fresh drinks at our table. 'I'll check on you two later,' he says.

'This pie,' River swoons between bites. 'It's totally what I nee—' He stops talking, his eyes locked on the people being seated in the booth behind me. Slowly, the color drains from his face, and his fork clinks against the glass plate as he drops it.

'Fuck, fuck, fuckety, fuck, fuck, fuck,' he grumbles

into his fist. He sits back in his seat, now rubbing his hands over his thighs with a heavy sigh.

'What's going on?' I ask, a little worried about his sudden outburst.

Before he can answer and sooner than I can think of any follow-up questions, a female voice interrupts us.

'River!' The woman seems thrilled to have bumped into him. He, not so much.

He clears his throat excessively. 'Caitlin,' he says flatly. 'And uh, Derek.' That last name seems to roll off his tongue violently. 'This is just fucking perfect,' he says under his breath.

'How are you?' The tall brunette moves from her table to ours, forcing River to slide over and allow her to join us. He scoots to the wall uncomfortably, visibly trying to keep a distance between them as she invades his space without concern.

'I've survived. Thanks for asking, five years later. How are you? Things look...' He glances to their table, where Derek is softly rocking a baby carrier in the center of their table while ignoring us. 'Is that a baby?'

'Yeah.' Caitlin beams, pulling her hands to her chest as if she just adores this kid. 'Little Phoenix.

He's three months old and just the best baby ever. So adorbs; he's Derek's mini.'

Adorbs? I'm not enjoying this woman already and not just because she's making my company uncomfortable in a way he's starting to sweat.

River's head snaps her way, horror on his face. 'You named him Phoenix? Seriously?'

She nods her head with a confused look. 'Just because we broke up doesn't mean I didn't still love the name.'

He nods exaggeratedly. 'Right yeah, that makes sense, 'cause using a name your ex suggested isn't weird at all.'

Caitlin shakes her head as if River is an annoying child. 'You didn't invent the name Phoenix, Riv. Plus, it was so long ago. Who's even still thinking about that?'

As a witness of this not-so-welcome reunion, I'd say River's still thinking about whatever the 'it' she's referring to is. While he's stunned into silence, she turns her attention to me.

'Who's this?'

'This?' River asks as if he's so distracted in his own head that he's forgotten I'm even here. He motions my way. 'This is uh...'

Based on his reaction to her I'd say things didn't end well between them, and they were serious enough five years ago to name their future children. Also, they don't run into one another often. He needs my help here.

'Hi!' I chirp, extending a hand her way. 'I'm Jade, River's girlfriend.'

His eyes meet mine, and although a hint of panic is visible at first, his shoulders drop as he relaxes.

'Girlfriend?' Caitlin asks, suddenly interested, shaking my hand over the table.

I realize I'm a lady, and handshakes aren't really my 'thing', but this woman's hand went limp as she took mine as though she was expecting me to kiss the ring she's wearing. *You're not the Pope, sweetheart.*

'I was beginning to think you'd never move on,' she says, nudging River's shoulder with hers playfully but the way leans away from her like she's got a contagious disease says he's not in a playful mood around this woman.

'Because I've spent five years circling you like the sun?' he huffs. 'No. You're not even a thought in my mind, woman, just old news no one wants to read. For the record, I've had plenty of girlfriends over the last five years. Double digits, easy...' His speech slows as he realizes this probably isn't the look he was going for.

'It hasn't been that many, hun,' I interrupt. 'By the way, did I just say girlfriend? Ugh, I'll never get used to this,' I lie. 'I mean fiancée. Darling River proposed recently, but the ring didn't fit. We're picking it up next week, and I can't wait. He designed it specially for me, spent a fortune, and it is *to die for*. Emerald cut, a full carat, and absolutely flawless.' I gush over the ring I hoped I'd be wearing by now – the one I expected Conner to be interested in buying. I have a photo of it on my fridge. You know what they say, manifest the things you want. I'm desperately trying.

River's face lights up with a grin and he gives me a slight nod, encouraging me to continue the act.

'One carat?' the woman asks, slowly removing her hands from the tabletop. Her barely there glare of a diamond on her finger inspired me to go big and River looks relieved I did.

'Yep,' he says. 'Only the best for the most beautiful, amazing woman on the planet,' he says, taking my hand and pulling it to his lips, kissing the exact spot an engagement ring would go, just like Conner did the day he proposed. But this feels different. We're just acting out a scenario here, yet it feels more real now than it did when Conner did it. How's that possible?

'That's great,' Caitlin says, obviously not meaning

it. 'I'm so glad you finally found your person. If anyone deserves happiness, it's you. Shall we make this reunion interesting and have a little double date?'

'No,' River practically barks, making Caitlin jump and the baby behind me fuss. 'No, no, we uh, we're celebrating our first anniversary.' He motions between us frantically. 'It's kind of a big deal, and the last thing I need is to be staring at your faces.' His gaze shoots towards the irritated man sitting directly behind me.

'If you don't mind...' He scoots Caitlin's way, practically shoving her out of the booth and onto the floor, but somehow she saves it. 'We're going to finish this at the bar. Where no children are allowed, and it sounds like yours needs you...' The baby fusses louder, and Derek looks completely clueless as he glances back at Caitlin.

While she's preoccupied, River starts grabbing things from our table. His drink, his fries, the pie plate, nodding for me to grab my stuff too. If he breaks into a sprint, I'm going to insist on hearing this story.

'Sorry,' I apologize. 'We didn't realize they're playing, uh...' I glance through the transparent wall overlooking the bar area. Every television is filled with some game. '*SportsCenter*,' I say. 'Wouldn't want to miss that.'

'You're going to watch *SportsCenter* during your anniversary celebration?' Caitlin asks, her eyebrows shooting up her forehead.

'Of course I am. I'm his soon-to-be wife. We do everything together,' I say, bumping my hip to his.

River nods, our hands now full of food and drinks. 'She does all the things – clean, dirty, and then some,' he brags, leading us away from our original table and into the bar, somewhat walled off from the rest of the place.

'It was good to see you,' Caitlin calls after us.

'Pffttt... It was better not seeing you,' River says under his breath. 'I can't believe we just ran into that woman.' Once we've got our food back in front of us and are seated at the bar, he turns my way. 'Or that you just did what you did. How did you know...?'

I'm a little surprised at what I did too, honestly. It was one of those follow-your-gut moments, and I went with it.

I hold up my fork, going for more pie. 'When you lost all color to your face, I figured she was a person you weren't on the best terms with, and it was quite obvious she was an ex. Running into exes is like hell on earth. I couldn't let you go down like that.'

He grins shyly. 'You have no idea how much I appreciate that.'

'It's no problem,' I say casually. 'I have this rule, no matter what the truth is, if I run into an ex, I'm happier than he is. Basically, I talk until he seems irritated. So, I went with that technique. If she's happy, you're happier.' I glance back through the glass wall to see Caitlin staring our way. 'Just play the part, sweetheart.' I link my arm through his, planting a kiss on his cheek.

'Are you serious?' he asks, surprise in his voice. 'You're just going to help me out? What happened to Conner is the best man ever?'

'Conner has gone radio silent. That's actually why I invited you here tonight.'

'Oh yeah?'

I nod. 'We can talk about that later, though. For now, dish on Caitlin. What's the story, morning glory?'

'Nope,' he says through a nervous chuckle. 'I've forbidden myself from ever reliving that story. Let's just say Caitlin and I were in a relationship for a few years in college. Things were...' He hesitates as though he's picturing it and it's not great. '*So* good, progressing the way relationships do. Or so I thought. Unexpectedly a string of lies and misfortunes created the perfect storm, along with the most volatile break-up I've ever had. Until tonight, I haven't seen her since.'

'Yikes,' I say, pulling an onion ring off the stack. 'So, we hate Caite. I'm on board.'

He laughs softly, shoving fries into his mouth possibly to prevent any more talking. For the next few minutes, the two of us focus on our food and drinks.

Finally, I lift my drink. 'We need to make a toast, considering she's over there watching us.'

'Excellent idea.'

'To your heartbreak and living through seeing her again. Love bites, that much I know.'

River lifts his drink, tapping it to mine. 'Def Leppard themselves couldn't have said it better,' he says, casually glancing around the room, a sadness falling over him when his gaze reaches Caitlin's table.

This woman broke his heart. It's all over his face. I hardly know the guy but I already don't like her just because she hurt this sweetheart of a man. Is this how he feels about Conner? If so, I guess I get it now.

9

RIVER

'Wanna share an Uber?' I ask, figuring, why not? Save us both some money.

'That's almost as good as the coupon you refused to let me use.'

'You saved me from catching up with a part of my life I never wanted to rethink. The least I could do is pay for our anti-date. Which, by the way, is something I usually avoid at all costs, voluntarily paying. You must be special,' I say with a wink.

We're standing outside the restaurant; she's in her squirrel-skin coat and looks adorable in the ridiculous thing. Even her purse is quirky. Red lips. I love it.

'I'm the most special girl ever, don't you know?' she asks with a laugh.

'Has your boyfriend ever called you special?' I'm just curious.

'*Fiancé*,' she corrects me. 'And no.' The words leave her lips softly, almost regretfully.

I frown, shaking my head with disappointment. I want to tell her to dump that tool, but she's still holding on to him like she's all in, and I'm not sure why, considering the red flags are waving in the wind like a damn tornado is approaching.

Once our car arrives, we both get into the back seat, strapping on our seat belts.

'To her place first,' I say, wanting to ensure she gets home safely.

'I didn't expect you to be such a gentleman if I'm honest.'

'Why not?' I ask. 'Am I not when I'm at the bar?'

'No, you are, to me. But I thought you were being polite, so I didn't spit in your drink.'

I laugh out loud. 'You do that?'

She looks guilty as fuck. 'I mean, I work in a bar wearing a bikini top and grass skirt. I can't say I haven't.'

'If you have, they probably deserved it.'

We go back to silence, but she speaks after sitting through a couple of red lights. 'Remember when I said I invited you to dinner to talk about something?'

'Yep.'

'Well, there is something. You're a guy near Conner's age, and I need guy advice. For scientific purposes.'

I side-eye her. 'You're a fan of science, eh?'

She shrugs. 'I had one of those chemistry kits as a kid. And a microscope. Does that count?'

'As did I. Squished ants under a microscope aren't pretty.'

She grins. 'I guess that makes us both amateur scientists. So, question one, how old are you?' She's got the notes app opened on her phone as if she's writing all this down in proper scientific form.

'Twenty-nine,' I answer honestly.

She cocks her head. 'Is that like a forever twenty-nine or a legit I'm almost thirty, shit?'

'Not sure which of those is worse, but for "science", I'll go with the latter.'

'You're older than Conner, but I think you'll still work.'

'Older also equals wiser. I won't be doing the stupid shit he is because I've already done it.'

'I do see a slightly more mature River when we're alone.'

She noticed that, did she? I'm not all jokes and ridiculousness. Not when I vibe with someone romantically. Not that this is what she and I are, but I kind of wonder if we could be.

'Tit for tat, girl – how old are *you*?'

'How old do you think I am?' she asks with a coy smile.

'Would you like me to guess your weight next?' I laugh and then shake my head. 'No way am I playing that game. I know you're at least twenty-one because you're a barkeep.'

She lets out a slightly tipsy laugh. 'A barkeep?' she asks. 'What century do you live in?'

I balk. 'What is everyone's problem with the word barkeep? Mercy makes fun of it too. I think it's a cool as fuck word. It makes you sound like a badass who takes no one's shit. I mean, why bar*tender*? That puts you at the same status as coat-tender, chicken-tender, tender-ly. I don't see you like that at all.'

'How *do* you see me?' she asks.

She gets distracted in conversations as easily as I do. 'Let's put all loaded questions on the back burner, and you answer my question first. Age, woman?'

'Twenty-six. A total adult.'

'Legally.'

She chuckles. 'You say that as if you fall into the same category.'

'I do. Twenty-five, possibly even to seventy-five,

I'll likely never be what others consider an "adult". I tried it once, and no, thank you.'

'You *look* like an adult; that's something.'

'Oh, physically, I'm completely a man,' I say, lowering my voice to get my point across. '*Ev-er-y* part of me...'

'Ahh,' she says with a wide grin. 'There it is. You're a teenager in a man's body. Are you also the guy who laughs at farts?'

Her eyes are a little glassed over from earlier drinks, and she's way more easily amused than usual. My ego likes that she thinks I'm funny.

'I'm the guy who will laugh at the *word* fart. Fart. Balls. Boners. All funny. Why exclude them from our vocab? They're hilarious, so I sprinkle them into conversations along with other ridiculousness that I won't spill right this second because I can't show you just how weird I am yet. A little at a time; a man must have some secrets.'

'In total transparency,' she says, lifting a finger. 'I laughed my way through sex ed in middle school with a couple of boys, and we got sent to in-school detention for a private class taught by the weirdo football coach/PE teacher, Mr Knix. He fumbled trying to put a condom on a banana, and only managed to get it half rolled on, then couldn't get it off.'

She realizes what she's said. 'The banana,' she quickly corrects herself. 'He couldn't get the condom off the banana.' She slaps a hand to her forehead playfully, obviously a bit tipsy and cute as fuck.

'How were your condom skills?'

'It was like I'd done it in another life. They were all impressed.'

I nod, attempting not to picture that, but the more I'm with the woman, the more I do.

'We're like one soul, girl. I got detention for a month when I was thirteen because I sketched out elaborate genital drawings copied from the health book. The principal called my mom to "chat" about my newfound hobby, and she assured them that I'd be grounded. However, my parents were pretty open with us kids about things like that, so those drawings are now framed in my dad's office. Like medical genitalia maps drawn by a kid who'd never visited a vagina.'

This has her in complete giggles. 'Would this make you an "expert" in the subject?' she asks, pulling herself together.

Could this conversation be a slippery slope? Hell yeah. If she didn't have a fiancé she's tied to. That said, I'm still answering her question.

'Are we talking an expert in drawing them or in

general? 'Cause the drawings were bad. But face to – *ya know* – I know what I'm doing.'

The look on her face is part amusement, part shock that I said what I said, and – maybe this is just me hoping – but a little bit of wonder? She laughs, then stops, then laughs again. 'Is it hot in here?' She shrugs off her coat.

'I think it's the spicy conversation,' our driver, Jacob, says, glancing at the two of us in the rearview mirror.

We both grimace, knowing a stranger is super into our somewhat 'spicy' conversation, but that's the risk you take hiring a guy you don't know to drive you around.

'Maybe we should stick to my science experiment,' she suggests.

Ya made it awkward, Jacob. Well done, dumbass. While I internally lecture myself on thinking before speaking because I'm sure I didn't help the conversation stay clean and shiny, she gives me the rundown on all the Conner bullshit that happened last week. This is a Jade I'm not used to. She's no longer gushing over him. She's more crushed he's not speaking in more than emojis. I don't blame her.

I scrunch my face, genuinely disappointed in the guy. 'Those aren't even sexual, and this guy's your fiancé?' I balk. 'If you were my girlfriend, you'd get sugar, spice, and everything nice. *Not* emojis.'

The two of us stare at one another awkwardly. Fuck, what is wrong with me? First, I talk about being an X-rated child artist, and now I say the words, 'if you were my girlfriend'? *Jesus, River. You'll be lucky if you ever see this woman again.*

Jade raises an eyebrow. 'Isn't that an old nursery rhyme for how girls are made? Boys are snakes, snails, and puppy dog tails?'

I blow out a breath. Thank God she's going to pretend I didn't say any of it. I nod, confirming she's right.

'Yes, and that makes zero fucking sense. I shriek like a girl when snakes are involved.' I shoot her a playful glare. 'Tell no one about that, calamity Jade. I like to pretend I'm scared of nothing, and as my friend, you're required to uphold that lie.'

'Cross my heart and hope to die.' She does the movement with the words. 'I'd never let anyone know long slithering reptiles make you shriek.'

I roll my eyes playfully. 'Does boys being made of snails not freak you out? Ew – snails are just slugs with homes on their backs. I am not a slug. And don't even get me started on the puppy dog tails. If someone out there is legit collecting puppy dog tails, it's highly likely they've also got women in freezers in their basement.'

'You've thought this through,' she says, clearly amused.

'I've got one of those overactive minds. They call it ADD. Overthinking some of these "stories", I realized nursery rhymes are just a bunch of creepy bullshit that someone thought was genius to teach kids lessons, and they're scary as fuck. I mean, look at Jack and Jill. Hey kids, wanna hear a story about a sibling pair whose physical labor killed them both in a tumble down a steep hill? It *rhymes*...' I sing out the last two words, clearly intoxicated.

Jade giggles loudly, making our driver glance back at us in the rearview mirror again.

'Our conversation is off the rails, but I like it. You're fun, River. I do have one question, though.'

'Shoot.'

'*How* has some woman not locked you down yet? You're so...' She thinks about her words here, and when she's thought too long, I take over, worried that whatever leaves her lips won't be flattering.

'Pretty sure the words you're looking for are unconventionally charming,' I say, leaning into her and bumping my shoulder to hers. 'Now, do you want to know what I think about Corndog and his emoji attack or what?'

'*Conner*,' she corrects me. 'I'm not ready to badmouth him.'

I smirk. 'Well, I am, so prepare yourself.'

We're headed through the Highway 26 tunnels into the city, and when we emerge, the driver turns up the radio for a Neil Diamond song I'm familiar with, 'Love on the Rocks'.

'I'd like to dedicate this song to your relationship. Blast it, Jacob.' Our driver humors me and turns the song up, revealing that he's a music fan, too, and has decent speakers.

'I don't even know this song!' Jade yells over the music.

'You don't know Neil Diamond? My God, woman. He's a legend. I'm going to need to introduce you to some stuff.'

'Aren't you a little young to be head of the Neil Diamond fan club?' she asks, totally enjoying this.

I laugh. 'My dad's in the fan club, so whenever we got out the karaoke machine – I'm from a musical, sometimes obnoxious family – he'd belt one of Neil's songs out, and I learned to love him. The guy is like Wayne Newton legendary; they're Vegas-performance famous.'

'So is Celine Dion,' Jade says. 'Does that mean you're singing "My Heart Will Go On" next?'

'Blech, no. But maybe one day I'll serenade you with Britney Spears, another Vegas God. Who doesn't love her?'

Jade nods her head. 'Now, *she* is a legend of your time.'

'Until I was eighteen, I fell asleep to her on my ceiling. Seriously, though, this was Neil's number one song, and I feel like it could be the theme to your current "engagement".'

With the buzz settling in nicely and her suggestion of me singing along, I impress the girl with my ability to remember nearly all the lyrics. After a few lines, she and Jacob encourage me to continue. Jacob is singing along too, so he and I do a full-out duet performance in his Uber car, bouncing in our seats. Jade doesn't know the words, but her laughter fills the car, and something inside me is so thrilled with this. I've never seen her this happy around Conner. But then again, he's probably never sung a ridiculous song to her like I am. We all moan when the song ends and moves on to something less cool.

'Now that that's over, let's return to my thoughts on Corndog. I think your relationship has been on the rocks since day one. Why didn't you break up before he left?'

'Because we're in love,' she says as if trying to convince herself.

I shake my head, flashing her a suspicious smile. 'Not after two months. You were in the honeymoon phase of infatuation.'

'No way,' she argues. 'I'm in total love with the guy.'

'Alright, what do you love about him?'

She opens her mouth to answer, but nothing leaves her lips, causing her to slump back in her seat with a huff.

'If you truly loved the guy, you wouldn't have hesitated. You deserve someone way better than Conrad Francis Walsh III.'

Confusion fills her face. '*How* do you know his whole name?'

Shit. Now I have to come clean with her, or it'll blow up in the future and fuck me over. 'I didn't know how to tell you this and want you to know I didn't exactly agree. I thought he was nuts and wanted him to get lost.'

'When was he nuts?'

'The night before he left. You were distracted by

customers, and he legit asked me to "keep an eye on you" while he was gone.'

'What? Like a stalker?' she snaps. 'I don't need a babysitter. I'm not a child.'

Perhaps after we've both been drinking wasn't the time to tell her this news.

'I'm sorry I blurted that out. But you should know what kind of guy he really is,' I say, reading her reaction. 'My sister was this love blind at one point and wasted a decade of her life on the wrong man. Now she regrets all of it. But I'm no expert on any-thing, love included. All I know is that there are three things you can never get back; people after death, words spoken, and time wasted.' I lift a finger with each one. 'You're a nice girl, sweet, funny, gor-geous, all that shit. I think Corndog is wasting your time.'

Her brows stitch together as she thinks this over. 'But he proposed.'

'Yeah, that part I haven't figured out yet. Personal-ly,' I say, taking a breath, ready to let the truth fly as usual, but for some reason, I think twice about it this time. I don't want to hurt Jade – not even a little. 'I think he wanted to get laid this summer, and being in mourning, you probably responded just as he'd hoped to all his love-bombing bullshit.'

'You think he love-bombed me?' she asks, worry on her face.

'He was the perfect man, swept you off your feet, then once he got what he wanted, it all stopped. That's love-bombing, and yeah, I think he did that.'

'How didn't I see it?' she asks herself.

'It's those damn rose-colored glasses we wear as we fall in love. Some things aren't worth forgiving, and this is one of them for me. But that's just my take. I know you love him, so despite what I think, this is a decision you'll have to make alone.'

She sighs heavily, pointing out the window. 'This is me,' she says to the driver.

I get out of the car once he's parked at the curb, extending a hand to her while asking the driver to stick around to drive me home.

'How much do I owe you for the ride and advice?' she asks.

'Uh, nothing?'

'I thought you said you were cheap?' she asks playfully.

'Usually, I am. But there's something about you, calamity Jade. I can't put my finger on it yet, but after tonight, I'll buy you dessert, drinks, and appetizers any day of the week. Just say the word.'

She purses her lips as if deep in thought. 'Okay,

well, since you wouldn't let me use my coupon for dinner *or* pay for our Uber, how about this?' she asks. 'One of my mom's favorite movies is playing at an old theater in the Hawthorne district. Her, my little sister Laney, and I used to go every year. Since Mom's no longer here and you're a fan of things older than you, maybe you'd like to join us, unromantically? My treat.'

The truth didn't scare her away, and she's inviting me out with her again, with her sister. Unromantically, of course, but I feel like that's something.

I rock back on my heels, standing on the sidewalk facing her. 'I could probably squeeze that into my busy schedule. You've got my number, text me details, and I'll meet you there.'

'Great!' she says with a smile. 'It's not a date.' She laughs.

'Perfect,' I say, backing away as she opens her gate by typing in a code. 'Oh!' I say, stopping her in her tracks just after she's in the courtyard of her building. 'Tongue. Moisture droplets. Never symbol. Send that back to Corndog. There's no way he won't reply.'

'Dirty, I like it. I haven't tried that yet.' She pulls her phone from the pocket of her fur coat, tapping the screen. 'Update you with the results when I get them?' she asks, flashing me her lit phone as proof she's sent them.

'I won't hold my breath, but yeah, send me his response. I'm curious.'

'Thanks for dinner,' she says. 'And all the laughing. I'm excited to see you again for the movie.'

She's excited to see me again? That's not a bad sign.

'You're welcome. I'll see ya,' I say, meandering outside the gate until she disappears inside her building, then heading back to my Uber. She's like no one I've ever met, and I want to know more.

10

RIVER

Part of my night last night was amazing. The rest, Jesus, when will invisibility become a thing? What terrible fucking luck to run into Caitlin. Five years spent avoiding that woman, and the one night I'm out with a legit friend of the female sort, she walks in with trash magnet, Derek, the guy she ran to when things between us went wrong.

My mind was legit blown with the baby thing, to the point that I only slept peacefully for maybe an hour last night. The rest was spent in chaotic night-mares that followed the *Groundhog Day* pattern, cir-cling as our relationship progressively declined on a loop. Worst. Movie. Ever.

Then there was the part where I couldn't stop

thinking about Jade. But when I'd convinced myself not to go there because she's engaged and trying to fix things with her fiancé, on came the nightmare again. Round and round that went.

I've had about fifteen cups of coffee to keep myself awake today. Currently, I'm running on caffeine, booze, and all the tiny pretzel bread sandwiches a guy could want. Mom wanted to go catered for this little photoshoot/rehearsal, and since she offered to handle it, I'm not disappointed in the snack bar she's paid a fortune for. However, she did make me handle the drinks.

'You look tired, Riv,' Mom says as she looks over the food table, picking out a few things.

'Long night. I'm exhausted,' I say.

'I know that feeling,' Rico, her drummer, says. 'It's rough. I got some blow if you wanna—'

'*No*,' I cut him off as he's reaching into his jacket for something. 'And considering your age, you better just say no too, dude.'

'My age?' he bellows, clearly offended. 'You think you could do this at my age?' He storms onto the stage, making himself comfortable behind his drum set and banging out a solo Phil Collins would be proud of.

I'm in no mood for attitude today, so I'm not arguing with him. 'You win at the drum wars, Rico. Considering you freaks agreed to this gig with a ridiculous rider, I get at least one rule. Here it is. Listen closely. *Do not die of a cocaine overdose on my time.*' I wave a finger at all four band members, stopping at Mom. 'If I find out *you* did "blow", this documentary will come to a screeching halt, young lady.'

'I've never done cocaine,' she insists, with a chuckle that says otherwise, and I really, *really* do not want to know.

We're in downtown Portland at the Crystal Ballroom. A popular small concert venue that's hired Mom's alter ego, Penny Candy, to play at their New Year's Eve party. It's a giant old ballroom (venue capacity is about 1,500, but that's crammed in shoulder to shoulder, front to back) on the third floor with bouncy wooden floors meant for dancing, a lifted stage, huge windows covered in black-out drapes, and even a balcony at the far end of the room. The rounded dome ceilings are the most impressive – enormous crystal chandeliers and ornate molding, including creepy faces that observe the room from all angles. Vintage elaborate Victorian-style circular paintings are dotted along one wall. It's pretty incredible, like a piece of the past that hasn't yet crumbled away to eternity or been replaced by overpriced condos. Our current society doesn't make buildings like this anymore. If only the walls could talk, I'd be interested in what they had to say.

I'm not sure how I finagled them into it, but this show will be our closing scene for the documentary. We'll announce a US tour starting next year live on the news, as Portland was chosen for one of the national news station NYE check-ins. This is a massive deal for Mom and me – the guy behind the camera and the creative brains of this thing. It'll be my solo documentary debut and her attempt at a career comeback with a bang.

Today the place is empty as this is just a rehearsal that I've turned into a combined photo shoot, hopefully to get her new album cover shot. I say empty, but where the band goes, as do a dozen other folks who cater to their every need. Photographers, lighting folks, band members, personal assistants and spouses, make-up people, hair stylists, venue employees, caterers, and randos I've never seen, so truthfully, it's a pretty packed house.

Despite what Mom wanted, we aren't going full-out original Penny Candy here. That would be like fishing for a Gen Z'er with Gen X on the hook.

They'd never bite. We're going for nostalgia meets the 2020s. Mature, but still with that hint of when the world worshipped her.

For now, I'm standing at the food table, my usual position of choice at parties, making myself busy with these sandwiches and coffee while overseeing everything getting set up to shoot.

'Hey,' Staci, Penny Candy's guitarist, approaches the photographer, Dale, who is busy setting up his equipment near the stage. She's aged pretty well. They all have, really. Staci is tall, slender, and brunette with a Paula Abdul aura; my mom is her version of Debbie Harry.

'We ain't exactly in our twenties anymore,' she says to Dale while I eavesdrop. 'You're shooting this from our best sides, right? Don't be shy if we need to snap a thousand photos to get a good one. Keep that in mind, kiddo.' She bumps her fist against his shoulder as she awaits his answer.

Dale glances back at me, lifting a single eyebrow. I nod, shoving my lips out, hoping he gets my 'say whatever she needs to hear' telepathy.

'Yeah,' he says. 'Best sides are my specialty.'

'Excellent,' Staci says, happy with his answer.

'Riv,' Mom calls from the stage on one side of the

room. 'It's too quiet in here. We need mood music for the photo shoot.'

'Yeah,' I say. 'That's why I brought a band in.' I motion at the band members meandering about. 'Maybe you guys should consider playing something if you're bored.' That'll at least keep them from doing blow and annoying the crew.

Mom turns into someone else entirely when she morphs into Penny Candy. Suddenly, I'm her personal assistant. She and her band are a little demanding, considering they haven't had a release in twenty years. In the rider to get them even to do this gig, I had to shop at five stores to supply just the drinks I was in charge of. They wanted Evian water only. Blackberry Clearly Canadian, which I had to special order a month ago from Canada. Crystal Pepsi, which no longer exists, so I've filled some Pepsi bottles with Sprite, printed old labels from the internet, taped them to the bottles, and called it good. They've yet to notice, and one bottle is nearly gone already. Last but not the one to forget, as Rico reminded me twenty times via text this month, is Fireball whiskey, an entire case. That shit is nasty.

Mom insisted we all did shots when we got here, and I've never been one to turn down a free shot, until they got to number three, and I had to fall out because if I didn't, my throat was going to turn to lava and hack it right back at them. I didn't expect to swallow a mouthful of fiery hot cough syrup this early in the morning. It may have burned off my taste buds, as it's all I'm tasting now despite the three sandwiches I've eaten.

'How's it going, Riv?' a familiar voice asks as Dad stops next to me, having just arrived, still in blue scrubs, as he's got a couple of patients in the birthing unit today and is on call 24/7.

'Why can nothing be easy? Look at this list.' I hand Dad my iPad. 'Every single detail includes unrealistic "requirements". They forced me to rent a freaking smoke machine. Were they this high maintenance back in the day?'

He shakes his head. 'Back in the day, venues offered this stuff voluntarily. They'd made it far enough into the industry to be seen as royalty. Their presence alone guaranteed the concert venues would make bank off them. That's how they discovered they liked the perks of a rider.' He smirks as he reads through the list. 'They're reliving their youth, son. One day you'll get it.'

'I guessed that when I saw Mom's request to "recreate original gold album cover" and "get a photo of the band holding this".' I grab the decades-old MTV music award from the table and shake it in the air. 'Should I tell them this thing would be considered an antique nowadays?'

'No,' he says swiftly, handing back my iPad. 'In your mother's mind, she won that yesterday.' His gaze is on her as he speaks, a smile curling at his lips with each passing second. They've been together for thirty-something years, and he still looks at her utterly smitten, as if she's his entire world.

I've always wanted to experience feeling that way about someone else. At one point, I thought I'd found it. But life kicked me in the balls that time and took a second shot last night at dinner.

My parents met while Dad worked as a backup dancer in the music industry. He was well-known and appeared in countless music videos with various artists. Even to this day, he keeps up on all the dancing TikTok trends and never fails to entertain fans of the 'DancingDrJohn' account.

He doesn't have as many dance partners these days, so guess who's been recruited to participate in the videos not filmed in his office with his staff? Me, Mom and Dax. It's our weird thing. Music and dancing have been a part of my life since I was just a tiny sperm building my strength to win the battle that brought me here. Please don't ask me to go against you in a dance off 'cause I'll undoubtedly dance your face off. Dad's talent was passed down to me, but sadly Hollyn didn't get it. Dax has been working with her to spare her some embarrassment during the first dance for their wedding. She's got some work to do and only four more months to do it.

Finally, the band stops fucking around, and somehow they've been wrangled to the stage and encouraged to start playing. The lights dim, the sound and light guys take over, and Rico, the greasy, aging man with a head full of curly black hair, permanent forehead wrinkles, and multiple gold chains around his neck, wastes no time and beats out the intro to one of their most popular songs. Mom immediately transforms into her performing self, dancing around the stage, lost in the music.

For the next couple of hours, I order people around, and Mom bosses me around, micromanaging my every move, but by the end of the day, I feel like we've gotten somewhere even though Dad has had to wake me up multiple times as I nodded off.

It's well-known in my family that I could sleep through a marching band in my apartment. So dozing off here, where a band blasts music through the speakers ten feet from me, is no problem.

'What's wrong with you?' Dad asks from his spot on the bench next to me where we're watching (or sleeping) through the rehearsal.

'I didn't sleep much last night,' I say, dragging my hand down my face. I wave down one of the many personal assistants meandering about the room, none of them mine, but since I'm the boss here, they come to my every wave.

'Can I get you something, Mr Matthews?'

'Mr Matthews is my father.' I throw a thumb his way. 'Call me River. Can you bring me the biggest cup of coffee you can find? Four sugars, a shot of creamer.'

'Sure thing,' the perky young man says, spinning on his heel and heading towards the food and drink table.

'Why didn't you sleep?' Dad asks.

I rub the side of my face, realizing I didn't even shave this morning; I was that tired. 'I, uh, ran into Caitlin last night.'

Dad's eyes go wide. 'Ouch,' he says with a grimace. 'How'd that go?'

I sigh heavily. 'About as well as you're picturing. She brought the tool bag, and they have a fucking baby.' I realize after I've said it that I sound incredibly irritated by this. Why? It all happened so long ago.

Dad's face says it all. I'm not about to tell him the details because those are fuzzy even for me. My heart has told my brain to block it out, but it hasn't quite happened yet.

'The whole damn thing played in my head night-terror style while I slept. It was like reliving it all over again.'

He rests his hand on my knee as he used to when I was a teen as he'd prepare to give me some speech he was dreading.

'Before you say anything, I'm cool.' I wave his concern away, standing from the bench to wake myself up. I pace a few steps back and forth, pulling my hair into the black elastic band always around my wrist and securing it at the back of my head. 'I'm completely over it, but momentarily it did feel like a brick was thrown through my sternum with the shock of finally having a run-in with her five years later. I knew it would happen eventually but didn't expect what I felt when it did.'

'What did you fee—'

I hold up a hand. 'Bad things, Dad. Terrible, horrible, really nasty things. I also felt like a freaking loser, so I'm trying to block it out.'

Dad crosses his arms over his chest as he reclines on the bench. 'You're not a loser. Caitlin chose the life she did. You probably got lucky.'

'Maybe,' I say, not sure luck is a part of that story at all.

'My lack of sleep was a tad more complicated. I bring life into the world, and currently, those lives are being stubborn as hell. Thanks for asking,' he says sarcastically, a smirk on his face. His way of changing the subject has always been to talk about work. No guy wants to discuss a woman giving birth beside him.

'To womankind, you're kind of like God,' I joke.

He lifts a shoulder, smirking as if he agrees. 'Only difference is, I didn't father the children,' he laughs.

I scrunch my face at the thought of it. Brand new nightmare material, my dad fathering every baby he delivers. Gross.

'Is that a wrap?' Mom asks after they've gone through their entire set several times.

'That's my line, Mom, and not until I've looked at the photos.'

'Let's do another shot to celebrate,' she says, not meaning a photo shot. The four band members gather around their case of Fireball that I will end up with afterward because they're not exactly the drinkers they once were.

These photos turned out great. I think we even have cover material here. Wow. I may actually finish this documentary on time.

11

JADE

What a night. I lay in bed and thought about everything River and I talked about for a long time last night. Our conversations often seemed to wander into flirtatious zones, but he eventually answered my questions. Now I'm stressing if he's right about Conner, and I'm just a huge idiot.

Another part of me wonders why he didn't kiss me that night so long ago. There was a chance we could have been more, but we both missed it. Now I'm curious if it's still there somewhere. He's so much fun. I never laugh as much as I do when he's around. But that feels wrong considering I have a fiancé. Like the time Monica told Chandler a guy at her work was the funniest man she'd ever met and Chandler proceeded to be offended then told every joke he knew. Would Conner be offended that another man makes me laugh? At this point, I doubt it.

This morning, I'm headed to a restaurant in SE Portland called Jam. When Laney and I moved out, my parents created this once-a-month breakfast outing as a family catch-up date. Just the smell of the place reminds me of my mom, and as I drive, I dread walking in to see her missing from our table again.

As usual, nearly every chair is occupied. Jam is always busy, probably because the food is so freaking good. The interior is open, bright, and cheery with mint green walls, a bar counter at one end, tall house plants separating seating areas, giving patrons a bit of privacy, and local artwork covering the walls. The ceilings are high, and all the HVAC, piping, and ceiling joists are visible. I wonder what this place used to be.

'Jade!' my sister hollers without shame, waving a hand my way.

They're sitting near the windows, with cups of steaming coffee in front of them as they scan the menus in their hands. I sit at the chair beside Dad, where a full cup of joe and a menu awaits me.

'I'm *so* glad you guys can read my mind,' I say, pouring sugar and vanilla-flavored creamer into the hot black liquid before me. As I stir, I glance through the menu. Seconds after the first sip of bean juice, our waitress arrives, taking our orders.

'Are we all caffeinated enough to feel alive yet?' Dad asks after the server leaves.

'Nearly there,' I say, coffee cup practically to my lips again. 'You two started before me, so feel free to chat amongst yourselves.'

He chuckles, turning his attention to my sister sitting across from him. 'What have you been up to, Laney?'

'You mean, besides her telling you all my business...' I ask with a snap, halting my coffee drinking to stab at her with a little sisterly irritation.

Laney rolls her eyes, ignoring me altogether. 'Let's see...' she says, setting her cup on the table. 'Work, work, work, bought a pink taser – remind me to show you – more work, overtime, got my hair done.' The required hair flip after announcing she had it done cracks me up. We all do it. 'I also had my eyebrows reshaped. The left one finally grew back after the last place made it look like I'd lost it in a barbecue accident. What do you think?' she asks, her eyes on me.

'Can't even tell anymore,' I say, sincerely impressed. Her eyebrow took months to grow back. I was starting to worry it never would. I'm actually re-lieved for her. 'They look good.'

'Wait. Back up. You bought a taser?' Dad asks worriedly. 'If you're having an issue with a guy, say the word, and I'll take care of him.'

'I'm not fourteen. My daddy can't handle my problems anymore. That would be weird,' Laney in-sists. 'Besides, Jade carries around a bottle of mace that I know for a fact she's used at least once. Why aren't you worried about her?'

He laughs, but it's not humorous. 'Because if I ever get a call that one of you needs to be bailed out of jail, I'm almost certain it won't be Jade.'

I smirk her way, enjoying being the favorite child for a moment. Or at least the one he knows is mostly well-behaved. Luckily, there's no time for her to argue as our waitress approaches our table.

Oh my Lord, the sweet smell of pancakes and fruit fills my head. I didn't realize how starving I was until my plate was placed in front of me. I got my fave: fancy maddie cakes – aka three lemon ricotta pancakes topped with house-made blueberry com-pote and lemon curd. It's like a dessert for breakfast. So good.

After we've silenced our hunger by allowing our food to distract us from words, we all start to liven up.

'Do you also need a taser?' Dad asks, studying me as he works on his Bennie Hashbrowns – fancy hashbrowns topped with bacon, ham, spinach, two poached eggs, and hollandaise sauce. It's complemented with buttered sourdough toast that Dad slathers a spoonful of my blueberry compote across.

'Not yet. But I'm a good girl,' I tease Laney.

'You're boring,' she retaliates.

'I am not boring.'

Dad laughs under his breath like he always does when we girls fight. He has one brother, and no sisters, so the sister vibe took him a long time to get.

'Jade has an attack parrot that barks at dogs; she's far from boring,' he says, coming to my rescue. 'How was your non-date?'

Laney practically drops her fork from her mouth. 'You had a *date*?'

Right. I never told her. Oops.

I shake my head to correct her. 'I had an *anti-date*. With a *friend*. It was nothing.'

'What friend?'

'Just a guy from the bar whom I've befriended over the months. He's harmless and sweet, so I figured he could advise me on Conner since he's about my age.'

'And the verdict is?' she asks, as though she can't believe I went to someone besides her for advice.

'He thinks I could do better.'

Dad nods his head as if he agrees while he eats. 'I like him already. Does he think the better is him?'

'Um...'

Laney's eyes are burning through me as I consider my answer. Things did get a little flirty in the Uber last night, and I *did* pretend to be his fiancée. Are those hints that he likes me? Nah. I think he's just being nice. But maybe he does? We did have that 'moment' in the street a few months ago where I thought he would kiss me, and I'll be honest, I'd have kissed him back. But that moment fled, and now I'm engaged.

'I'm going to plead Magic 8 Ball and go with, ask again later.'

'I will ask continually until you spill everything,' she says. 'You know this. Now when do I get to meet him?'

I freeze, my fork midway to my mouth. Inviting him out with me and Laney was probably a terrible idea. She's obnoxious at times. But I asked, and he said yes, so we're in it now.

'Next week? I sort of invited him to the movie with us to pay him back for last night.'

'Pay him back for what?'

'The advice. And pie, drinks, appetizers, and the Uber ride home.' I shove the halted bite into my mouth so I can't keep talking. Why is talking about River making me uncomfortable? I don't want to tell them about our conversations.

Dad clears his throat before sipping his coffee and changes the subject. 'Any new emojis?'

'Just a couple of question marks on some I sent, which I will not reveal because they may have suggested something dirty.'

That's right, Conner didn't understand River's emojis, or at least he pretended he didn't. This whole thing is stupid. Like a fight you'd have with a boy in middle school. I grab my phone from my purse to glance at what I sent back to his confusion.

'What are the most recent you've sent?' Laney asks. If she could take my phone and do this for me, she'd love it. But since I won't allow that, I have to explain or she really will continue to pry for information until she has it.

'Praying hands, a phone, a swearing face, wind, and a black hole.'

'Which means?' Laney asks.

'Uh, praying you call so I can swear at you, ya blowhole.'

A laugh bursts from Dad, filling the whole room and turning some heads. 'That's a good one, though if he didn't understand the dirty stuff, he'll never get that message decoded. What was his response?'

'Stop sign, hospital.'

'Let me see that thing,' Laney says, snatching the phone from my hand and tapping the screen frantically.

'Laney, *no*.' I reach for my phone but she pulls it away from me.

'*Trust* me...' she insists, but I do not trust her in this scenario. When she's done, she hands the phone to our father, who pulls his reading glasses from the neckline of his shirt to see better.

'Sword, heart, man, coffin, and she signed off with my name. *Perfect*,' he says sarcastically. 'I've just threatened to kill a guy without saying the words. I'm sure that won't come back and bite me in the ass.' He's amused, though. His tone says he's proud, and his nod confirms it.

'Laney!'

'What?' she asks as if innocent. 'He didn't respond to the thing I shan't say aloud because our dad is in the room, so maybe he'll respond to a death threat from him.'

Shockingly, my phone rings almost immediately.

Both Dad and Laney glance at the screen where Conner's contact flashes. I throw up a finger, toss my napkin onto the table. Grab my phone from where Dad set it on the table, and bolt out of the restaurant to the parking lot.

'Hello?' I answer as if I don't know who it is.

'What the hell?'

'My God, Conner. You're alive! I thought maybe you'd been kidnapped and were trying to get help via emojis. But you're fine?' Yes, I'm putting on a bit of a show. My tone is angry and a little mixed with shock that Laney was finally the one to smoke him out of silence.

'You thought I'd been kidnapped? We talk every day.'

'*No*, we emoji every day. Talking consists of words, either written or spoken.'

'Jay,' he says, clearly already tired of this conversation. Or maybe just tired of me. 'I promise, I'm just busy with school. Residency is no picnic. I don't have time to flirt via text or have long, drawn-out, giggly conversations anymore.'

'Then *say* that, *Condor*. I've been worried.'

He groans a forced laugh when I use his nickname. 'You don't need to worry about me. I'm completely fine, just back to my real life, and that has me stressed, a little traumatized, and I don't want to lay it all on you.'

Back to his real life? Holy freaking spaceballs. River might be right. He wasn't serious about *anything* while he was here. I was literally something for him to 'do' while on summer break. Now that he's back to his real life, he's no longer got time to woo me, his *fiancée*. Fuck. Now I'm mad.

'How about laying anything on me? Tell me about your day, or ask about mine. *Anything*, Conner. Whatever happened to the sweet good morning and goodnight texts you used to send? You swooned me with that, and now that we're engaged, all those sweet things just stopped. Then we had the whole Masterblake incident. What am I supposed to think of your "real" life?'

'First of all...' His tone says we're fighting. Our first, besides the day he left, which had me so disheveled I didn't know how to respond. It was like he was a different person to the one I'd gotten to know. Does that guy even exist, or was it all an act? I clutch my chest suddenly because something hurts.

'Blake isn't exactly Satan on my shoulder,' he says, defending his asswipe friend. 'He's more of a free-spirited, try anything once, live in the moment kind of guy, and he certainly doesn't watch his words.

He says what he wants, but he's not influencing me. Truthfully, it's nice to be around that kind of honesty. It makes my days go by fast.'

'He's a *mean* truth-teller, though, Conner. He insulted me when we "met", and you said nothing. In fact, you just stood up for him, and *I'm* the girl you supposedly want to marry.'

He sighs heavily into the phone. 'I had a few drinks in me, Jay. I'm sorry. I apologize for both Blake's and my behavior that night.'

He's apologizing for them both? Right now, I really wish I wasn't the kind of girl to forgive people easily. But I am. I am because I've lost so many important people, and I'd never want to live with hate towards anyone and then have them die.

'Fine. I accept an apology from you, but Masterblake can kiss off.'

'Fair enough,' he says, sounding relieved. 'I'm walking to the cafeteria for my first meal in ten hours. Tell me things. How are you?'

He wants to talk. *Now?* While my dad and sister stare out the window, discussing and probably making up words that each of us is saying because that's one of their favorite games – muting the TV and making up their script. They're shockingly good at it.

'Conner, I'm fine. Life is exactly as it was before you left. However, currently, I'm at my monthly family breakfast, and I feel like I can't leave them to catch you up because it's already weird not having my mom here. I can't bail too.'

'Oh,' he says. 'I guess I've been so busy I haven't considered that you have your own life there. I get it. I'll try to get better at calling when I've got a minute. Alright?'

He'll what? I feel like I need to ask him to repeat himself, but I'm also sure I've heard what I've heard. I just don't believe it.

'Oh-kay?'

Perfect response, Jade. He'll never know you're questioning everything about your life right now.

'I promise, Jay. I love you.'

I practically drop the phone. 'I. Love. You. Too.' I say each word slowly with a hard stop and shut up just before the rise of a question mark alerts him to the fact that my emotions are everywhere.

'Talk later,' he says gently, hanging up first and leaving me speechless with the phone to my ear long after he's gone.

The sound of a fist pounding on glass wakes me up, and when I turn towards the window, Laney is sitting at the table with her hands in the air.

Right. Breakfast with my family. I feel like one of those frozen computer screens you swear at before doing the one thing you probably shouldn't do: intentionally forcing it off and rebooting it. Did Conner and I just have a hard reset?

12

JADE

I'm relieved to be at work tonight. You can't spend too much time thinking about one topic because the place is always buzzing with people and conversation. That doesn't mean Kai isn't interested in knowing exactly what is happening in my personal life. 'Did you two talk yet?' were the first words out of her mouth when we finally got a chance to breathe. I tell her all about the phone call at breakfast, including how pissed it made me, and I'm not a girl who gets mad easily. Someone's got to really push my buttons to activate pissed-off Jade.

'He *apologized*?' Kai asks, somewhat stunned. 'Was it for the weeks of being a douche or just the one night you complained about?'

I hadn't even thought of that. I guess it sort of sounded like it was just for that one night.

'I was stunned he'd called at all, especially with the threat of my father murdering him, so I'm not really sure. But he promised to call more.'

'You were stunned by his fear of death? Are you kidding? Your father is scary as hell. I for sure wouldn't want to be on his bad side. He's in a biker gang,' she reminds me.

'He's in the same gang Thomas is in. Are you scared of him?'

'I'm scared he'll fall and break a hip,' she laughs. 'Thomas doesn't count; he's elderly and adorable. Anyway, we're off-topic. *Did* Conner follow through and call you this morning?' she asks, her tone demanding an answer. She's pulling her long hair over one shoulder and readjusting our required flower behind one ear.

'No,' I say sheepishly.

'Text?' she asks, turning to me instead of staring at herself in the small mirror we use to ensure we look good throughout the night without leaving the bar unless it's for our scheduled breaks.

He *did* text. But it wasn't impressive, and if I say it out loud, Kai will undoubtedly lose her shit. She's a little like Laney in that way. I'm the most 'timid' of our friend group, even though I'm not *really*, so she and my sister like to try to 'take care of things' for me. Like I can't handle it myself.

I shake my head. Lying is easier right now.

'*Lolo kanapapiki!*' she spurts with hate.

Uh-oh. I didn't even tell the truth, and she's pissed enough that she's swearing in Hawaiian. That's never a good sign.

'What did I do?' Adam turns, questioning her, assuming she's swearing at him because that's what these two do. They insult one another (jokingly) in languages I don't speak.

'Not *you*,' she jeers, then turns to me, planting both hands on my shoulders. 'Dump. Him,' she insists. 'Seriously, this isn't how love works.'

'Kai... I want to give him a chance. He *proposed*. I feel like that's a big deal.'

She grabs my left hand and holds it in front of my face. 'But are you *really* engaged? Has he said one word about this wedding since he left?'

'No.'

'Any discussions about rings you might like?'

'No.'

'Does he even know you've already got your entire honeymoon planned out and have since you were twelve?'

She's right. I've been dreaming of the Bahamas since I was a kid, and I've done so much research I've got an itinerary that I update yearly. My love of everything tropical is why I love my job so much.

'No...' I say timidly.

'*Yeeooowww!*' A hand slaps the bar counter behind us as a catcall fills the room. 'Look at this hottie!' a male voice says. A voice I recognize but am not thrilled to hear. I turn, and it's confirmed – Declan, one of Conner's local buddies. I haven't seen any of his friends since he left. In fact, I've only met this guy a couple of times because Conner didn't really hang with his friends when I was around. We spent too much time in my bed, giggling at ridiculous things to include his friends in our world often.

'Is *every* guy he's friends with douchey?' Kai asks.

I only nod because so far, to my knowledge, the answer is yes.

'Hey, Dec.'

'*Big* Dec,' he corrects me with a laugh. A couple of buddies on either side of him laugh too. I forgot they have 'bro names'. It's so stupid.

'I'm never calling you that, so give up now.'

He frowns as if he's disappointed and hops onto a free stool beside him. 'How's our doctor boy?'

'She wouldn't know because *doctor boy* is also a

real buttpipe,' Kai answers for me, sidling up to me and grabbing what she assumes they'll order. PBR in the can. There are some people who we just know what their order will be, and usually, that's it.

Declan has a head full of curly hair, but only on top because he shaves the sides, so he looks a little like an eighties movie villain.

'That's a little harsh,' he says, defending his friend. He looks at me. 'You two are engaged; how don't you know how he is?'

I lift my shoulders. 'Seems he's not a big talker while he's away.'

'Big Dec' looks confused. 'He doesn't call you?'

'Not often. Does he call you?'

'Hell yeah, he calls me. I'm his PDX bestie. Mostly it's to tell me about the hotties at the club's he's—' Right then, mid-sentence, he groans as one of his friends elbows him in the ribs.

'*What* are you doing?' the nameless friend asks. 'That was supposed to be on the downlow.' He attempts to say this ventriloquist style, but he doesn't have the talent, so both Kai and I hear the words plainly.

'My God, drunk men are idiots,' Kai mumbles, setting the three PBRs on the counter. 'Go away. Preferably to the bar down the block.'

Declan grimaces as she walks away to help someone else. 'She's kinda bitchy.'

'She's also got ears like a bat and takes weekly Krav Maga classes, so I'd watch your words.'

'Please.' He waves a hand like he's not worried. 'You want an easy way to get my boy Condor to respond? Nudes. Send him some unprovoked. You are his fiancée; isn't that what lovers do?'

Nudes? His friends know he enjoys *nudes*? Not once has he requested them from me. So who is he requesting them from?

This is where Roman steps over. He can tell by the look on my face that I'm not enjoying these boys' company. His phone is in his hand, and the smirk on his face tells me he's overheard that last statement, or he's been listening the whole time.

'He likes nudes, does he?' Roman asks in his deep bellowing voice. 'How about dick pics? 'Cause I got some good ones. I took this one for my recent anniversary celebration. He's wearing a bow; isn't that cute?' His jolly laugh as he turns his phone Declan's way says he's enjoying this. I can only hope he's not genuinely showing them a photo of his dick, but if he is, I guess don't ask for nudes around Roman.

A grin fills my face as Roman winks at me. Declan and his friends all look horrified. 'I think we're just going to go find a table.'

'Good idea.' Roman nods, shoving his phone back into his pocket.

'Thanks,' I say softly as they leave the counter.

'No problem, sweetie. Just remember, I've been married three times, and I've learned that you don't only marry one person; you get all their family and friends as a bonus.'

Ugh. Could I deal with these people for the rest of my life? I probably *could*, but do I *want* to is the question. I feel like new engagements shouldn't be this stressful.

* * *

You up?

My phone dings on the nightstand next to me as I stare at my ceiling. Who could possibly be texting me at four in the morning? I grab it, scrolling to the text, wondering if maybe Conner has decided to make good on his promise. But nope, it's not him and to my surprise my heart races a little when I notice it's River.

Is your ceiling as boring as mine?

I'm surprised he's not out running the city. I thought that's what he did when he couldn't sleep. But I'm cool with this too. Finally, someone who makes me smile is texting me.

It is. How was work?

He's asking me about my night? Why's this so foreign to me? Oh, that's right, because my fiancé stopped doing it as soon as he left the state.

Work was… interesting. Drunk guys are something else.

LOL, don't I know it.

I don't consider you a drunk like the type I dealt with tonight. Roman had to get involved.

What are their names? I'll kick some ass.

LOL, no taking names and kicking asses. At least not yet.

I'll do it. I once spent a night in the clink because my
sister's boyfriend was a mega douche.

LOL @ the clink.

Is Corndog as funny as me?

No.

At first I hesitated sending that last word through.
Why do I feel bad saying that? It's the truth. He's not
traditionally the 'funny guy'. He's more the 'serious
about life and where he's headed' guy and I thought I
wanted that. He's driven. Now every time someone
talks about him, I'm finding out things about him
that I don't want.

You make me laugh way more than Corndog
ever has.

I wish I could see that right now. I've been a workaholic lately so making women smile hasn't been on
my priority list... until tonight.

He wishes he could see me smile right now? Well,
that's *not* a guy asking for nudes.

What the hell? I take a make-up free selfie, with a cheesy grin and send it through.

How the fuck do you look this good at four in the morning? I look like a wreck.

LOL, why thank you. Did you say wreck? Prove it, mister.

Ha! Fine, but don't compliment me, I'll think you like me or something.

Thirty second later, he texts a photo through. His hair is loose and swept to one side, and of course he's posed duck lip style.

YIKES!
LOL KIDDING! I don't hate 4 a.m. River.

We're moving into dangerous territory, girl. You have a fiancé.

No fiancé talk tonight. I'd rather fall asleep with good things on my mind.

I'm the good thing, aren't I? I fucking knew it.

I think I can see your head swelling from here.

Ha!

He didn't say what a usual douchebag guy would. 'Something's swelling.' How weird. River is a different kind of guy and it's a little refreshing honestly.

Goodnight calamity Jade. I hope you dream of whatever makes your heart happy.

Night, Riv. Thanks for the smiles. Truly.

13

RIVER

I pace just inside the theater, where I'm meeting Jade and her sister. It's an old vintage theater that only plays old movies, and for way cheaper than traditional theaters. I've been here a few times throughout my life, and it's a little like going back in time when movie-going was a big deal and not just something everyone did.

Why am I pacing, though? I'm not usually this nervous around anyone. Could it be that an incredible woman invited me to watch one of my favorite actors (John Cusack, God, there'll never be another of him) in a film she and I (and her mother) apparently both love? There's nothing weird about that, besides the fact that this movie was released in 1989, and we were born a decade later, so it probably shouldn't be on our faves list.

Sometimes, I feel like I was born in the wrong decade because the pop culture of the eighties and early nineties calls to me lover-to-lover style. Or maybe it's because my parents were at their peak, living exciting lives at that time, part of which Hols and I were on the road with them while Mom toured, so it's ingrained into me that girls (and guys) just wanna have fun.

A blast of cool air blows in as the theater's front door opens. In walks the lady of the night, wrapped in her coat of squirrels to prevent the nip of the incoming fall from freezing her to death.

'Hey!' she says with a smile. Next to her is a woman shorter than Jade by maybe an inch, a tiny build (much like my sister), with silvery blonde chin-length hair worn messy. A silver hoop is through one nostril, and she shares Jade's gorgeous big brown eyes. Instead of a fur coat, she's wearing a vintage-y motorcycle jacket, fringe included. This has got to be her sister.

'You made it,' I say. 'I was almost worried I was being stood up for the second time recently.'

Her face drops. 'You got stood up?'

I nod as if I can't believe it, either. 'Shocking, right?'

'Maybe she showed, thought you were lame, and dipped out,' her sister says.

Rude. That's exactly what Dax said. 'It's nice to meet you, too,' I say sarcastically.

Jade rolls her eyes. 'This is my little sister, Laney. Word of warning, she says what she wants without thought, so take little of it seriously.'

I laugh, extending my hand to her. 'We may clash,' I say jokingly.

A smile spreads across Laney's face as she takes my hand, gripping mine firmly, then she glances at Jade.

'What are the rules here?' Laney asks, motioning between Jade and me. 'Since you can't... can I?'

'Can you what?' Jade asks.

'Have him?' Laney says under her breath, leaning in so only Jade hears, but it isn't that quiet.

Mine and Jade's eyes lock. I'm a little curious about her answer to this, too, and I didn't even have to ask the question. Not that I want Laney. I do not. I can already tell we have similar personalities, so that's a hard no. It'd be like dating Mercy. Gross. Her big sister is another story. I've gotten my head out of nightmares about my ex lately by texting the adorable girl in front of me who moonlights as a hula girl bartender. Considering she has a fiancé, that's a problem.

'Um, yes? Er, noooo? I don't...' Jade stumbles over words. 'I mean, if he's into party girls who use and abuse men, then be my guest,' she says with attitude but attempts to make it breezy. Because her eyes are on me, I see right through it. Laney best not be her guest.

Jade flashes me half of an awkward grin, and only then do I realize I'm beaming a toothy smile like a fucking lunatic. She likes me. I knew she wanted me to kiss her that night! Damn it, I am a moron!

But I've gotta put her out of her misery of trying to answer this without making it weird.

'Laney,' I say. 'I've got a rule; I don't date friends' sisters. My best friend is marrying *my* sister, so thanks, but no thanks. No offense.' I gently tap her shoulder with the side of my fist before pointing Jade's way. 'I'm gonna go buy our tickets because, ya know, this is weird,' I say, turning to escape.

'No, no, no.' Jade scurries behind me, reaching my side quickly. 'This is on me, remember?'

'Weirder,' I laugh.

'Ugh.' Jade drops her head back with a frustrated

chuckle, then grabs my arm, forcing me to stop and talk to her.

'It's no big deal,' I say, my eyes on her but my brain on her velvety soft hand now holding my wrist. 'I know I'm pretty,' I joke, grabbing her hand and then winking obnoxiously.

Pink fills her cheeks, it's adorable. 'You're very modest about it too.' She pulls her hand from mine, shoving it into her coat pocket.

'Well, I'm single and agreed to watch a movie with two gorgeous women, and the prettiest one has a fiancé. My looks might be the only good thing I got because I'm obviously not a great decision-maker.'

'Hey,' Laney says, as though she's offended.

Jade shoots her a 'shut up' glare. I'd know it anywhere because it's the same one Hollyn gives me. Often.

'I want to pay,' she insists.

This is that important to her?

'Alright. I'd never usually turn that down, so why start now? But be warned, I'm buying a giant tub of popcorn, and Joey doesn't share food – besides the pie recently.'

She laughs, her eyes lingering on mine for a moment. 'Laney's buying our snacks. That's how we roll.'

Finally, she breaks our stare as she approaches the ticket counter, only a few feet away.

'Three for *Say Anything*,' she says to the ticket salesman.

'Two adults, *one child*,' Laney says, meaning it in the worst way possible based on her tone. She crosses her arms over her chest. 'That was for the pretty thing. By the way, our mom used to pay for dinner, so I hope you brought your wallet.'

'I did indeed bring my wallet. How much could a couple of girls the sizes of you two eat?'

'Laney, act as if you've met people before,' Jade says as she overhears her sister.

'*What*? If he wants to hang with you, he will have to get used to me.'

'Are you two like besties?' I ask as Jade hands us our tickets.

'Pretty much,' Laney answers.

Jade shoots her a glare. 'I'm the only woman who could ever put up with her,' she jokes. 'But yeah, she's the spare to my BFF heir.'

'*Kai* is the spare,' Laney says, leading the way to the snack counter. 'She has to be because we're blood related. I'm your built-in best friend. It's literally what Mom and Dad had me for, to be your friend so they could get a break.'

When she turns to make her candy order, Jade and I laugh.

'She's absolutely lovely,' I say jokingly. 'I'm so glad to be the third wheel on this weird sister date.'

'And I'm so glad you're here.'

That was cute. 'So, what's your candy vice for a trip into the past via movie screen?'

'Peanut M&Ms or gummy anything.'

'You're a sweet and salty girl. Nice, I'm a fan too. But I gotta go popcorn with so much butter and salt that I'll risk a stroke as I leave the theater later, partnered with a giant sugary, caffeinated soda, to wash it down with.'

'But what *kind* of soda?' she asks. 'If I had to guess, I'd say Mountain Dew.'

'Gross. Guess again.'

'Um, Pepsi?'

'Barq's root beer,' I announce with importance. 'The kind with caffeine. I'm a man with a childlike food and drink pallet. I'm not even ashamed. This morning I had a cupcake for breakfast. Because I'm apparently a grown man who buys cupcakes.'

Jade's laughing like she was the other night now. She has the best laugh. Jolly and girly. It's so cute, it's contagious. 'Your favorite soda is root beer?'

I nod. 'Is that weird?'

'Only because it's also mine...' she says.

Interesting. 'We seem to share some favorites. I wonder if it means anything?' I joke. 'What's that called when two people have everything in common? The perfect match? Soulmates?'

'A match made in heaven?' she says with a shy grin. 'I'm sure that's not what this is.'

'You're probably right,' I agree, but not really. Truthfully, I've never vibed with a woman this easily. 'There's no way we're soulmates. That would be cray-cray.'

Jade nods, but there's something going on her head that I can't quite read yet. Hesitation? But is it about what I've just said, or something (maybe some*one*) else? When we're seated, Jade is between Laney and me as she didn't feel I'd be safe from her sister attempting to feel me up, which is a little disturbing. Laney's a fine-looking girl, but I think I have a crush on her sister. Her *engaged* sister. Fuck.

Midway through the movie, Jade leans into me. 'What's your favorite eighties movie?' she whispers. The lean wasn't necessary; I can hear her just fine as we're practically the only people in the theater.

'Besides this one?'

'This is on your list?' she asks excitedly.

'Yep. Next up would be *Ferris Bueller*. How can

you not enjoy watching a teenager outsmart adults? As a teen, I wanted to *be* him.'

She grins. 'You are a total Ferris. I can't believe I'm just seeing it. You're smooth but funny, charming, and I bet you could spin a story anyone would believe.'

'*Sssshhhhhut. Up*,' Laney orders in a loud whisper.

I laugh, holding a finger to my lips. 'Quiet, the movie police have spoken.'

Jade giggles, turning back towards the screen.

Ferris, huh? Mercy calls me Spicoli, which I was alright with, but Ferris is way cooler. I guess it just took the right girl to see it.

As the movie ends, Jade sighs heavily. A satisfied sigh that says she just swooned at Lloyd's gesture for Diane precisely like the rest of the theater did. Me included.

'This is what I thought love was like when I was younger. Over the top, romantic, and so corny you'd remember every detail for the rest of your life.'

'Dude, I'd let John Cusack serenade *me*, so I get it.' I wink at her, enjoying my ability to make her smile easily. 'Back then, people had to make more of an effort than they do now. The interwebs and social media have ruined us. Now we text break-ups and post every detail of our lives. Nothing is innocent, and hardly anyone goes out of their way to bring someone joy. If you find someone who does, never let them go.'

'That's an excellent suggestion,' she says. 'Aren't you just full of wisdom?'

'Hang on.' I grab my phone from my pocket. 'Let me just call all my friends and family so you can say that again.'

'Say what?' she asks innocently.

'That I'm wise, they'll never believe you,' I kid.

She laughs to herself.

'Where are we eating?' Laney asks as we exit the theater, sort of killing the moment between Jade and me, which might be for the best considering the situation.

14

JADE

'Why *can't* love be like the final scene of an eighties rom-com? Someone tell me why?' I ask as River drives the three of us to a burger truck he 'just knows we'll love'. His words, and considering he's impressed me with his food taste recently, I trust him. But the movie is sticking with me, along with the flirting River and I did pretty much since I walked into the place. I can't think about it too deeply, or I'll wonder if he was suggesting something I shouldn't be considering right now.

'Maybe because the innocence of the eighties is gone?' Laney snaps. 'Back then, people were friends with their neighbors and slept with open windows.

Kids came home when the streetlights came on, and no one knew where they were because there were no cell phones. Now we live in a world full of sex offenders, serial killers, the dark web, and all kinds of toxic bullshit. Kids can't even play outside anymore unless constantly supervised, and even then, let's hope their guardian isn't a super creep.' She groans with frustration. 'Can you *please* watch one of the true-crime episodes I constantly send you? You and your walking around downtown at night will one day get you killed if you don't.'

'Yeah, Jade.' River continues the lecture jokingly. 'Don't get murdered; it'll greatly inconvenience your sister. Alright?'

Finally, Laney laughs. 'That's right. I mean, what would you even wear?'

My jaw drops. 'To my murder?' I balk. 'You think I've got an outfit planned for that?' I ask. 'This is a weird conversation. How did we even start talking about this? Let's change the subject. River, tell us about this food truck,' I say. Earlier, he bragged that he knew all the best food trucks and visits them so often that they know him (and his order) by name.

'Bun Jovi,' he says with a goofy grin. 'Get it?'

'Like Bon Jovi?'

'Yep. The owner's name is Jovi, it's a hamburger joint, hamburgers have buns...'

Of course I get it, but watching him explain it is funny. He's excited to get to this food truck.

'Seriously,' he continues. 'Jovi is the coolest guy you'll ever meet. Big guy with an accent I can't place. It could be backwoods southern, who knows? What I do know is that Jovi is a burger genius.'

Ten minutes later, we pull up to a food truck, in an iffy part of the city lit by a super old streetlight flashing intermittently. Creepy, but the truck has LEDs around the top, so it's less horror film and more amusing with a giant photo of who I assume is Jovi, the owner, drawn cartoon Bon Jovi style with a burger in his hand.

'River!' The man matching the cartoon on his truck greets him by name, just like River said he would. '*Two* dates tonight? You're living the life, my man.' He reaches out the window, and he and River fist bump one another.

'Actually, neither is my date. I'm just entertaining two beautiful women.' He waves a hand Jovi's way. 'This is Jovi, the proud owner of Bun Jovi, also known as the best burger truck in the world.'

'Ha-ha! Yes! River is my best customer!' Jovi says; the accent River previously mentioned is very prominent. 'You know what... uh-oh,' he says, checking his phone then nodding at River. 'Tonight's the night you become a man.'

'Oh, really?' River asks, raising his eyebrows.

'The coronary express,' Jovi says. 'You promised next time, and this is the time, brother!' He extends his fist to River, who, a little less enthusiastically, responds with another fist bump.

'Shit,' he says under his breath, not an ounce of the excitement Jovi has in his tone. 'Was that *this* time?'

'Wait!' I say, stopping whatever weird deal is about to be made. 'What is the coronary express? Drugs?'

River and Jovi both laugh, then Jovi leans out the food truck window, pointing at an item on the menu. 'The coronary express, the one burger that promises heaven with how good it is, and hell if you finish it. It includes two pounds of beef, multiple kinds of cheese, smoked bacon, lettuce, tomato, ghost peppers, habaneros, and a sauce that's recipe will be buried alongside me.'

I glance at River. 'According to the menu, your upcoming death costs twenty-two bucks. Do you have a coupon?'

He chuckles, shaking his head. 'Nope, but I made

a promise,' he says with a shrug. 'I'm not a man who breaks his word. I gotta do it. I understand if you'd rather not see this side of me.'

'We're staying,' Laney says gleefully, glancing at her sister with a smirk. 'Dinner *and* a show, plus he's paying. Why wouldn't we stay?'

He confirms his order of the coronary express, and we girls get regular-sized burgers. Then we head to the patio furniture on a deck attached to the back of the truck. Laney and I sit beside one another, and River sits across from me.

'This won't even be the most embarrassing thing I've ever done in front of people,' River says.

'Oh yeah?' I ask, afraid to know what other promises he's kept for people he has casual relation-ships with.

'I entered a hotdog eating contest at the state fair when I was eighteen.'

'How many wieners did ya swallow?' Laney asks the question in the most perverted way possible, but River laughs.

'Twenty-eight. In ten minutes.'

'*Wow!*' I say. 'You are full of fun information tonight. With every moment we spend together, I wonder a little more why you're single.'

'He-he,' he smirks. 'It's by choice,' he says. 'Mostly.' His tone is less than thrilled with this fact. But I can't imagine a woman turning him down for anything. He's incredible to be around.

It takes two people to bring out our burgers, mainly because River's requires an entire man to carry. They set the food in front of us, the staff back off, and Jovi chants for River. They're going to cheer on his death. That's cute.

'Eat it. Eat it. Eat it.'

'That's what she said,' I say under my breath, making him laugh.

'Eat it!' Laney hollers.

River looks at me nervously. 'I can't possibly not do it now. I've got fans.'

With his new fan club's encouragement, River attempts his first bite but can't even get his mouth around the thing. He does his best, and the crew and Laney cheer. He raises a fist into the air.

'I got this!' he says to his cheerleaders.

But after ten minutes, I can tell he doesn't got this.

'Someone distract me,' he says, the meat sweats kicking in causing him to lift the bottom of his shirt and wipe the sweat from his brow. Laney and I glance to one another, both our eyes on his very chiseled abs.

'Ai-yi-yi,' Laney says, fanning herself while River isn't looking. Thank God. How embarrassing would that be. Though she's not wrong. River is beautiful in a very underwear model kind of way.

'Let's play a game,' he suggests, his mind on his challenge rather than Laney and my ogling him while he sweats out an upcoming coronary.

'Truth or dare!' Laney exclaims. Of course. Her go-to game. No birthday party we went to as kids was complete without it. It's how I had my first kiss.

'Dare!' River answers immediately, even though we haven't established any rules. 'You should know I've never turned down a dare, and considering I'm attempting to die via cheeseburger right now, please go easy on me.'

'Never turned down a dare, huh?' Laney asks. 'What a man you are,' she teases.

I raise my hand, and Laney and River look at me, confused. Slowly, I lower it realizing I'm not in the third grade with a question. 'Sorry, that was nerdy. But I've got a dare. Sort of.'

'Let's hear it,' he says between bites.

'Tell us about the most out-there dare you've ever done?'

He wipes his hands on his napkin with a smile. 'Let me think.' He taps his forehead with each word, sipping his drink. 'Got it. You ladies ready for this?'

Laney and I both nod. 'Lay it on us, Evel Knievel.'

The smile creeping on the side of his face is cute.

'I like that you were raised by parents who also kept the eighties alive. That Evel guy was straight nuts. This dare isn't quite his level, but it has always stuck with me, and only three other people on this earth know.'

'Oooh,' I say, my soda cup in my hand. 'Must be good if it's a secret dare story.'

He nods, taking another bite of his burger. When he's done chewing, he takes a deep breath and starts telling the tale of the man who does any dare.

'About a month after Caitlin and I broke up, me and a buddy, Dax – you've met him – we decided to hike the Pacific Coast Trail. We'd been doing overnight weekend hikes for a few years to get into shape, so we weren't novices or anything. We had good gear and experience. Hiking the full trail would've been too much, so we started in southern Oregon on the California border. The plan was to hike to the Washington border, then have my dad pick us up. It would take us a couple of weeks, but I'd hoped it would clear my head of all the shit I'd been through with my break-up. But all this trip did was add a new horror to my nightmares.'

'I'm intrigued,' I say, my chin resting in my hands. Laney seems into it, too, but she's more focused on her food than I am.

'As you should be,' River teases, taking another bite of his burger. 'About three days in, we were lying in our tent, side by side, trying to sleep, when we heard footsteps. We both lay there, wide awake, nudging one another with each new noise. It sounded like someone was circling our tent, crunching branches and leaves on the forest floor but never getting closer. It was unnerving. Eventually, Dax got up and attempted to sneak to the tent door. It took him a couple of seconds to psych himself up, but finally he did. He unzipped the door and blasted out with a spotlight in his hand.' He pauses, working on his burger and keeping us in limbo for so long Laney can't stand it.

'And *then*?' she says impatiently.

'Nothing.'

'Nothing?' I ask.

'Zilch.' He holds his hand in an O. 'There was nobody and nothing out there.'

'But you heard something.'

'We did,' he confirms.

'What do you think it was?' I ask.

'What the hell does this have to do with a dare?' Laney talks over me.

'I'm getting there,' River says with a chuckle. Clearly, he wants to tell this story in a certain way. 'It was for sure a dude because we found a trail of boot-prints over-stepping one another around our tent. He was circling us, just like we thought. As we hiked the next day, we concocted a plan in case it happened again. I would sneak out of the tent this time because I'm smaller, quicker, and probably quieter than giant Dax, so we agreed we'd try it.'

'Did it happen again?' I ask.

He nods. 'Again, nothing.'

'*What?*' Laney's voice is high-pitched. 'You're making this up.'

'I'm not,' River says. 'Cross my heart and hope to die; it happened.' He turns to the burger he's only a quarter through, eating between sentences.

'Continue talking,' Laney orders.

'Alright, *bossy*,' River says as though she annoys him. 'That next morning, Dax and I started fighting. Over nothing, really. We'd hardly slept two nights in a row, hiked all day, and were exhausted. We couldn't understand what we had heard. No way could we be having the same dream. And how could there be actual footprints if nothing was there? We argued back and forth, like brothers, as we hiked. He blamed me for being heard exiting the tent, and I blamed him. He started mouthing off while walking in front of me, something about how maybe I could get out faster, but he'd have to protect me from whatever it was, so he might as well go first tonight. That pissed me off, so I reached down, grabbed a pebble, and chucked it at the back of his pack. Brotherly love style.'

Laney laughs. Yes, she'd for sure do this to me.

'Only it didn't hit his pack,' he laughs. 'It hit him in the side of the neck as he turned around to "apologize", which, for the record, he never did. "If you think you're so damn tough, I dare you to sleep outside the tent tonight." Those were his words. Not exactly an apology. And I swear on everything – that dare almost got me killed.'

Both mine and Laney's eyes go wide. 'You did it?' we ask in unison.

'Of course I did it. It was a dare, and I'm a guy who needs cool stories to tell my future kids so I can pass this nonsense down through the generations.'

'Perfect reasoning,' I joke.

'So, you lived to tell the tale. Nothing's even happened yet,' Laney says, clearly not impressed. 'When's this story get good?'

River shoots her a glare. 'I'm getting there, Miss Impatience.' He returns to his burger for a while, looking increasingly tired of it with each bite, but he's halfway through.

'Dax had what looked like a hickey on his neck for the rest of the trip, which gave me ammunition for endless jokes that he did not think were amusing. With every single step of that day's hike, I prayed to the universe that there was a god, then prayed that we'd hiked far enough away from the original two spots and nothing would happen that night. I was bargaining with God, scared out of my mind that this "thing" would be some forest cannibal, just waiting to get us to the right place and then turn us into a stew he'd feed to his village of forest people.'

Laney points his way, but her eyes are on me. 'He watches true crime!'

'I watch horror; there's a difference, as no one *really* dies.'

'Technicality,' she says, clearly not agreeing.

'Anyway, Dax was bitching all day that I insisted on hiking at full speed, with few breaks, so we were really under one another's skin at this point. Finally, at dusk, I chose a spot for our tent, and we set up camp. The fire was maybe five feet from the tent, facing the door, so if we heard this "person" getting close to me, I could jump up and shove him, her, or it, into the fire.'

'Willingness to commit a homicide; mark that down as a red flag,' Laney informs me nonchalantly.

River shakes his head, confirming he wouldn't really. I hope.

'Dax slept inside the tent, leaving the door unzipped in case he needed to flee. I set my sleeping bag just outside the door. It went tent, a foot of dirt, me, couple more feet of dirt, the fire, then pitch-black scary as fuck forest.'

'Descriptions like a painting, got it,' I say, genuinely able to visualize this entire scenario. The way he smiles at my reactions says he's enjoying those as much as he is telling it. I have to say, he's hooked me, quite possibly in more ways than one.

'Something woke me just after I'd nodded off, and I jolted up, grabbing the spotlight and shining it around the outside of the tent. Dax woke too because apparently, I'd "screamed like a girl" and scared the fuck out of him. I remember exactly none of that, probably because I was trying to restart my heart before I died of fear. Once we realized nobody was there but us, we started to settle and just sat by the fire. I say sat, but really we kneeled there, ready to run for our fucking lives. Then it happened,' he says, just like you would if telling a scary story around a campfire. 'The sound of footsteps started—' He stomps his feet on the deck below us for dramatics. 'And no matter how I shined that damn spotlight, I couldn't find a person.'

'Bigfoot?' Laney asks.

'No,' River says without hesitation. 'Sticks were snapping, and leaves were crunching, and still nothing. We stood back to back, each with a spotlight in one hand and our hiking hatchets in the other, looking for where these footsteps were coming from. How could we *hear* them and not see anything? My fight or flight senses were on high, and bravely I ventured away from Dax a bit, yelling for whoever was messing with us to "stop being cowards and show themselves!" We must have stood there for ten minutes, saying absolutely nothing, just listening for a response from something we couldn't see but could hear.'

'This is straight nuts,' I tell him. 'I would have died of fright.'

'Right when we'd convinced ourselves we were losing our minds, at the same time, somehow, something hit me in the shoulder blade. I spun to face Dax. "Did you just throw shit at me?" I hollered. "Did you just toss another rock?" he roared back. "If this is your idea of a joke, I will kill you, Riv," Dax threatened, but I knew he didn't mean it. Remember, we're exhausted and scared out of our minds in the middle of a dark forest where no one else should be,' River explains.

'I'm telling ya, people are the scariest monsters on this planet,' Laney says.

'Especially if they're in the middle of the fucking forest at night,' River says. 'I was triple scared now. Terrified. We were still days of hiking from where my dad was picking us up, so if something happened, we'd be in real trouble. There isn't exactly cell service in the middle of nowhere. Dax and I were so worked up that I was ready to murder whoever this was, and Dax was ready to kill me as he suspected I was pulling some prank on him. "Show yourself!" I screamed it so loud this time that it echoed back at us. If anyone was in those woods that night, they heard me. Seconds after the words left my lips, a huge crash occurred behind us. We spun, looking across the fire towards our tent. Dax shined his spotlight that way, and a giant branch – must have fallen fifty feet to the ground – landed directly on top of our tent.'

'Whoa... you could have been killed!' I exclaim,

completely invested in this story now. 'Both of you! What did you do?'

'We fucking ran until we could no longer physically run, then we hobbled into civilization and called my dad to pick us up like a couple of pussies.'

'Did you research this after?' I ask. 'Has anyone else had this experience before?'

'Yeah, Jade,' Laney says, not impressed with my suggestion. 'Loads of hikers go missing every year when an invisible camper throws a branch onto their tents after tormenting them for nights. It's like a *Blair Witch* thing. He made this up.' Laney still isn't a believer, but I think he's telling the truth.

'I didn't make it up,' River says. 'When we got home, I *did* research it. There are quite a few stories like this from other hikers in that area. People hear things and see footprints but never actually *see* anything. Hikers have gone missing in this forest.'

'Pretty sure hikers go missing in every forest at some point,' Laney says.

'You're right, but this trail in particular has some creepy, spooky vibe. We hiked back a few days later with my dad and another friend – armed this time, just in case – to get our stuff. We weren't messing around either; we probably would have shot a guy if someone had shown up. But nothing weird happened while they were with us, so now it's my "I saw a spaceship" party story.'

He is so freaking interesting. I could sit and listen to him talk all night long, and as slow as he's now working on the last quarter of this death burger, I think I might.

15

RIVER

The burger was a bad idea. I need to learn how to say no. But noooooo, I had to go and eat a giant, flaming hot burger in front of two beautiful women, and now I feel like I literally might die. If I don't, at minimum, I will spend some time in my bathroom this evening. I peel my hoodie off over my head, sitting it on my lap because I feel like I'm on fire.

'What are you doing?' Jade asks, instantly concerned. 'It's freezing out here?'

'Is it?' I pull my shirt away from my chest, creating a breeze. 'I'm hot.'

'How could you possibly be ho—' She stops midword as she touches my arm. Suddenly she stands, sliding her hand to the side of my neck. Her touch sends chills through me, but I try to stay calm so she won't notice.

'Getting hotter,' I say jokingly. My mouth can't keep anything cool.

'She's in mom mode,' Laney says.

'Mom mode?' I ask as Jade pulls her hand from me.

'I'm not in "mom" mode, but you are super hot.'

'I know, right?' I try to seem smooth, but the fact that I'm sweating like a snowman in a desert is probably giving me away. Right now, I am not 'hot'.

Jade smirks. 'As in possible fever hot.'

'Fever?' I feel my forehead as if I'll be able to tell. 'I haven't had a fever since I was in high school. I thought that was a childhood thing?'

'It's a humanity thing. You are eating a burger that promised misery. Maybe that special sauce is poison,' she jokes.

What is in that special sauce?

'Jovi!' I holler, and he appears like a genie. 'You put rat poison in this thing?'

'No,' he laughs. 'But it's going to feel like I did. We don't call it the coronary burger for nothing.' He glances at my plate and smiles, pulling his phone from his back pocket and snapping what is probably the worst photo ever. 'Congratulations, you've now got a twenty-two-dollar credit and your photo on the wall of fame.'

'I feel like that wall is more shame than fame,' Laney says not impressed even a little.

God, I think she's right. I groan, shoving the nearly empty plate out of the way and dropping my head onto the tabletop with a thunk.

'I gotta go home. Like, yesterday.'

'First you have to bring us home,' Laney reminds me.

'I can't believe I'm about to say this, but we are not having three-way, I respect your sister too much for that.' I side-eye her, watching her smirk to herself.

'You drove us,' Laney insists.

'Oh yeah...'

'Shit.' *I* drove them. *Great idea, River. Show off your cool car and now die in front of them. You're really pulling out all the stops tonight.* I reach into my pocket, fish out my keys, and set them in Jade's hand. 'You know how to drive a stick?'

'Yeah,' she says hesitantly.

'Good, 'cause you're driving. Which I can't believe I'm even suggesting 'cause I hardly let anyone drive that car. She's my baby.'

'Dork alert; his car's his baby. Not exactly a red flag, but close,' Laney says, not so under her breath.

'Laney, he's sick.' Jade sticks up for me. 'Come on, help me get him to his car.'

'I got it.' Jovi and another employee, men much larger than Laney and Jade, throw my arms over their shoulders and practically drag me to my car as the girls follow.

Jade fumbles with my keys, and without moving too drastically and upsetting whatever is already angry inside me, I press the button that unlocks my beloved BMW 328i, a car my parents bought me in high school. I fell in love with it the moment I saw it. Before I can get in, my stomach objects, and I veer off to the side of the food truck, my head in the bushes.

'People don't believe us about the misery thing,' Jovi tells the girls. 'As far as I know, everyone survives. He'll be just fine in a couple of days.'

'And if he's not?' Jade asks like she's an angry mother.

'He signed a form saying I'm not responsible.'

'He did? How did I miss that?' She seems confused. Thankfully, they give me some time to expel the burger trying to kill me, and when I'm done, I practically crawl back to my car.

Jade sits in the driver's seat with the car running, her hands on the wheel. 'I'm nervous.'

'Why?' Laney asks from the back seat. 'It's just a

car, and you've been driving for a decade. Put it in gear, and let's see what this thing can do.'

I raise a hand Laney's way. 'Do *not* see what it can do,' I order. 'We're not replaying *Tokyo Drift*. I already feel like I'm dying, and I will jump out of this car while it's moving before I puke in it.'

'I'll go slow; just tell me where.'

I type my address into my dash GPS as she speaks. That way, I don't have to talk.

The GPS starts ordering her around, and slowly she lets off the clutch, jerking only once, smoothing out and driving like I'm an instructor at the DMV.

'You could at least go to the speed limit, or this will be the longest drive home,' Laney gripes from the back seat.

'I can't risk making him sicker. How about you sit back there and shut up?' Jade snaps back.

I can't help but laugh at how these girls fight like Hollyn and I do. Those are the best relationships. It's sibling love at its finest.

* * *

Things have progressed by the time she gets me to my apartment. We had to stop twice so that the burger could exit, and each time, as I kneeled on the side of the freeway, hoping no one plowed into us, I regretted that burger a little more.

As I get out of my car, I glance into my building. There's no way I'm making it to the third floor easily. This much I know. When we reach the callbox outside the front doors, I jab Dylan's apartment number and lean against the wall.

'What are we doing?' Jade asks. 'Which floor do you live on?' she asks, looking up at the building. 'I feel like we need a plan.'

'I thought the plan was to drop him off so he could die peacefully, and we Uber home? Or did I make that up on the way here?'

'Your sister is terrifying,' I say to Jade, who agrees with a nod.

'Yeah?' Dylan's voice echoes through the dark street.

'Dyl,' I groan. 'I'm dying and need your help.'

'Shut up,' the man says through the intercom.

Right then, I bolt for the trash cans a few feet from me. Thank God this burger was free because I'm paying for it now.

'Hi there,' Jade says behind me, into the callbox. 'River's seriously sick; he chose to eat a burger that promises misery, and it's pulled through. My sister and I are here with him, but I'm unsure if we can get him to his apartment. Could you help? Please?'

A beat of silence says this isn't a great time, but eventually, a voice echoes through the empty city street. 'Give me a sec.'

Jade doesn't come near me; instead, her sister speaks loudly from where she is. 'Your boyfriend is on his way down.'

'Ha-ha.' I don't laugh. 'He's as much my boyfriend as you are my girlfriend.'

The front doors of the building burst open, and Dylan, dressed in a two-piece matching pajama set from the 1940s, walks my way. 'Virus or booze flu?' he asks, sliding his arm around my waist and pulling my arm over his shoulders.

'I defeated the coronary burger,' I tell him.

He laughs. 'Or did the coronary burger defeat you?'

'Shhh. I'm going with victory as I'm trying to look good in front of the ladies,' I whisper.

'You've got puke on your shirt, so think what you want, but you're way past that dream,' Dyl says, amusement in his voice. 'I got it from here, girls.'

'What?' Jade asks. 'I can't leave him. Not like this.'

'Yes, you can,' Laney says. 'We have plans.'

'Plans? It's like midnight.'

'And we're doing a cleanse at 3.33 a.m.'

'When did you *plan* to tell me this?'

'I'm telling you *now*.'

'Well, cancel it, because, as I told you after our last "cleanse", I'm never doing that coffee enema thing again.'

I raise my eyebrows. This conversation is getting weirder by the minute.

'It's not an enema. It's a spiritual cleanse to rid our souls of boys of the past and call in Mr Right.'

'Please tell me River didn't hook up with a couple of witches?' Dylan asks inquisitively, looking more than amused by this. 'But if he did, count River in,' he says as he practically drags me into the building. 'The guy has an ex that I'm sure he'd be all-in on tormenting her voodoo doll for a while if that's what you're suggesting.'

Both Laney and Jade stare my way. 'You have a voodoo doll of Caite?' Jade asks as she makes her way inside behind us.

'Nah,' I say, giving a slightly crooked grin to imply it's just a joke. In all seriousness, I do, but it was a gag gift from Dax after she and I broke up. I've never actually used it, but I can't say the thought has never crossed my mind. Since the girls refuse to leave, I throw an arm over Jade's shoulders and let her and

Dylan drag me up the stairs. Laney follows behind, offering the assistance of a hand on my butt so I don't fall ass over tea kettle to the bottom. She's not the most subtle girl.

'Who's Caite?' Laney finally asks.

'The evilest woman alive,' I groan.

'I met her the other night,' Jade explains to Laney. 'She was so "it's good to see you, who's *this*" that I pretended to be his fiancée. No big deal.'

Laney bursts out a laugh. 'No big deal besides the fact you're already someone else's fiancée.'

Dylan side-eyes me. 'You sure know how to pick 'em.'

'Shut up. It's a long story.'

Finally, after what feels like a hike up Mount Hood, I'm in my apartment. 'You ladies, make yourself comfortable. Remote's on the coffee table. Watch anything you want, just turn it up real loud.' Those are my last words before locking myself in my bathroom, dreading what might come next.

16

JADE

River's locked in his bathroom, and Laney is flipping through channels, the TV so loud I can hardly think, but he requested it loud, so I'll respect his wishes considering this is his apartment and he's sick. Though, this isn't how I expected tonight to turn out. We were having so much fun, and now I'm worried about a guy I hardly know.

I considered leaving after his neighbor, Dylan, promised us he could handle it, but that just wasn't enough to put my worrying heart at ease. I'm one of those worriers. For example, I slept on his couch for a week when Thomas got sick last year, ensuring he survived walking pneumonia. He needed round-the-clock care, breathing treatments, medications, fluids, and a *lot* of the Game Show Network. I missed a week of work.

That's when I discovered my favorite game show, *Supermarket Sweep*. It's like mixing shopping with road rage. I've seen every episode, and even though I know they won't, I secretly hope someone creates a spin-off one day called *Supermarket Sweep –XTREME*. It could be bumper cars meets shopping. I would sign Laney and me up in a second.

Anyhow, I'm a caretaker. It's in my blood. Mom was a nurse, and when we were sick as kids, there was no place else I wanted to be than home with her nursing me back to health. She was my hero, with so much compassion and empathy that she was the best part about being sick. As she was home with hospice care, I visited every day in her final weeks. For her last week on earth, I slept in my childhood bedroom, as did Laney, so that we wouldn't be far away when the moment came to say goodbye. I hardly slept that week, worrying that the next minute might be her last, and I didn't want her to go without knowing I was there. Imagine two twenty-something women sleeping in bunk beds. They weren't as magical as I remembered them.

No, Jade. You can't think about this, or you'll go down a dark 'why me' path, and River's night will get much worse with a crying woman attempting to nurse him back to health.

Think of anything else. I pick up a Rubik's Cube from his coffee table, but it's already completed, and that's such an accomplishment that I don't want to ruin it. On one wall, there are shelves holding hundreds of DVDs and CDs. I think movies and music are his thing. Every genre is present, but it's dominated by two decades. The eighties and nineties. He really is a fan. I wonder where he keeps his Magic 8 Ball? He seems like the type.

His apartment is kind of cool. It's in an older building, but with an updated floor plan open living room/kitchen with an island separating the two. The TV on his wall is giant, and besides empty drink containers and mail, it's relatively clean. An oversized leather sectional takes up the wall of windows facing the street, with a square wooden coffee table in the middle. The rug on his floor is a bright blue shag carpet. I love it.

I meander through the place, glancing into a room with the door open, the glow of multiple computer screens illuminating it. It's filled with electronics, stacks of CDs, soundboards, and equipment I think is for music, cluttering the corner-shaped desk.

I wonder what he does for work and if this is where that happens.

I hear the door of the bathroom crack open, and when I turn, he's peeking out. His hair hangs loosely from the bun until he brushes it away from his face, and he doesn't look like he's had a great time.

'Please tell me you heard none of that because I think I just flushed my ego down the toilet. If you did, I can never look you in the eye again.' His cheeks are pink, and even though I'm sure it's from whatever just went on behind that door, he's embarrassed we're here now.

'Do you want me to leave?'

'No,' he says quickly.

Whew. Because I didn't want to go yet. 'Can I get you anything?'

'Water?' he asks. 'There's bottled water in the fridge.'

'Coming right up,' I say, rushing to the fridge and grabbing the water. 'I'd suggest drinking it slowly.'

He takes the bottle from me. 'You don't *have* to stay. I'd be more than happy to die alone.'

'You're not dying, and I'm one of those women who can't leave if someone's not okay.'

'Why?'

'I suppose it's only fair to tell a humiliating story

considering what's happening right now to you. You know, to make you feel better.' I take a breath, prepping myself to tell the story I cringe at when my dad tells it. 'I once puked on the classmate standing before me during our school spring sing.'

River scrunches his face.

'Yep. I threw up in her hair and continued singing as if it had never happened. I didn't address it, didn't help, and definitely didn't stop the show because once I'd puked I felt fine again. There are multiple home videos of it too. Eventually, once the music teacher noticed a kid bawling, the whole show screeched to a halt, and I felt terrible. When my parents asked why I didn't run off stage to vomit, I had no answer because I was eight, and all I wanted was for the floor to open up and suck me in. Then they asked why I didn't help?' I sigh heavily as I always do when I tell this story. Am I really the person who damages someone then ignores it? I didn't want to be that girl so now I'm overly caring. Fall on the sidewalk in front of me, I'm stopping to help and I've got Band-Aids in my purse.

He laughs to himself. 'That is bad.'

I nod. 'Even though that girl and I had multiple classes together through the end of high school, she never spoke to me again, and no one ever spoke of it.

It was my take-it-to-the-grave secret, but now you know. I can't know you're sick and not help, that was the lesson I learned that day.'

'But you were sick,' River says.

'I felt better after and should have helped her, the girl in front of me trying not to throw up on everyone around her once she realized what had happened.'

River's jolly laugh makes him groan then rub his hand across his stomach like it still hurts with any movement. 'Does Corndog know this story?'

I shake my head. 'No way. He's in school to be a doctor, I can't ever tell him I ignored a girl who needed help after I caused a situation. That's like the essence of his business – helping people. I ran away, and I'll never do that again.'

Laney appears in the hallway with us; her phone is lit in her hand. 'I hate to break up this little love fest, but I've got an Uber on the way. I'm going to grab our ex boxes and a few other things I need, then I'll be back.'

'Lane, maybe tonight's not the night to cleanse our souls?' I suggest, noticing River's pale complexion again.

'It *has* to be the night, full moon and all. It's in the rules.'

River glances between us, still leaning on the

bathroom door frame with the door only cracked about a foot. 'Is your sister a witch?'

'Sometimes,' I joke.

'I'll be back,' Laney says, not caring that this is the very wrong moment. 'Find his burn box,' she says, exiting his apartment without a response that this is even alright to do.

'Since your stuck here until we summon whatever demon your sister is inhabited by and I am so embarrassed I may avoid you for the rest of my life after this, I need to ask you a favor?'

'What?' I ask.

'Can you please go into my top dresser drawer and grab me pretty much any bottoms you see. Mine are uh—' He glances back into bathroom with a grimace. 'This is quickly becoming the most humiliating night of my life. Mine are... compromised,' he says apologetically. 'Questions aren't allowed at this time, literally, grab anything.'

'Okey-dokey,' I chirp, hoping to put him at ease that he hasn't ruined my night and save him from any more embarrassment. If I pretend everything is normal, maybe this moment won't become a core memory for either of us. Actually, I kind of hope it does. I could use some more crazy stories and I haven't had a night this exciting for a long time.

I head towards the one dark room I haven't glanced into yet, assuming it is his room.

The room lights up as I flip the switch. It's mostly clean and organized, resembling a twenty-something bachelor's bedroom. Impressively, he *has* a bedframe, not just a mattress on the floor. A wall of those expensive 'adult' lightsabers (the 'collectors' editions that aren't considered 'toys' and cost hundreds of dollars) tells me everything I need to know about River. Deep down, he's still his teenage self and perhaps even dorkier than I thought despite his casual, cool exterior. Which is something I think I like. Life is already sucky; why make it worse by being too serious about everything?

On the wall facing his bed is another colossal TV above the dresser I'm looking for. Things are strewn about as if he actually lives here, and I wouldn't want to eat a meal off the floor or anything, but I've been in worse. I once dated a guy who lived in his parents' basement (which I've got zero problems with – live with whoever you want). But this guy had fifteen gerbils. You can imagine how it smelled. We didn't last long.

On the other hand, Conner is one of those sparkling clean, don't move anything, he washes his sheets after I sleep over, kind of guy. I once laid his toothbrush on the bathroom counter, and he lost his shit. In a Ross Geller-type rage, he threw the toothbrush into the toilet with a live demonstration of how much bacteria lives on the counter. That should have been a red flag, but I was lovestruck. If only Laney had been there to announce the flag on the field.

Not one piece of art (besides the light sabers he probably considers art) is on River's walls, but he does have a lovely collection of colorful Post-it notes, all with things jotted onto them – NYE, Crystal Ballroom, Rico/Rehab, mother of the bride dress, best man speech, bachelor party (epic), hula girl. Hula girl? Is that me? I glance up at a line of bright orange Post-its with the words 'WALL OF IMPORTANT SHIT'. I laugh to myself. *I'm* on his wall of important shit? That's interesting.

A hamper in one corner proves laundry is not his favorite chore. His bed is partially made like he quickly threw the gray comforter over it before leaving this morning. A few shirts, still on hangers, are set on the bed. Did he question what to wear tonight? If so, that makes me feel better about the pile of rejected outfits I went through before settling on the one I'm in. From the looks of my room when I left, you'd have thought this was a *date* date.

Bottoms, Jade, that's what you're here for. Hurry. He's in his bathroom, Donald Ducking it.

I pull open the top drawer and grab the first thing that catches my eye, Day-Glo zebra print. I take a better look, laughing to myself when I notice they're boxer briefs, in adult man size. I glance at the others. Floral print. Colorful leopard skin. Polka dot. A green and red 'Christmas' themed pair with a 'present' pictured in the groin. And so many more.

He's as weird as I am with clothes, and I love that. I may or may not have a thing for obnoxious thongs. I've got sexy ones, comfy ones, lacey ones, and even a pair of crotchless ones that the gerbil guy gifted me on our second date, which happened to fall on Valentine's. I'll never wear those, so I don't know why I don't just throw them away, but I don't.

The next pair I grab is black with a magenta-colored heart positioned over where his manhood will go. I know in my gut these are the ones I'll be bringing him. They're absolutely perfect.

To the far right of the drawer, I spot a stack of neatly folded sweats in three colors: black, navy, and gray. I'm sure these are the bottoms he hoped for, not the underwear in my hand, but I'm going with both.

'Knock, knock,' I say, simultaneously knocking on the bathroom door.

He opens the door a crack, extending only his hand. I hear him laugh after he closes himself back in to change.

'Woman, you're testing me,' he thunders with humor. Then suddenly, the door swings open as he flips the light off and walks into the hallway.

'I'm warning you right now, I've got no shame on a good day; tonight, it's completely left the building. I'd do a spin to model, but the room is already doing that for me, so if you need a good look, you'll have to circle me like the sun, girlfriend.'

'Girlfriend?' I repeat, attempting to keep my eyes on his, but he's literally standing in front of me in only the boxer briefs I just handed him and he is more beautiful than a girl could hope for. 'I didn't realize we'd gone full on "that's mah crew" with our friendship,' I say somewhat mindlessly, my eyes wandering his body.

'After *this*?' He motions to the bathroom, then to his nearly naked self. 'You just rifled through my underwear drawer. You're starting to know me better than I know myself.'

River is tall and thin but not 'skinny', with actual abs and solid shoulders. Muscly shoulders. Yum. What girl doesn't love that? All the better to protect you with. My gaze lowers. *Wow-sa*. This is my second time witnessing model-quality abs up close – the first earlier tonight when I excused him using his t-shirt as a sweat rag as I was distracted by these same abs. I want to touch them. Hell, I want to lick them. But I won't.

Jade! Stop. Staring. I shouldn't be ogling another guy. I know this, yet I can't look away. I don't want to.

A tattoo peeks out from under his left arm, and I want to know what it is, but I can't spend any more time admiring him like this. When my gaze hits his belly button, it's all over. I'm certain his underwear is sitting low on his hips, revealing that hip V that's hot as hell, on purpose. The purpose – seeing if I'll notice. Mission accomplished.

Do not follow that barely there trail of blond trail hair to where it disappears beneath the waistband of those ridiculous boxers, Jade. Ignore where that V is pointing. You are engaged; you'll look like a hussy.

As he clears his throat, I realize I've been caught.

'I can tell you're impressed,' he says, half an adorable smile on his face. His cheeks are flushed, and his hair is swept to one side. Suddenly, I see him like I never have before. 'Are you proud of yourself? Now you've seen me at my absolute worst *and* in my underwear. The only fair thing to do now is show me yours.'

An unexpected giggle that usually only surfaces after a few drinks leaves my lips. 'I'm never showing you my underwear,' I say, tossing the navy sweats his way. They hit him in the chest, dropping into his hands as he's not quite fast enough to catch them mid-flight in his current room-spinning state.

'Honestly, I didn't expect you to come out in them. I didn't even have to dare you. Now that I see them on, I chose well. They're *very* nice. As is the man in them. All the best, er, *wrong* places are perfectly emphasized.' I motion a hand over his 'wrong/best place' and then cover my eyes.

'Are you blushing right now?' he asks, balancing one hand against the wall as he carefully and slowly pulls on his sweats.

'No,' I say, peeking through my fingers and lying through my teeth. Yes, I'm probably blushing for good reason. This man is beautiful.

'Conner doesn't look this good in his tighty-whities, does he?'

How could he guess he wears those? In Conner's defense, they aren't white. They're black, but still, they are that style, which is not exactly sexy. Not like what I'm pretending I'm not still admiring now.

'I can't answer that,' I say. 'But you should probably wear a T-shirt to save me from further embarrassment. Tell me where your shirts live, and I'll get you one.'

A smirk crosses his face. 'Not until you admit you're enjoying this. Anti-dating me is everything you expected and then some, right?'

I laugh. 'It's definitely been an adventure that I don't hate.'

'Come on, calamity Jade. You saw what I went through earlier; humor me, woman. Tell me you're not headed for the hills once you leave my apartment because truthfully, even with you fully clothed, I think you're starting to enjoy being stuck with me while Dr McDorky ignores you.'

'I will admit, I'm quite enjoying being "stuck" with you.'

He grins. 'You staring through your fingers is the best part of this. I get it. I'm sure Conrad hasn't quite hit puberty, considering he can't even make a phone call to break up with the woman he's leading on, so there's no way he's got the sparkle I do.'

With this, I frown. 'He did call.'

River *was* headed to the couch but stops in his tracks. '*When?*' he asks without turning to face me.

'A few days ago.'

I swear he groans under his breath like this disappoints him. 'On that note, take a good long look while I head to the couch, where I will probably die later. Then you can dream of me after you've married mister wrong.'

He's pretty sure Conner is unsuitable for me like he's never questioned it. Why isn't it as easy for me to see it?

He moves through his apartment as though he's walking through a funhouse, dropping onto his couch face down like he's passed out mid-step. One arm and leg hang off the edge limply until he grabs the remote Laney left on the table and flips the channel. 'You don't have to stay,' he says, his mood suddenly low.

I sit at the far end of his sectional, attempting not to let my eyes wander down his still-bare chest.

'I thought you *wanted* me to stay?'

He raises a questioning eyebrow like I didn't read through his quick 'no' earlier when I asked if he wanted me to go.

'I do want you to stay. But if you made up with your boyfriend, maybe you shouldn't be sitting here with a guy in his underwear who thinks you're gorgeous.'

I suck in the tiniest breath. 'You think I'm gorgeous?'

He opens his eyes, a shy smile surfacing. 'I don't

say things I don't mean. I'm also pretty sure you know you're gorgeous.' He closes his eyes again, his face making me wonder if his next words physically hurt him of if that's just the cheeseburger doing more damage. 'Did you guys make up?'

'I don't really know?' I lift a single shoulder. 'He said sorry and swore it wouldn't happen again, but he still isn't making an effort like he promised he would. For instance, he was supposed to call today, but nothing.'

'You deserve better,' River says firmly.

'What's considered better? I mean, he proposed, he's in medical school, he's handsome, smart—'

'Evasive, doesn't appreciate you, requested a man he doesn't know keep an eye on you and call with the "real issues", and hasn't even bought you an engagement ring,' River continues my sentence without missing a beat. His words surprise me.

'What?' I ask. '*Real issues*? Did he actually say those words?'

River looks at me apologetically. 'I want to lie and say he didn't say exactly that because I can see that it's hurt your feelings and that's something I never want to do. But truth is, he did. Also, he gave me his business card so I could follow through, which I would never, because I like you too much to do anything that asshole has requested.'

My heart slows in my chest. Conner's passed me onto another guy while he 'lives his real life' in Boston without me. That jerk. Has he meant anything he's said since we met? I can't show River how much this pisses me off – that'll just prove I'm the biggest idiot ever to only really realize all this now.

'Thank you for telling me the truth,' I say matter-of-factly.

'You're too pretty to lie to,' River says, squinting open one eye and glancing my way, half a grin on his handsome face.

Even sick, the guy is charming as hell. I can't believe he just said that twice. Now I'm unsure whether to accept this by returning the compliment or blowing it off because, technically, I'm taken. *Technically*, technically, he already knows by my wandering eyes earlier. Newly engaged Jade would likely shut him down right now. But *this* Jade, the girl whose fiancé has been jerking her around for weeks, appreciates his honesty and wants to give it back.

'That's sweet, River. Shall I be candid?'

''Tis the only way to be,' he says. The poor guy speaks mostly without motion; even his eyes are closed. He can talk freely without the cheeseburger threatening a comeback as long as he doesn't move.

'Even on your deathbed, you're pretty too. I've always thought so.'

'Have you now?' He once again opens one eye with a smile. 'Prettier than Corndog?'

I laugh to myself, refusing to answer.

'Say it...' he jokes.

'I can't,' I laugh nervously. 'It feels wrong to say when I've committed myself to the guy. But, if you're going to twist my arm, I suppose my answer would be: Y for you're. E for extremely. And S for sexy.' With each of the letters, I lower my voice. Afraid to say the words any louder in case it's a cardinal sin to be attracted to someone while engaged to someone else and I tempt God to throw a bolt of lightning my way. 'Does that answer your question?'

He sits up, leaning his head on the back of his couch, his eyes on me. 'Message received, Captain Acronym. Poor Corndog. I bet he never thought a guy with a man-bun would be wooing his girl right now with only my body and honesty.' He rests his hand on his stomach, grimacing. 'Ugh. I don't think this cheeseburger is done with me yet.'

'You know what you need?'

'A time machine so I can go back and fix all this?'

All this? I wonder what he's talking about.

'I can hunt for Doc Brown if you want, but you need fluids, Advil, and Pepto. Got any?'

'I got fluids.' He lifts the water bottle from the table where he set it. 'The other things I keep at the drugstore three blocks that way and buy as needed.' He vaguely points behind him towards the street.

'So, you're prepared for anything,' I joke. 'Is this drugstore open twenty-four hours?'

'Yep.'

I grab my coat from where I laid it when we walked in.

'No,' he says, lifting his head. 'I can't possibly let you wander the city streets at this hour for me. Hang on.' Gently, he makes his way off his couch, walking towards me in a sort of zombie shuffle. A couple of moans later, he opens his front door and stops at the door across the hall. He leans forward, resting his head on the door frame. Piano notes drift from the apartment, stopping suddenly with his knock.

The door swings open, and the neighbor from before appears. 'Sort of in the middle of entertaining my lady,' Dylan says to River, giving him a look that says, *Get it? Now go away.* They seem like friends more than neighbors.

'I need medical intervention via the pharmacy.

Jade here wants to do me a favor and walk there –
alone – now. Can you please assist her?' River asks,
never removing his head from the door frame.

'No assistance necessary,' I insist. 'I have mace,
and I'm not afraid to use it. I've got a plan! First, I
mace, right in the eyes. Then, I'll knee the guy in the
balls. While they're incapacitated, I'll run to safety;
the earlier tap of my emergency call button on my
phone, while I maced them will have 911 on the line,
and help will already be on the way.'

Dylan and River slide their hands to cover their
manhoods like it pains them even to hear that part of
the plan.

'Ouch. I think that'd work,' River says.

'You're a little terrifying,' Dylan says, his eyebrows
raised as though he thinks I'm nuts.

'I walk these streets nightly; I'm not scared.' With
horror, I realize how that sounds. 'Because of my *job*.'
I try to explain myself, but that only makes it worse.
'As a *bartender*.'

Jesus, Jade, pull it together.

When I'm done explaining my situation poorly, I
notice the grin on River's face. At least he's amused, I
suppose.

'Give ya twenty bucks to escort Jade to and from

the pharmacy and make sure nothing happens to her.'

'Who's going to make sure nothing happens to me?' Dylan asks.

River lifts a shoulder as though that's not his problem.

Reluctantly, Dylan nods. 'Does Cassie need to babysit you while we're gone?'

'Nah,' River says, shuffling across the hall towards his apartment. 'I'll be waiting on my couch. I'll leave the door unlocked.'

'Please don't die while I'm gone?' I request.

'If the Grim Reaper shows, I'll ask him to wait – just for you.' He winks as he closes the door to his apartment, leaving Dylan and me in the hall. Besides my father, I'm not used to having a man worry about me like this. Conner should be treating me this way, but he isn't that concerned, especially if he asked River to call him only with *real issues*. That pisses me off. But I don't have time to think about it; I've got a sick man to nurse back to health.

17

JADE

Dylan doesn't speak much while I shop; he just follows me like my bodyguard, which, in a way, is precisely what River asked him to do. Once I've bought everything I think may help River's symptoms, we exit the store.

'How'd you and River meet?' Dylan asks on our walk home.

'I work at Black Tide Tiki, and we have this ukulele performer, Mercy. She's friends with him.'

'Oh, yeah.' Dylan smiles. 'Mercy's my best friend. We work together. I don't do well in hot, humid conditions, so I never go when she plays Black Tide.'

'You must be her overly sweaty friend she once referred to.'

He lowers his chin. 'She said I was her sweaty friend?'

Oops. Clearly, I've hit a nerve. I probably shouldn't have said that part out loud. *Walk it back, Jade. Don't get Mercy into trouble with your incessant talking.*

'No. *Noooooo.* She just said you hated the heat, so I assumed it's because you were one of those men who sweat a lot.'

Truthfully, she called him 'Sir Sweats-A-Lot', but I swear she said it with love.

'Considering you work in an establishment that serves alcohol, I'm surprised River hasn't embarrassed himself in front of you before tonight.'

'He has. But he's also a great listener and makes me laugh.'

'Were you two on a date?'

'Kind of...' I pull my coat tighter around me, the crisp night air biting at any exposed skin.

Dylan bellows a laugh. 'Kind of counts. Welcome to Riverland; you're off to a rough start.'

I laugh. 'We were more on what we call an anti-date. I'm engaged.' I'm inclined to flash a diamond as proof, but I don't have one. 'But that's not going great either, so River is distracting me until I figure some things out.'

'Ah,' Dylan says like it all makes sense. 'The situation sounds very River.'

I wonder what that means. 'Tell me about him.'

'About River?' he asks.

I nod.

'Oh...' He smirks. 'I can tell you all about River. He's a movie guy, a cameraman, and a producer who shoots commercials and music videos. I think he's also still working on a documentary about his once-famous mother. He's obsessed with all things eighties and nineties. He's overly honest and refuses to "grow up". He used to date a lot, but they rarely turned into anything serious, though not for his lack of trying. He's full of quirks and jokes, and it will take just the right woman to love all of him.'

'Ya think?'

Dylan nods. 'I *know*. You chose the right person to distract you from whatever you're going through because he's great at lightening the mood. If you need someone to cheer you up, he's your guy. If you end up in River's circle, he'll be the most loyal friend ever. Despite being distracted easily by shiny new things, or his mother requesting his presence at all hours of the day and night, he'll never let you down when things get tough, and he's way more normal than his "class clown" exterior portrays. River's a guy you can count on.'

'Back up a sec. His once-famous mother? Who's his mom?'

Surprise fills Dylan's face. 'He hasn't already told you? God, with as much time as he spends with her, I'd have suspected that was the first thing he announced to people. His mom is Penny Candy, the singer. She was big back in the late eighties and nineties, and she's now trying to make a comeback with River's help. You ever heard of her?'

My jaw drops, and my steps stop. 'No. Freaking. Way!' I say excitedly. Not only have I heard of her, but she was one of my mom's favorite musicians. Penny Candy albums were always in her visor holder amongst the rest of her teenage faves (Madonna, Mariah Carey, Toni Braxton, Debbie Gibson, etc.). *All* of them. She grew up as such a super fan that I've seen photos of her from the eighties in full Penny Candy style. She would die of excitement right now, knowing this.

'Are you serious? Penny Candy is River's mom?'

'Yeah,' Dylan says with a curious grin. 'I'm honestly surprised he didn't tell you.'

Finally, once the starstruck part of me calms, I

start walking again. This is incredible. Wait until Laney finds out!

'Well, until now, we haven't spent much time together outside my job, and as I'm only just realizing, I do most of the talking. About myself, it seems.' I drop my head back against the collar of my fur coat. 'God, that's so rude, isn't it? I hardly ever ask about his life. I always just saw him as a fun customer. Now I'm wondering things about him. Like what the real story is on the whole Caitlin thing.'

This piques Dylan's attention. 'He told you about Caitlin but not Penny?'

I nod. 'He didn't exactly want to, but we went out for pie recently, and they had a run-in. Besides her being his ex and things ending badly, he wouldn't elaborate.'

'Even I don't know the details of Caitlin. At least not from the horse's mouth. I once got the hearsay version from Mercy and was told never to mention her name, and I've followed instructions.' The grimace on his face says it's bad. Like, *really* bad. Great. Now I *have* to know.

'Thanks for walking me,' I say as we approach different apartment doors.

'No problem. Good luck with all that,' he says

motioning towards River's apartment, then disappearing inside his own.

I stare at River's front door. He said it would be unlocked, but I can't just walk in; that feels weird.

Tap, tap. I knock lightly twice, then turn the handle. 'It's me. Jade Monroe.'

Why am I announcing myself by first and last name like I'm visiting a stranger?

River's lying on the couch, one foot propped on the armrest; the other leg has flopped off the sofa, and his head rests in his hands behind his head. I set the bag of medical supplies on the counter along with my purse. He's still not wearing a shirt, so hopefully that's helping his fever come down because it's not helping me not take a peak while he's asleep.

I shake out of my coat, laying it on his couch, then gently rest my hand on his cheek, checking his fever. Still there. Hmmm. What would my mom do? Duh. I need a cool, wet rag. I flip on the light in his bathroom. All his earlier clothes are piled on the floor as if he stripped out of them in a feverish rage. I glance around the room, deciding to get to know him via his possessions. That's not a crime, is it?

He's got a counter full of potions, hair products, and anti-aging cream for men? I set that one back down. Nothing in the medicine cabinet is problematic, so that's relieving. The top drawer contains condoms of every size, color, and type. Interesting. At least he's responsible, but isn't he a hopeful guy thinking he'll go through those quickly?

After pulling open a few drawers under his sink, I find one full of hand towels and washcloths. I grab two, running them under cold water. One I wring, fold, and put in his fridge for later. The other I lay across his forehead gently. He doesn't even stir.

He's right, his ceiling is as boring as mine; I'm laying opposite where he is on his section. Where is Laney? I pull my phone from my pocket to check on Laney.

'I'm on my way,' she says instead of saying hello. 'Is he still alive?'

'Yeah. But he's sleeping. Hey.' I leave the couch, walking to the kitchen island, where I sat the bag from the pharmacy down. 'What's better for a fever? Tylenol or Advil?' I ask, pulling things from the bag. 'I think I remember Mom using Tylenol for fevers. Pedialyte helps with dehydration in adults, too, right?'

'Jade.' Laney says my name seriously. 'You've gone full-on mom with this guy. You *like* him! I mean, I don't blame you, he's hot as fuck, especially compared to Conner, but you're sort of engaged. Remember?'

'How could I forget? Everyone reminds me constantly, and I check my phone fifty times a day, hoping he's said something sweet like he used to before he left, but he's very business now. Hello, how was your day, is the extent of our conversations and just barely that.'

'No phone sex?' She balks.

'Nope.'

'Ugh, dump him already and go for man-bun.'

'Laney, I can't. My stupid conscience wants me to figure out what's wrong first, and I haven't achieved that yet.'

'Borrow mine.'

'You don't have one,' I say.

She laughs. 'Oh yeah. Thank God, I say.'

'River's just being a good friend, that's all.'

Laney laughs. 'He wants to *do* you, moron. It's so obvious he's into you.'

Right then, he stirs, restlessly turning, then sitting up suddenly with a gasp. The washcloth falls from his head to his stomach, and he looks at it, confused. He glances around the room, his gaze settling on me – more confusion.

'I gotta go. My patient is awake and possibly delusional. Get here soon, would you? I could use help with this,' I hiss into the phone, glad I couldn't focus on her last statement.

'Hi,' I say with a wave. 'I came back. The wet rag was an attempt to get your fever down. How do you feel?' I sit down next to him, once again placing my hand on the side of his neck.

'Half dead and a little surprised you didn't flee when you had the chance. Did everything go okay?' he asks, more worried about me than he should be, considering he's sick.

'Everything was fine. What about you, though? Feeling better?'

'I'm alive.'

'I was hoping you would be.'

He laughs to himself. 'What time is it?' he asks, brushing his hair back again.

'It's way late, and if you want to go to bed, I completely understand.'

He side-eyes me. 'Truthfully, having someone here is nice. I've spent a lot of time alone lately. Mercy and I used to be roommates, but she's now across the street with Brooks. Plus, no way would she have cared for me like you are. You're a natural.'

18

RIVER

'I'm doing my best,' she says. 'Feel like testing that gag reflex by downing these?' She shakes a bottle of pills in her hand. 'They'll help your head not feel like concrete and possibly bring down your fever.'

'What if my main symptom is that I feel like ass? Does it help with that?'

'That probably depends on whose ass you feel like,' she laughs.

'The one sitting next to me looks pretty good. Can I feel that one?' I ask playfully, entirely joking, before swallowing down the pills and leaning my head against the back of my couch.

Jade laughs to herself. '*River Muriel Matthews*. You

dirty bird. No, you can't feel my ass because I am engaged. Remember?'

'What if you weren't engaged?' he asks.

'Um... I suppose it would then be an option.'

'You're unmarried and don't even have a date set, so technically, you're still available. And *Muriel*? *Really*?' I ask, my laugh echoing against the inside of my skull painfully.

'When I don't know someone's middle name, I use Muriel. I'm a *Friends* fan, and it's funny.' She lifts a shoulder, inspecting the pill bottle in her hand. 'These don't specify ass, but I think they'll still help.'

She's got her long hair pulled into a ponytail, but strands have escaped after she walked to the pharmacy, now framing her face. Jade is gorgeous. This Conner fella is a fucking moron. How can he not want to save this with her? I would do absolutely anything.

'You don't *have* to stay here and take care of me. Really. I can handle it.'

'No more saying that. I'm here, and it's where I *want* to be. Plus, Laney is headed back over with everything we need to burn some boys' souls, apparently. She's really good at making things weird as they can be.'

'I noticed that pretty quickly.' Once again, I laugh,

forgetting it hurts my head. 'So, Conner apologized. Does that mean everything is alright between you two now? Update me, what's going on in that pretty head.'

'Well, you caught me ogling your mostly naked self with heart eyes earlier, a moment I had no control over. And yes, Conner apologized and even says he loves me at the end of our calls again. But when I say it back...' She frowns, fidgeting with one of the rings on her fingers as if she's nervous about finishing her sentence. 'I don't know. I'm not sure my heart is on board anymore. Love is complicated, and after losing so many people in my life so close together, maybe I don't even know what it is. Usually, I'd talk to my mom about this, but I can't.'

I know my mom is a massive pain in my ass nine times out of ten, but I don't know what I'd do if she died. I can't imagine what it might be like to miss her the way Jade is currently missing hers.

'You know, I've got time. And the only working sense I've got left this evening is my hearing. Tell me about her.'

'About who?'

'Your mom.'

'You want to hear about my mother?'

'Why not? She's important to you, and I can tell

you miss her. Let's pretend I'm meeting her. Who am I meeting?'

She changes position, sitting with her legs crossed beneath her, facing me, a few feet away.

'I'll make you a deal,' she says. 'I'll introduce you to my mom if you introduce me to yours.'

Great. She knows. 'Figured me out, did ya?'

'Somehow, I had no clue. Dylan told me.'

'It's true,' I say. 'I'm never escaping the Penny Candy fandom. She is indeed my mother.'

'Want to hear something weird?' Jade asks.

'Always.'

'*My* mom was *your* mom's biggest fan.'

'Shut up,' I say, squinting open one eye. The room is mostly dark, with just a couple of lamps glowing on either side of the couch. 'Are you serious?'

'Completely,' she says with a grin. 'If she were still here, I'd be setting up a playdate between the two of them right now. She'd fangirl so freaking hard.'

Another thing oddly in common. How come I didn't know any of this before? 'Tell me more. What was she like?' I ask, feeling she needs to talk. Besides that one night she cried to me about her mom's illness, I don't know much, and she vaguely talks about her all the time, so I want to learn more.

'She was amazing. Sweet as sugar but took no

one's shit. I don't remember a single time she wasn't happy to see Laney or me – even if we were in trouble, she'd start her lecture with a hug. Rarely was she in a bad mood; she was more super-chill and light-hearted. She saw life as an adventure and wasn't afraid to hop on the back of Archibald with my dad and go for a ride through the city.'

'Archibald?'

'Oh,' she laughs. 'My dad's Harley.'

'He *named* it?'

'Well, in his defense, they're deeply in love.'

'Your dad is having a love affair with his chopper?'

'And with a cat he feeds human food on the dining table while he eats, along with my mom's yappy dog who rides with him now. But don't worry; he wears a helmet.'

'Your dad or the dog?'

'Both.'

I laugh out loud even though it makes my head pound. Jade's funny. 'I think I'd enjoy seeing that.'

'He gets a lot of attention when they ride together. It was mom's idea but when the dog loved it, my dad fell in love with him too.' Her mood fades a little. 'Speaking of love,' she sighs. 'Mom would have been so excited I'm getting married.'

Maybe she's attached to Conner because her mother approved of him? That would make sense. She misses her mom, and if she lets Conner go, she'd lose another piece of her.

'What did she think of Conner?' I take the chance and ask.

She drops her head, shaking it slightly. The purple glow of the Roku screensaver on the TV makes her look like an old-school video game character. I swear she's pretty in any lighting.

'They never met. He and I only met just after she died. But I think she'd approve. I mean, I'm a bartender marrying a future ER doctor.'

I wonder what her thoughts on me being a struggling artist are? I'm for sure not bringing in doctor money. 'His job matters then?'

Quickly she shakes her head. 'I didn't care what his job was. I fell in love with how he listened to me and said the right things. But, every day, I'm learning new things about him, and I'm beginning to wonder if he's just a smooth talker who possibly conned me and ended up in over his head, you know?'

'The boy is standing in quicksand.'

'Can I ask you something?'

'I'm an open book.'

'When did you first know he wasn't right for me?' she asks almost innocently. I didn't expect this one.

Telling her this is risky. Have I been flirting pretty much every time I see her? Yes. But I don't *mean* to. The words just leave my lips. But beating around the bush is getting me nowhere here. I'm sure there's something between us. I might as well be my truthful self.

'Pretty much the moment I met him.'

'How?'

'He made fun of my hair and called me bud, sport, or champ, which makes me want to punch him. He seems like one of those nepo babies who has everything handed to him on a silver platter and then acts like that alone makes him more important than others.'

'I can't exactly deny that he was born into money.'

'So was I,' I say. 'I'm not a douche to women because of it. I just don't understand the guy. He's not even broken-hearted to be away from you. If I had a girl like you, you'd have come with me because I wouldn't have wanted to live without you.'

'Really?' she asks, her voice soft.

My God did I say all that out loud? The burger has really affected my head.

'Yes, really,' I confirm.

She bites her bottom lip, bewilderment on her face. 'Were you going to kiss me that night I cried to you about my mom?'

We're finally going to talk about this lost moment, are we? I wondered if we ever would, and here it is.

'Yeah,' I answer honestly. 'But my friends were right. Drunk dudes shouldn't be kissing sober girls.'

'Not even if that sober girl hoped the drunk dude would?'

I lift my head, catching the cold cloth as it drops from my forehead. 'You *wanted* me to?'

'I don't cry in front of people, especially guys. I was serious when I said I'd rather run into a dark, scary forest. But that night, when you walked up on me, even though my back was to you, I knew it was you because I like your cologne.' She chuckles to herself. 'There's just something about you. I felt like I could trust you, and I don't get that feeling around many men. I work in a bar; typically, I see the worst of mankind. But you always made me smile, and that night you read my mind with how you said little and just... held me. That was what I needed, and while it was happening, I thought I felt something between us, so I concocted a plan to get you alone and possibly ask you out. But then you left, so I chased you out and gave you the green light. But the moment passed without you kissing me at a moment where I was setting you up to do exactly that. I assumed you'd placed me in the friend zone for some reason, and I didn't want to push my luck because I liked being friends with you.'

'I like being friends with you too, but that doesn't mean I've "friend zoned" you. The best relationships start with friendship.'

She nods as though she now gets that. 'Then my life blew up, and I felt like a zombie doing what I thought was right. What I thought would distract me from losing so many people I loved in so little time. Every day Conner is gone, I question whether he may have been one of those thoughtless decisions I made because I needed the attention. The day he proposed, I hesitated with my answer for so long, the poor guy was sweating bullets. I'm always worried about other people's feelings, so I felt like I couldn't say no in front of my whole family and totally destroy the guy's ego. Plus, like the obvious moron I must be, I sincerely thought he was serious.'

I don't really know what to say here. We've both just admitted there are feelings between us, but that doesn't change the fact that she's engaged to someone else. And I'm not a guy encouraging any woman to cheat on her boyfriend. I do have *some* morals. But I have to say something. Something to make her feel better that she's possibly made the wrong choice, and fixing it won't be easy, but will be worth it.

'When I was twenty-four/twenty-five, I too was in love with the wrong person and fought for her even when it was a burning hot mess.'

'Caitlin?'

'Yeah. Letting go was fucking hard because I was *so* sure she was the one even though everyone around me was telling me she wasn't. I spent a year trying to get her back, and it was only when she introduced me to her "friend" Derek that I finally realized she truly was moving on without me and my friends were right. Love shouldn't hurt.'

Jade's face probably reflects my own. Sadness. You don't want your friends ever to have broken hearts as much as you don't want them to be right about something you were sure they were wrong about.

'That's when you decided to risk your life and hike the haunted trail with Dax?'

'No, that happened when my mother finally forced me out of bed about a month after we broke up. I thought it would be good for my mental health. Boy, was I wrong.'

I can't believe I told her the story I made Dax promise to take to the grave. This woman knows more about me than my sister does, and I want to tell her everything she doesn't, good, bad, humiliating, all of it. I want to make up for not kissing her that night, by kissing the hell out of her right now, but I may have missed my chance when Conner swooped in and suddenly I've never regretted anything more.

19

JADE

'Hellloooo?' Laney's voice rings through the apartment as she knocks while opening the door, letting herself in. Totally unlike me, who was afraid to just walk in, she's met this guy once and is completely at home in his apartment. She stops near the kitchen island, looking at us both with an eyebrow raised. 'Did you two just see a ghost or what?'

Maybe the ghost of possible relationship opportunities that have passed. I can't believe we both felt the same and missed the perfect moment. Then fate jumped in and turned my world upside down, so I never really thought about it again until we started hanging out recently.

'No,' I say, glancing at River. 'Just realized we have

much more in common than we thought.' I flash him a smile, getting one in return. Excellent answer.

'Perfect, you're new BFFs, whatevs,' Laney says, completely unimpressed, dropping a bag full to the top of things she's spent the last hour scouring the city for. She pushes the coffee table out of the way and sits on the floor in front of us, her nearly bursting bag in front of her. Before she digs in, she rubs her hands together excitedly. 'Ready to burn some bitches?'

River and I exchange glances. Perhaps bringing Laney into our world was a bad idea, though she is excellent at ruining moments, and right now, I don't trust myself around River alone after that conversation.

'What else would a man who just ate a poisonous burger want to do at three in the morning, with a set of good and evil sisters, than burn some bitches in my apartment? Believe it or not, worse things have happened here.'

I'm not sure what we're in for here, but Laney swears she's found a way to get the response your heart wants painlessly and quickly. She was telling me all about it on the phone the other day, while I responded with 'wow, that's cool' over and over because when she's on a rant, I'm not about to disagree with her and considering a boy just did her wrong, I didn't want to test her. I didn't realize she wanted to actually do this.

We're sisters, so I trust her with my life, but not always her plans. She's been known to have some wild ideas. Like the time she set up a speed date event for herself by asking each of her Tinder matches to meet her five minutes apart so she could quickly weed out the losers. None of them knew that practically every other man in the joint was also there for her. If a man did this to a woman, he'd have gone home with no one. But once these guys figured out what was happening, they didn't disappoint. She ended up dating three of them for months.

'Are you sure this is safe?' I ask, opening the door to River's balcony for ventilation when I realize she's seriously grabbed the small metal trash can she usually keeps in her bathroom, and has a lighter. I don't think River would be pleased if we burned down his building.

'My friend Becca did this the last time a guy burned her, and she's now engaged to Mr Perfect. He was literally the next man she met. I'm willing to take the risk. Are you two?'

Riv and I both look a little worried. Mr Perfect was literally the next man she met? Huh.

'She gave me detailed instructions that we will follow, so what could possibly go wrong? I've got everything we need.' This is where she starts pulling things from her bag of tricks. 'Spices, fire, and a fire extinguisher. Plus, the boxes of memorabilia of all the boys that have done us wrong.' The trinkets of relationships past you keep to reminisce about later. Instead, we're going curse or maybe do magic, but that's how things go with Laney.

'Where's his box?' she asks, glancing around the dimly lit room.

'I don't have a box,' River says.

'Yes, you do,' Laney insists. 'Everyone does. Now stop being a pussy and go get it.'

'He's sick, Laney. If he doesn't want to do this, he can be in charge of the fire extinguisher,' I say, setting that in front of him.

River leans into me, the fresh, clean scent of his cologne I love clouding my brain power. 'In another life, I bet Laney spent her time in a state institution,' he jokes in a whisper. 'I have a box. It's in my room, on top of the closet, in a black box with a big white X painted on top.'

I grin as he rolls his eyes playfully. He does have one.

'I'll be right back,' I say, hurrying to his bedroom.

It takes me a minute to find something to stand on to reach the top of his closet, but when I do, there's a small black square box, a white X painted on the top, just like he said. I wonder what he's got in here? I shake it, but it feels empty.

'Thank you,' he says as I hand it to him and sit beside him again. I accidentally sit a little closer than intended, and our hips touch, but neither of us moves.

'Are you ready to smoke your true desires out of the universe?'

'Yeah, I'm not at all terrified,' River says flatly. 'How's this going down?'

'We burn shit; how many rules did you think there were?' Laney snaps, sprinkling different spices into the metal bin.

He glances at me with a smile. 'You two are total opposites. Word of warning, we've got about ten minutes to get this done before the sprinklers go off. Keep it short. Burn our shit. Break or make the curses and get our closure. Then we're done. Oh, and keep your voices down. My head is pounding.'

Laney starts us off. 'Goodbye, Lawrence,' she says while lighting a photo of them at the Rose Festival last year. That was actually a fun day. I went with them, and he won us both stuffed starfish at the bottle ball toss. Spike nearly immediately mutilated mine, but I'm a little surprised that the starfish isn't what Laney is burning. Maybe she already did?

'I'll never again date a man with a God complex,' she says, passing me the lighter.

Ugh. I reach into my box, grabbing anything. 'The Valentine my high school boyfriend, Ezra, dumped me with. "Please be..."' I read his words scribbled across a homemade pink heart with lace edging before opening it to read the rest. '"Someone else's girlfriend."' I sigh. 'God, I'm good at picking boys.'

'*What?*' River snatches the valentine from me, looking it over. 'That guy's a tool. Be gone, Ezra,' he says, tossing the card into the fire.

He fishes around the box in his hands, careful not to move too much, even though I suspect the meds are finally starting to work as he's got a bit more color in him than he did before. Finally, he pulls out a pair of bright pink thong underwear.

Laney laughs.

'Those don't really match your collection,' I joke. Yes, I'm still thinking about his underwear drawer.

'They're not mine.' They dangle from the tip of his index finger over the fire. 'Crazy in the head does not equal crazy in the bed. Lesson learned.'

'Ew. You kept her panties?' Laney asks, a mix of disgust and fascination all over her face as they burst into flames.

'Not kept, *left*. As in, she left them. I was young and thought it would be funny to keep them, but I now realize that despite never wanting to grow up, I have, and it's time to dispose of both of them and the memory. The girl gave me a scar.' He points at the back of one arm where a tiny half-moon scar exists, only visible if you're looking for it.

Note to self: ask to hear the story of crazy in the head girl.

'A sex injury,' Laney laughs. 'Be careful with this one,' she warns me.

If anything with every story he tells each are enticing me into his bed a little more.

We continue cycling through the three of us, and after a couple of turns each, we're laughing so much at each other's terrible relationships that I snort laugh, earning a side-eye from River. I'm overly tired, and it's showing.

'Pretend I didn't just do that. Who's next?' I ask.

'I've got one thing left,' Laney says, pulling out a small vial of liquid.

River scrunches his face. 'Please don't tell us what this one is.'

She rolls her eyes. 'It's the cologne of a guy I once had a fling with. It turned out he was married. I hope the next time he wears this; it'll burn his skin.' She pops the top and pours the tablespoon of liquid into the fire. It roars, forcing all of us to lean back, hoping no eyebrows were just lost.

'Cologne is flammable, you psycho,' River scolds her, like she's a child.

'Ah, really? I was hoping that was my curse manifesting. Damn. Somebody go.'

'I've got one thing left,' I say, glancing at River. 'You?'

'Also, one thing,' he says.

'I'll go.' I pull out the magazine ad, full of gorgeous engagement rings I'd consider wearing.

'The dream ring list?' Laney gasps. 'Are you finally giving up on him?'

River looks my way.

'Wow, suddenly this is heavy.' Laney keeps talking. 'Which one did you want again?'

'This one.' I point to one near the center of the page. Even River pays attention. A simple emerald-cut diamond solitaire. Not quite a carat, but so beautiful I've had dreams about the perfect man giving it to me. Would he go big? Or intimate? I guess I'll never know.

'I realize you two think I'm an idiot, but I swear I'm not. I know I need to dump Conner. Everyone is right; he's not the one. It's just so hard to do because I've lost so many people recently, and I thought he was the real deal.' I sigh, tossing the ad into the now-growing fire, flames lapping over the edge of the metal can. 'Never say yes to a man who proposes after two months, gets your name wrong, and doesn't have a ring.'

'Fuck Conner,' Laney cheers.

River quietly rests his hand on my back. 'You alright?' he asks, speaking softly into my ear.

'I will be. Go ahead, your turn.'

He looks into his box with a frown. 'This, uh.' He swallows hard, rubbing his hand over his chin. 'Well, I won't get into the story, but don't fall in love with a woman who's only looking out for herself,' he says, reading silently through the words on the card in his hand.

'Can I see it?' I ask, wondering if this is what I suspect it may be. I read it aloud. 'Together, with their parents, Mrs & Mr Ken Schiller and Mrs & Mr John Matthews, Caitlin Elaine Schiller and River Jonathon Matthews request your presence as they celebrate their marriage.' I gasp.

'You were *engaged*?' Laney asks with shock.

'Don't act so surprised; I'm a hell of a good guy when you get to know me,' he says. 'But yeah. When I was young and stupid, I was engaged and didn't see the forest through the trees.' He takes back the invitation. 'She called it off the day of our wedding.' After one more look, he tosses the invite into the burning can.

He was left at the altar? That is heartbreaking.

'I'm so sorry,' I say, unsure what else to say. I thought Caitlin was just an ex-girlfriend, not his almost-wife.

He lifts a shoulder as if it's no big deal, but I witnessed him around her, and it is a big deal. That woman truly hurt him. For a second, we all stare at the fire burning our memories and, hopefully, the ties that connect these people to our souls. But instead of it fizzling out, as we expect, it grows, setting off the fire alarms.

'Shit!' Despite being sick, River jumps up, steadies himself, then grabs the extinguisher before we burn the place down. Once the fire is out, he stares at the ceiling, perplexed. 'Nice to know the sprinkler system doesn't work.'

We see the front door swing open through the haze of the extinguisher and smoke.

'Riv! There's a fire.' Dylan stops midway into the

room, a nice enough guy that he ran over to save his friend from a fiery death. He glances around at the three of us. '*This* is what you wanted to do? Burn down the building?'

'The fire is out,' River assures him.

Suddenly we hear sirens racing towards the building.

'They don't know that, so come on,' Dylan says, ushering us out of the apartment. But I notice last minute that River's shoeless and shirtless, so I grab my coat and shove it his way as we walk out the door.

'Put this on. You don't need to get sicker.'

'The squirrel-skin rug?' he argues, moving the slowest of everyone in the building now headed outside. 'These things' souls are probably following you, hoping to get back into their skin.'

'Disturbing image, thank you. Now wear it,' I command, helping him get it on. It's a tad tight, but it works for now.

'You really should consider the nursing thing,' he says, an arm thrown over my neck as I lead him downstairs behind the rest of the building.

'Good patients make nursing easy,' I say. 'My mom used to say that.'

'Have I been a good patient?' he asks curiously. 'I let ya nearly burn down my apartment.'

I laugh. 'I apologize for that and so much more. That said, yes, you're a pretty good patient. You have little in the way of complaints; you've complimented me, made me feel better about myself, called me pretty, and never lost your sense of humor. It's been a night I'll never forget.'

Unexpectedly, my heart gallops when he slips his hand over mine. 'I feel like shit, and yet I've never been happier. Kick that asshole to the curb and never settle, Jade.'

Why can't it be that easy?

20

RIVER

We spent thirty minutes in the street last night after our little bonfire. I got an earful from my landlord, who, unfortunately for me, lives in the building. Laney left pretty much immediately after we evacuated the place. Jade was so tired I sent her to my room to sleep until morning so she didn't have to go home alone in the dark again. She finally agreed, only after insisting she put my laundry in the dryer, and that's why I'm on the couch. The girl did my laundry. Who does that?

I've finally nodded off into a peaceful, fever-free sleep – thanks to Jade – when there's a knock on my door. The sun greets me as I open my eyes, shining through my half-closed blinds. I glance at the clock on my wall. Eight a.m. Great. Who's this early bird at my door? When I hear a key in the lock, I'm suddenly wide awake and dying a little when I glimpse her purple highlights as the door cracks open.

'Go away!' I holler, hearing Jade stir in my room immediately.

I know yelling 'go away' to my mother won't work, but maybe it'll stall her long enough for me to explain what's happening to a woman I'm trying to impress and so far feel I'm flailing around in the ocean with.

'I'll go away when I'm good and ready,' Jade hollers back, sitting in my bed and glancing at me. Perhaps she wasn't sleeping as soundly as I suspected.

'Not *you*,' I say, pointing towards the front door.

'Riv?' Mom calls when the door finally pops all the way open. Her key is stuck in the deadbolt, so she drops a few brightly colored reusable grocery bags to the floor while she yanks the key from it. 'This apartment is such a shit hole,' she mumbles. 'I don't understand why you'd want to live here.'

I hear the footsteps of Jade exiting my room. This is about to blow up.

'Rivy?' Mom calls my name brightly after the key

extraction is successful and marches to my office, where I usually am.

Jade is now standing off to the side of my living room. 'Rivy?' she mouths with a grin.

I wave her away, but there's no way she's going after that.

'Mom.'

The look on Jade's face is pure joy when she figures out who's invaded my apartment.

Mom glances from my office towards my voice. 'There you are! What is this I hear about you being —' She stops speaking mid-word. 'Lord, sweetheart, you look like death.'

'Yeah, I had a bit of a rough night. *What* are you doing here at dawn?' I ask, attempting to sit up slowly to not anger the food poisoning back into action.

'I came to discuss a rumor I'd heard, but clearly, now is not the time. What's wrong? Alcohol poisoning? The bubonic plague? Herpes?'

'Herpes? What in the hell do you think that is?'

She ignores my question. 'Do you need an ER or not? I can take you. Are you hungry? I went grocery shopping early and brought some of your favorites.' She glances back at the bags now on my floor.

'No hospitals, *no* herpes, and no food. I'm never eating again. I'm fine; things are settling down.'

'You're sick and alone; you're not fine. Why didn't you call me earlier?'

'I didn't call you at all,' I remind her.

She leans over me, pressing her lips to my forehead.

'Will you stop?' I moan, gently pushing her by her shoulders to an arm's length away.

'Quit acting like a baby who's too old for his mother and let me help you!' Mom jokes loudly. As she turns towards the kitchen to take care of her shopping purchases, she spots a silent Jade, watching her baby me. How embarrassing is that?

'Oh, hello,' Mom says to her with surprise, glancing back at me, 'who is this' plastered on her face.

'Mom, this is—'

'Are you with his insurance company?' she cuts me off, guessing instead of listening. 'I knew I'd purchased him the big plan, but I had no idea it included home visits. How nice is that.' She gushes while she talks over me. 'Thank you so much for taking care of my baby boy! I'm here now. Does insurance cover your services, or is River supposed to pay you? Because I can cover it. How much is it?'

'Mom!'

Finally, she snaps her head my way. 'What?'

'She's not the help. I invited her here. *Yesterday*.'

Her eyebrows shoot up her forehead as she glances back at Jade. 'Oh?'

Dear God, she is assuming we had sex. If the next question out of her mouth is 'how was it?' I will somehow summon the energy to swiftly lead her back to her car and away from making me seem like a massive momma's boy.

I wave Mom my way, encouraging her to lean in so I can yell at her in a whisper and not seem like an asshole in front of Jade.

'What is it, sweetheart?' She leans towards the couch.

'Get. Out,' I say as sweetly yet firmly as possible under my breath.

The look on her face is of pure confusion.

'But I brought all your favorites...' She motions towards the kitchen where Jade is now happily unloading the bags, watching our every word. 'String cheese, Cool Ranch Doritos, chocolate milk, maple syrup oatmeal, and mint chocolate chip ice cream, the green kind.'

Jade laughs. 'Yep, I see that childlike food pallet you mentioned. By the way, this is my favorite too...' she says, displaying the ice cream container.

Of course it is. For a second, my eight-year-old

heart spins at the fact that Mom found the recently elusive green mint chocolate chip ice cream, but my stomach quickly rejects the idea.

'Can we not talk food right now?'

Mom leans in again. 'Do I need to pay her for "services" or what?'

'You think I need to pay a woman to come over?' I ask, completely offended. 'She is neither a prostitute nor a caretaker. So, no, you do not need to pay her,' I command with as much energy as possible. 'Her name is Jade, and we're...' I hesitate. After our conversation last night, I'm not really sure what she is to me.

Suddenly Mom stands, throwing her hands into the air. 'Oh, my God! *This* is Jade? Oh, honey, I was unsure you actually existed, but you are beautiful!' She smothers Jade in a hug that would terrify even me, but Jade eats it up, hugging her back and flashing an enthused grin.

'No, *you're* beautiful,' Jade says after Mom finally releases her. 'I can't believe I'm meeting Penny Candy. I'm a huge fan, and my mom absolutely worshipped you.'

Am I in a coma right now? Or did I actually die, and heaven's a bit wonky?

'How in the hell would you know who she is?' I ask my mom, confused.

'You'll never guess who I ran into yesterday evening,' Mom says, helping her put groceries away. I can tell from here Jade is completely starstruck, watching my mom's every move with a grin plastered on her face.

'Billy Joel?' I guess only because I know she'll make me, and I want to get this conversation over with quickly.

'Nooo...' she laughs. 'I haven't seen Billy since our trip with him and Alexis to Jamaica a few years back. Did I ever tell you we put on an impromptu show at an oceanside bar? That was such a fun vacation.' She stares into space momentarily while reliving it. 'Anyway, I'm off track. Would you believe me if I said *Caitlin* stopped by the house?'

Yep. I gotta be dead. There's only one world where this would be normal. Hell.

'Caitlin?' Jade asks, her eyes now wide.

'Oh, don't worry, sweetheart. I get way better vibes from you.' She pats Jade's back like she's comforting her. 'But yeah,' she continues, glancing out at me. 'I got a knock on the door, and when I opened it, there she was, as beautiful as ever, with the most adorable baby.'

Holy fuck. She went to my mom's house? With the baby? Why?

'Said she was in the neighborhood and thought she'd pop in,' Mom says, reading my mind. 'Isn't that sweet?'

Ah, yeah. How super sweet that my ex stopped by to introduce her baby to my mother. I should have thrown myself into that fire last night.

'She told me a little secret: I'm surprised you haven't told me yet.'

'Is it that I can't stand her? 'Cause, in my defense, I thought you knew.'

Mom shoots me a glare. 'No, it's that you have this gorgeous fiancée, Jade!' Mom turns to her, once again gushing. 'How have I never heard of you? He didn't even tell his sister; those two tell each other everything. Hols is who suggested I come over and get some answers.'

Freaking Hollyn.

'Why would you hide her from us, Riv? She's adorable. Though, you both look tired. Long night?' she asks with a giggle.

Jade's eyes go wide as she glances my way.

'Let's see that ring, sweetheart?' Mom asks, grabbing Jade's hand, lifting it to get a good look, then dropping it suddenly as she turns my way.

'*River*. What have I told you your entire life?'

'Always wear clean underwear because you never know what might happen.' I blurt out one of the many things she's told me my entire life.

Jade laughs, but Mom is not so amused.

'Men do not propose without a ring. Boys who haven't thought it through do.'

These words affect Jade visibly as she glances at her ringless finger. She frowns, then something changes, as though she's had a revelation.

'There is a ring,' she says suddenly, grimacing my way behind my mom's back. 'It was just, uh, too big. It's being sized. It'll be ready by the end of the month.'

'The end of the month?' Mom squawks. 'Noooo. That is far too long for a newly engaged woman not to be able to brag to her friends about the love of her life. What jeweler is it with? I'll make some calls, and you'll have it by the end of the day tomorrow.'

'Um,' Jade mumbles. 'I can't remember the name of the jeweler, hun. Do you?'

'Bejeweled in Vancouver,' I say, making up the name of a shop that only exists across state lines and in this conversation. That'll buy me some time to straighten this out.

'I'll call them this afternoon,' Mom says before

turning to Jade. 'How do you feel, honey? Are you sick too?' Before she can answer, Mom's got her lips pressed to her forehead, checking her temp the mom way and leaving deep pink lip prints that I realize I'm probably sporting too. I have to end this.

After a few moans, I'm off the couch.

'Mom.' I take her elbow, leading her towards the front door. 'Jade and I hadn't announced anything yet. You know I don't want to jump into anything and have it go wrong again.'

'I was afraid you would feel this way when I told you she stopped by. Don't let Caitlin affect your relationship with Jade. If you need closure, find it. But you two are perfect together. I feel it in my bones.' Mom wraps her arms around my waist, hugging me tightly, leaning her head on my chest.

'Unless you want me to puke on you, I'd advise you back away slowly.'

'Hugs are healing,' she insists.

'So is chicken noodle soup, and Jade's been kind enough to order some for delivery this afternoon.'

'She read my mind. Good girl,' she compliments her. 'Now Riv, mark your calendar because we're having a family dinner tomorrow night with both my kids now engaged. Jade, if you're available, you're welcome to come. You're family now.'

Her smile is as cute as it could get. 'As much as I would love that, I work tomorrow night.'

'That's okay,' Mom tells her. 'There will be plenty of dinners, darling.'

'Time to go,' I hint blatantly.

Mom beams as she exits into the hallway. 'I'm so glad this is happening for you. I like her, Riv. Bring her by the house.'

'We'll see,' I say, closing the door and locking all three locks: knob, deadbolt, chain. I can't risk any more visitors at this point.

'I'm so sorry!' Jade says. 'I totally just made that worse because I was lost for words, starstruck, and confused, so I think I will go. Running away always helps in these situations.'

As she gathers her things and heads my way towards the door, I grab her hand. 'Jade, I really do like you. More than I expected. But I can't make a move until I know you're available, and I will leave that up to you. Absolutely no pressure.'

She laughs nervously. 'Yeah, no pressure. Alright. Well, I've got some things to sleep on today, don't I.'

'Call me later?' I ask, hopeful she isn't going to leave my apartment and run for the fucking hills after all this.

'Of course,' she promises as she exits my building, only glancing back once. As soon as I close the door, I hunt down my phone and dial my sister's number.

'Hey, dork,' Hollyn answers.

'I'm going to drive you out into the middle of nowhere, cover you in peanut butter, and drop you off for the wildlife to consume.'

She laughs nervously. 'You're homicidal, alright. May I ask why?'

'Mom stopped by,' I say flatly as I walk to my room, dropping onto my bed and staring at the ceiling. Jade's coconut shampoo is lingering on my pillow and I don't hate it.

'Right... I may have had something to do with that. Sorry, but what's the deal? Are you suddenly engaged? To *Jade*? I thought she already had a fiancé. Also, why would Caitlin stop by Mom's for a visit after five years? Did something happen? That's not your baby is it?'

'It's definitely not my baby. But yes, something did happen. I ran into the woman I've been avoiding for five years and had a stroke while Jade talked for me.'

'You *saw* her? What did you guys talk about? Why didn't you tell me?'

'We talked about nothing because I hate her. All I

could do was try to figure out an emergency exit. How do you not know that Caitlin's not my favorite person on the planet, much like your ex, Professor Dickbag. We aren't chatting it up in the grocery store. Now you've sent Mom here for answers at the worst possible time, Hols. I was *with* Jade the night I ran into Caitlin. She read the room and pretended to be my fiancée.'

'Ohhhhh. Fake engagement? Easily straightened out.'

'Is it? Because having a crush on a girl who's taken doesn't feel easy to straighten out.'

'You have a crush on Jade? Does she know?'

'Yes, she knows. I'm pretty sure the feeling is mutual.'

'Shoot. And Caitlin visited Mom to get the details because she thinks the engagement is real?'

'Uh-huh.'

'Oops.'

I hit the speaker button and lay the phone on my chest. 'Oops? *That's* your response? Oops, I spilled all the fucking tea to our invasive mother, who has probably already submitted a newspaper engagement announcement about a girl with a fiancé and me. I'm sure she'll enjoy explaining that to her family. Not to mention Jade was here when Mom arrived this morning. They've now met, and Mom feels she's the one "in her bones". Thanks for that.'

Hollyn gasps. 'She's *there*? No way. Did you guys, boom-chicka-bow-wow or what? I can't believe you'd do that with a girl with a boyfriend. That's one of your rules. No cheating.'

'The only thing I did last night was try to survive a nasty bout of food poisoning while Jade attempted to keep me alive. There was and will be no cheating. I swear to God, Hols if I could demote you to stepsister, I would.'

'Well, you can't, so ha. You better figure this out fast because Mom's already scheduled a family dinner for tomorrow night, and if you don't hurry, she'll have your wedding planned by the end of the week. Trust me; she's been trying to plan mine for months.'

I know she's right, and the thought terrifies me. Poor Jade already realizes the world she knew just weeks ago is no longer. The last thing she needs is to deal with my psycho mother trying to marry me off.

21

JADE

I can't believe I met Penny Candy and had no words! Well, I did have words, but they were all wrong based on River's reaction. She's so pretty, so bubbly, and loves River very much. But I'm confused about how she looks just like she used to. She's got to be in her sixties by now. God, my mom would have fainted. Then I lied to her, probably making everything worse for River, but I didn't know what else to do. I was starstruck in a way I've never experienced, and now I have to sleep it off because I am absolutely exhausted and don't want to think about everything I need to think about, including dumping Conner, which obviously I'm going to have to do. Love shouldn't feel like this. I just don't know how to do it. I've never dumped someone before.

Hours later, the smell of something wonderfully familiar wakes me from my deep sleep – a sleep filled with dreams of River and me. When I say dreams, I mean *sex* dreams. That's right. I'm probably going straight to hell, considering I'm taken and dreaming about doing another guy. What even brought it on, besides our subtle flirting, which I consider harmless because I don't plan on having sex with him? God, how could this happen? Rarely do I have sex dreams, never even about Conner. What does it mean? And *what* is that smell?

I force myself out of bed, Spike greeting me immediately from his cage.

'Hai, pretty lady!'

'Hi, Spike. Was someone here?' I ask, noticing my front door is wide open. I glance around my apartment, wondering if perhaps I should be watching Laney's beloved true crime shows so I'd know what the hell to do right now. Instead, I shuffle out the door (did *I* leave it open?) and into Thomas's open front door, spotting my dad and him sitting at his dining table.

'Sleeping beauty!' Dad says with a grin. 'Are you

ready to supply Thomas' laundry money this month?'

Sleepily I rub my eyes, making sure I'm really awake. 'I forgot about this.' Every so often, Thomas, Dad, and I have a poker night. He taught me to play as a kid, and I got pretty good. Lately, though, Thomas has also gotten very good. We only play for quarters, but last time we did, I owed him fifteen bucks. He said it paid for his laundry for a month.

'Quick question, though. What do I smell?'

'That'd be your mother's famous taco soup,' Dad says. 'Thomas made it. I thought I'd gone back in time when I walked in. It was a little heartbreaking and heart-waking at the same time.'

I nod, understanding completely. 'Why's my door open?'

'We didn't want to wake you, so we let the soup do it for us,' Thomas says with a sweet grin.

An hour later, I'm down six bucks, but the soup is warming my soul, so it's worth it. I'm also two beers in and starting to feel overly chatty. I toss a card for exchange towards my dad, who is playing the part of dealer this evening. He hands a new one back. Bingo. Three Aces.

'I've got a hot date tomorrow night,' Thomas announces as he waits for his card trade-ins.

'You're going on a date?' I ask, surprised to hear this. Thomas' wife died a decade ago, and to my knowledge, he's not dated since. 'Do I know her?'

He shakes his head. 'She works at the grocery store I go to. Real sweet to talk to, and not bad to look at either.'

Dad drops his cards face down onto the table. 'I fold.'

I glance at Thomas, who playfully glares. 'Just you and me, kid. You in?'

Could he have a better hand than me? It's possible. But I'm feeling lucky. 'I'm all the way in,' I say, pushing every poker chip I have to the center of the table.

'Oh,' Dad murmurs. 'She must have something good.'

'Or she's bluffin'.'

'My Jade would never lie. She was bitten by the truth bug at birth.'

If he only knew the lies I've been telling. Primarily to myself, but they still count.

'What?' Dad asks, knowing immediately something is wrong. I can't hide things from him, but I also don't want to tell them what's happening in my life because even I don't understand it.

'Nothing. Well, maybe not *nothing*. I do have one

question, and since you two are full-grown men, you'll probably have the best advice. Buuuttt, it's kind of X-rated.'

Dad scrunches his face but pulls it back together pretty quickly. 'You can tell us anything, Jadeybug.'

'What kind of man asks women for nudes?'

Both he and Thomas freeze. They glance at one another and then back to me, where Dad suddenly clears his throat.

'Did someone ask you for a nude?' he asks.

'No, but it was suggested, and I just wondered, is that love? Nudes?'

Thomas laughs, shaking his head. 'That's lust, sweetheart.'

I sigh heavily. That's what I thought. Conner is a playboy. Everything points in that direction, so why did he propose to me? Was it just a last-minute 'I forgot a gift' decision? I lay my cards down after Thomas goes all in with me.

'Damn it, girl,' he says, tossing his cards onto the table, obviously unable to beat me.

'Ha-ha! The laundry money is mine this month!'

'What's going on, Jade?' Dad asks, concern in his voice.

'I've just been doing a lot of thinking lately and spending time with someone who makes me sincerely feel good, and I realize Conner doesn't. Now I'm questioning if I even know what love is. And how do you know if you're in it? Or better question, how do you know if someone loves you? Like, for certain? Am I just a total dumbass?'

Dad laughs. 'If you are, so is everyone else who's questioned the same thing, and we all have. Is this other someone the "friend" you recently had dinner with?'

'It was dessert, drinks, and appetizers, but yeah. I like him, which makes me feel so sleazy since I'm engaged to someone else. Is what I'm doing cheating? 'Cause I don't want to be that girl.'

'You do anything with him, physically?' Thomas asks the question I'm sure my dad doesn't want to hear the answer to.

I shake my head. 'No. Just some harmless flirting, but we did talk about an "almost kiss" moment we had months ago – long before Conner came into the picture. It turns out, we both felt the same way, we just missed the moment, and he's one of those guys who would never touch me like that unless I was absolutely single.'

'Is he the guy suggesting the nudes?'

'Nooooo,' I tell him. 'In fact, if I told him about

that, he'd probably be pissed. He doesn't love Conner.'

'Then whatever you two have going on isn't cheating. It sounds like he sincerely likes you if he's trying to protect you from a boyfriend he doesn't like. That's the kind of guy you want.'

'But how do I know for sure? I don't want to make another mistake, Dad.'

He scoots closer, hugging me to him. 'We all make mistakes, Jade. Let's try something your mom used to make me do. Close your eyes,' he suggests.

I do as I'm told, closing my eyes, his arm still around my shoulders.

'What's your heart telling you right now?'

'My heart is screaming—' My phone blasts from my apartment, ringing loudly. 'Shit, be right back,' I say, racing to my apartment.

'Hullo?' Spike screeches with each ring until I answer.

'Hello?'

'Hey, babe.' My heart stops. It's Conner. I didn't even check before I answered because I was afraid I would miss it. 'Hello? Did I lose you?'

Possibly.

'No, I, uh, just woke up. What are you doing?'

'I had a night off, so I thought I'd give you a ring.'

Not a chance he's thinking about rings – wrong choice of words, Conner.

'Oh.' I sit down on my unmade bed. 'How are things?'

'Good. Busy, but good.' He doesn't elaborate, and he would if he wanted me to know the details. I'm not about to beg for conversation from the guy.

'That's great.'

The line is silent. Neither of us speaks because what's there even to talk about anymore? I feel like I don't know him.

'How are things with you?' he finally asks. 'Anything exciting happening?'

'Alexa, play love song,' Spike squawks.

'No!' I holler to cancel it out. I'll never understand why Laney thought teaching him to use Alexa would be funny.

'What?' Conner asks.

'Not you, Spike. He's ordering around Alexa again. Just a minute.' Before I can stop it, a song blasts through my echo dot speaker, causing me to drop my phone onto the floor. It skids across the hardwood floor under my bed as I sit in shock. Why would Alexa play this song? Of all songs, why the one from my favorite movie scene ever?

'What's going on?' Dad asks, walking into my

apartment and covering his ears; that's how loud it is. 'How do we turn it off?'

'Alexa, cancel music,' I say when I finally return from my momentary shock. The song stops immediately.

'Alexa, play music,' Spike yells again, causing the song to blast back on.

My dad laughs. 'I don't know how you live with him,' he yells over the music.

The only way to stop it is to unplug the damn thing. I storm across the room to yank the cord from the wall.

'Wait!' Dad stops me just before I do it, a single hand in the air. 'This is the song from that movie your mom loved. What was it called?' he asks, recognizing it because she forced him to watch it as often as possible.

'*Say Anything*. Laney and I just went and watched it recently. It was playing at the Hawthorne Theater.'

Dad sits on a chair in the corner of my living/bedroom and drops his head into his hands, suddenly letting out a sob he can't control. He's held it together for months since she died, but hearing that was too much. I squeeze in next to him, wrapping my arms around his neck and letting him cry it out while the song continues playing. Maybe it is loud enough to wake the whole building, or at least my direct neighbors, but he hasn't shown this much emotion since the day she died, so I'm not about to shut it down.

'Alexa, turn the music down,' Thomas says, grabbing my door handle to shut my door. He's pretty good at reading rooms. The music softly fades to a quieter level. 'By the way, this is what love looks like, sweetheart.' He nods my dad's way. 'When you can't imagine being away from someone, and when you are, it physically hurts.'

My heart sinks through my chest, and my head goes to one person. And that person isn't the guy probably listening to this entire conversation from under my bed right now.

22

RIVER

'There he is!' Dax says, standing from my parents' couch when I walk in with a beaming smile I already hate. 'The man of the night. You're engaged!' he says with a knowing laugh, shaking my hand obnoxiously. 'Congratulations! When's the big day?'

I told him over the phone this morning, and he laughed until I hung up. 'You're not funny.'

'I'm a little funny,' he insists.

'What is she doing right now?' I ask, wondering where my mother is and what this dinner is about. Why a family dinner the moment she finds out I'm engaged? Er, *fake* engaged.

'Hols is in the bathroom.'

'I meant my mom,' I groan.

'Oh, right, your mom. To my knowledge, she's in the kitchen chatting up Caitlin.'

Chatting up, *who*? No, no, no. This can't be happening. '*What?*'

He nods. 'Yep. She figured that since Jade couldn't join us, tonight would be the perfect night for you two to get closure so you could move on with your newfound love.'

Suddenly, I want to go back and attempt that coronary burger again and hope it kills me.

'No, she did not,' I say in disbelief.

He smiles wide. 'She sure did. I tell you what, coming over here always makes me glad my mom is normal.'

That's perfect. We'll leave. Let's visit Dax's mom, a woman who does not involve herself in his life and lets him be a grown man.

'We should go visit, I haven't talked to your mom in ages,' I say, heading right back out the front door, but instead, Dax grabs the back of my shirt, stopping me.

'You're in this now. We ain't going anywhere.'

I sigh heavily. 'Please, *please* tell me Derek isn't—'

'What up, Riv? Your parents got a nice house. Caitlin had mentioned something about that, but this is my first visit.' He chomps down on a carrot stick, glancing around the room with a nod.

'This is also your last visit, so enjoy it while you can.'

'He's here,' Dax says, a moment too late, scrunching his nose in disgust. Bro-code rules; we hate who the other hates. 'Got any cameras on you? You may need this recorded to remember it because you look like you're about to black out.'

Please, for the love of everything holy, let me black out. I breathe in through my nose and out through my mouth, ready to explode.

'Riv!' Mom greets me happily. 'What do you think of this one?' she asks, motioning to the dress she's wearing that hits her high enough above the knees that a public school would send her home to change. 'For Hollyn's wedding. Doesn't it just scream mother of the bride?'

Dax lifts a single eyebrow, shaking his head behind her back, obviously not on board.

'Veto,' I say. 'It screams prom, 1985. Can I, uh, talk to you?' I ask, grabbing her hand and dragging her upstairs to my old bedroom, which still looks exactly as it did the day I graduated – Britney Spears poster on the ceiling over the bed and everything.

'*What* are you doing?' I ask, nearly boiling over inside.

'Preparing dinner, what are *you* doing?'

I pace, my hands in my hair as I walk back and forth in front of my trophy shelf, all my baseball awards from childhood still looking shiny and brand new as if I just got them yesterday.

'I'm trying to figure out why you would intervene like this. You realize I'm a grown man, right?'

'*Obviously*. I gave birth to you, and I remember it like it was yesterday despite it being almost thirty years ago. You were such a cute bald baby. It was one of the best days of my life.'

One of the best days of her life, and now she's trying to kill me. 'Why's Caitlin here? And why the fuck would you let Derek in this house?'

She sighs, sitting on my bed and crossing her legs. 'You can't hate them forever,' she says. 'You're getting married; shouldn't you go into that knowing everything with your past has been resolved? Instead of holding all this bitterness in your heart?'

'Ugh,' I groan, dropping down in my old computer chair and leaning back. 'Mom, I'm not getting married. Jade and I are not engaged. It was just a ruse to get rid of Caitlin one night when we unexpectedly ran into her. Jade and I aren't even dating. In fact, she's getting married to someone else.'

Her shoulders drop like this is a huge disappointment to her. 'She already has a husband? *River!* We do not date taken girls.'

'Mom, I *know* this. It's exactly why we aren't dating.'

'Then why did she make up a story about a ring?'

'Because she saw your disappointment, was overly starstruck, and wanted you to like her.'

'That's cute, but still, she lied. You don't want a woman who lies to your mother, do you?'

'She lied because she's having a rough time right now. Her fiancé isn't who she thought he was. She recently lost her mother to cancer. And when she discovered you were my mom, it brought back memories of her own mom, who was some kind of super fan of yours back in the day.'

I feel like I'm twelve years old and in trouble for smoking behind the bleachers during lunch again. That argument was heated to the point Dad wanted to make me smoke an entire pack to teach me a lesson. The first one made me sick, so why would I want a whole pack? It's not like I did drugs. Every kid tries smoking, and I hated it, so lesson learned.

'How can she already be engaged and not wear a ring? That's the most exciting part!'

Of course she'd be stuck on that.

'Because the tool never gave her one.'

I almost died when she pulled that ring advertisement from her ex box recently. Not because I was surprised she had a photo of her perfect ring, but because it's the exact ring still sitting in the bottom drawer of the desk I'm sitting in front of that I bought for Caitlin. The planet has a million engagement ring styles; *how* could she have chosen that one?

There's a knock on the door frame, and Mom and I jerk our heads in that direction. Thank God, it's my father.

'Everything alright in here?' he asks softly.

'No. Mom's on crack,' I say, glaring her way.

'I am not on crack,' she snaps back. 'You told me you were engaged.'

'But I didn't. The woman I never wanted to see again, who is now sitting downstairs with her happy little family, that fucked me over in front of everyone I know, did. Do you not remember what she did to me?'

'Of course I remember. You spent weeks in this bed, refusing to do anything. How could I forget?'

'If you remember it so well why on earth would you invite her over here for dinner?'

'I'm a firm believer in closure. When your dad and I got serious I called all my old flings and let them know I was no longer taking booty calls. It's what made everything between us more serious.'

The last thing I want to hear is stories about her booty call days. 'Pretending she didn't exist was my closure.'

'You can't ignore your past, Riv or it'll continue to haunt you. You need to look this girl in the eye and tell her how she made you feel.'

I clutch my chest, pain searing through it. 'My God, I'm having a heart attack at twenty-nine. Are you happy now? You've killed me.' Dead would be easier right now.

'You're not having a heart attack,' Dad says, sitting on the chest at the end of my bed and taking my pulse. 'You can't die before your wedding anyway, son. That's too tragic of a story, especially considering the first one.'

I smirk. 'If you think you're funny, you're wrong.'

Dad laughs.

'Am I too old to be adopted into a family that doesn't get involved in my business?' I ask. I've never felt the way

I do right now. I literally want to jump out my bedroom window and take off running *if* my legs aren't both broken from the fall. 'Jesus, and here I thought Dax breaking my "bro code" was bad. Seems like what I *really* needed was a "mom code".' After this nightmare night, I might need a new best friend, sister, mother, all of it.

Mom rolls her eyes. 'Had you told the truth, you wouldn't be in this mess.'

'I never lied to you. You assumed things, and then you meddled. I'm nearly thirty. I don't need help with my love life or lack thereof. If I ever get engaged, you would be the first to know, and the news won't be brought to you by my *ex*-fiancée.'

She nods, finally looking like she's sorry. 'I did think it was a little weird, but then I walked into your apartment to see Jade there, so I thought it was true. And you two didn't help by playing along.'

'River?' Caitlin's voice stops all of us where we are. I don't even want to look that way, so instead, I drop my head with a moan. Jesus, let's invite up every girlfriend of my past and do this, shall we?

'What?' I say furiously.

'Can we talk?' Caitlin asks, sweetly, as if she's got absolutely nothing to do with this but in all reality, she's the reason this is happening.

'I guess if we have to. I wouldn't want you to have ruined my life a second time for nothing.'

'We'll just leave you two be,' Mom says, dragging Dad out of my room and closing the door like I want to be alone with this woman.

Caite walks around, looking at old photos with nostalgia on her face. This isn't the first time she's been in here. We've had sex in this room. Great, and now I'm picturing it.

'I can't believe they kept your room the way it was. When I moved out, my mom turned my room into a home gym within days.'

'You're quite the star of your own show, aren't you?' I ask, my tone bitter, just like Mom suggested. 'Do you have any idea what you've done?'

She turns to me, a questioning look on her face. 'I wasn't thinking, and after I ran into you, I thought it might be nice to visit with your mom again. I had no clue that nothing you two told me at the restaurant that night was true.'

I run my hand over my head, unsure what to say here.

'I didn't expect you'd feel the need to lie about a fiancée the first time we ran into one another.'

'Pfft, bullshit. You didn't realize it because you've never been the type of girl to see anything beyond how things affect you. For instance, I was in my tuxedo, and guests were seated. Our honeymoon was paid for, and my bags were packed when I learned you weren't coming. *To our wedding*. My dad had to announce that everything had been canceled because I couldn't even speak; I was so torn up. Any idea what that does to a guy who legit thought you were the one?'

Guilt crosses her face. 'I didn't know. I'm sorry.'

'Excellent, all better. Caitlin's sorry,' I say, tossing my arms out in frustration. 'How about we acknowledge the fact that you named your baby *Phoenix*?'

'So?'

'*So...* the whole reason we decided to get married then was because you were pregnant. With *my* baby. The one we agreed to name Phoenix.'

Her face drops with the mention of the baby we never had. When I found out she was pregnant, I rushed around and proposed because I loved her and thought it was the right thing to do. Then she miscarried a couple of weeks before our wedding at thirteen weeks. I thought we were doing everything right. I spent all my time with her, and behind my back, she spent all her time with her high school ex, Derek.

'When I lost that baby, I was distraught.'

'Well, I'm glad Derek could be there to comfort you, while I also was distraught and alone.'

She looks ashamed of herself, as she should be. This woman broke me in a way that made me never want to grow up, get married, *or* have kids. And that used to be my dream. Besides random short-term relationships here and there, I've been alone ever since.

'Again, I'm sorry,' she says. 'Losing that baby changed everything about me, and I figured it had done the same for you,' she says. 'Because of that, I know I shouldn't have left you when you probably needed someone most, but I did, and I couldn't exactly take it back. Everything was a mess, so I disappeared.'

Finally, she says the words I've needed to hear, even if it is five years too late.

'Honestly,' I glance at her feeling a bit defeated. 'That's the only part of this I'm thankful for. Next time you see me in a store or anywhere, I want you to pretend we've never met. Don't ask who I'm with. Don't stop to say hello. Just turn around and walk the other way.'

She stares at me blankly, swallowing hard. 'Fine. But I can't change my baby's name, Riv. I suppose I can suggest we call him by his middle name instead, considering you did come up with Phoenix, and I did sort of steal it...'

'If that kid's middle name is River, Caitlin, so help me Go—'

'His middle name is Derek, after his father. How crazy do you think I am?'

I laugh to myself. 'Trust me; you do *not* want the answer to that question.'

'I guess we'll just go then,' she says, opening my bedroom door but stopping in the hall and glancing back. 'I truly do hope you find someone, Riv. You deserve to be loved.'

I say nothing. Instead, I just try not to let my heart explode again as she walks away from my room, hopefully never to be seen again.

23

RIVER

The next day I'm lying on my couch, staring at the TV, and it's not even on. How in the hell did all this happen? It's all I'm thinking about. But I have to stop. I've got to get up and do something. Anything. I wonder what Dax is doing? I'm about to reach for my phone when it buzzes on the coffee table. There's absolutely nobody I want to talk to right now, besides Dax. It buzzes again. And again. Finally, I grab it, smiling at the name flashing across the screen as she texts me repeatedly.

Hi.
How are you?

Doing anything today?
I'm bored and need my favorite distraction.

I hope that's not all I am for her, a distraction, because she's all I want right now. I want to be pissed at
everything that's happened in the last twenty-four
hours, but all I can think about is possibly losing her
in all this. Seeing her smile might lift my mood.

Hi, pretty lady. Honestly, I'm not great and could use a
distraction myself.

You're having a crap day too? What's wrong? Please,
let me help.
You do so much for me. It's the least I could do. I'm
up for anything.

Nothing 'wrong', just have a meddling mother that
won't quit.

Up for anything, huh? That's a risky invitation. Of
course, in my current mood, I've got exactly no sug-
gestions, which doesn't help. But there's got to be
something we could do to get our minds off the pain
we call love.

Oooh, I'm sorry. At least you know she loves you!
I have an idea. Have you ever been roller skating?
It's like, the eighties-est thing to do.

Too much, she loves me too much. LOL
Have I ever been skating?
My mom is Penny Candy.
She used to take us and request her own songs.
Know a place?

LOL, that's funny. I do know a place!
My grandfather used to take me there when I was
little.
Do you want to go?

Yes, I do. Pick you up in thirty?

I'll be ready, but no cheeseburgers tonight.

LOL, that's a promise.

An hour later, we're sitting at the roller rink her
grandfather used to take her to; only it's no longer a
skating rink but an Office Max. I can't believe they'd
turn something so nostalgic into something so dull.

This place used to be where kids came to lose themselves in music and make new friends, and now it's filled with work shit. Yuk.

'I'm sure there's something we can do in here still. Wanna sniff some Sharpies?' I ask jokingly. I'm not a pen huffer, I swear, though if this place sold pot, I might be a buyer; that's how I'm feeling today.

'Well, this sucks,' she says, pulling open the door to the store anyway. 'I can't believe they'd turn this building into something as boring as an office store. This place was magical. It had flashing lights, neon carpets, walls of brightly colored lockers, and in the center was the DJ, a guy who danced while he played. I had my first French kiss here.' She points to a corner at the back of the building. 'Right over there, with a boy named Aiden Turner.'

'Sounds like a loser,' I kid, making her laugh.

As we walk through the aisles, I notice an office furniture section. Most of it's bolted down, but one chair is free. Hmm. That could actually work. She'll think I'm a lunatic, but what have I got to lose at this point?

'I have an idea. Sit down,' I say quietly, glancing around the store, hoping the only people who work here are teenagers and they'll think this is funny instead of calling the cops, because I'm about to disturb the peace in this joint.

'Sit down where?'

'Here,' I say, grabbing the back of the free-rolling desk chair.

'Alright,' she says curiously, sitting down and holding her purse that looks like a Chinese take-out bag in her lap. I love this girl's style, and considering I'm wearing a light pink cheetah print T-shirt and gray jeans with magenta-colored Converses that she hasn't even batted an eye at, I don't think she's scared by mine. This is refreshing, considering most friends make fun of my style.

I pull my phone from my pocket and search for a song I remember hearing at a skating rink when I was younger. Something not sung by my mother. When 'Rock DJ' by Robbie Williams blasts through my phone, she laughs.

'Robbie Williams!' she exclaims. 'He's like ex-boy band legend. Oh my God! Do *you* like boy bands?' she asks excitedly.

'Uh, Mercy claims I could *be* in a boy band.'

Jade's face is deadly serious. 'Is there something wrong with that?'

I smile wide. She's the girl. The girl of my dreams, and I want to be stuck with her forever.

'Seriously, I adore boy bands. Old, new, doesn't matter, especially the British boys. Ai-yi-yi,' she says, fanning herself. 'They're all so pretty. But what *are* we doing?'

'We're going skating, office chair edition,' I say, getting a running start as I push her through the aisles, one foot on the bottom of the chair, the other scooting us through the store like we're on a skateboard.

The giggle that leaves her lips is worth every dirty look customers shopping give us. As she rolls through the store, I dance like a lunatic, spinning her chair, catching her at the right moments (before she crashes into shelving), and most importantly, not mowing down customers.

'Hey!' an employee yells our way. 'What are you doing?'

I straighten up as if the guy is some authority figure and not a twenty-year-old, in dress clothes and a tie, with thick glasses and hair parted down the middle, wearing a nametag that says 'Jaeger – assistant day manager.'

'Dwight Schrute?' Jade says under her breath through a laugh.

I crack a smile because the guy could be Dwight's doppelganger, but I force it away because I'm not here to get in trouble. I'm here to make this girl smile.

'We are, uh, well, we came to go roller skating, but that dream is gone,' I say, motioning around the store. 'So we're making the best of it.'

The man smiles. 'I used to skate here as a kid. Wait right there!' he commands before rushing off, disappearing down one of the many aisles.

'You think he's calling the cops?' Jade asks.

I shake my head. 'He didn't seem mad. So, I'm not sure what he's doin'. Searching for his sex store-bought handcuffs he's yet to use, maybe?'

Jade laughs. 'There's a scene I never wanted to imagine.'

A moment later, the radio blasts a station playing Billy Idol's 'To Be a Lover'. As I shut my phone tunes down, the overhead store lights dim, and the skating rink lighting, apparently still installed, starts flashing around the room.

'Oh, my God!' Jade squeals. 'Part of it does exist!'

I can't help but laugh. This turned out better than I expected. I push her around the place until she insists she does me next. She only knocks me over once – partially my fault because I couldn't quit dancing in my chair – I mean, Billy Idol, how can you not dance? But it was totally worth it.

When we get to the store's back corner, where her kiss with Aiden Turner took place, she spins me around to face her. I hold my breath for a second, convinced this gorgeous girl is about to kiss me. The vibe is there, and I am suddenly nervous. Like I've never been kissed. But she kisses my cheek instead, and I'm not mad about it. Her lips send shivers through me. I can imagine what kissing her might be like – absolute magic.

'This is seriously the nicest, most fun thing anyone has ever done for me,' she says. 'If I had already broken up with Conner, I'd kiss the hell out of you right now.'

I heard two things. Kiss and Conner.

'You're breaking up with him?' I ask suddenly, my mood lifting almost instantly. This is the first I've heard this.

'I think so,' she says with a nod. 'Love shouldn't hurt. I've recently come to discover this.'

What did that asshole do? Besides all the douchey things I know about already. I hate the sound of her hurting, let alone him being the reason behind it.

'You're right; love shouldn't hurt.'

'Being with you doesn't. I just want you to know that.'

I grin, suddenly shy. 'It doesn't hurt at all.'

She deserves to know how love feels, or at least a proper engagement. Instead, here she is, thinking love is painful when that's not the case at all. At least not when it's right. I don't know about her, but being here, ridiculously pushing each other around in an office chair, feels so incredibly right.

The store has now flipped off the skating rink lights and turned down the music. Boo.

'Thanks for the memories, guys,' a voice says over the loudspeaker. 'But back to business.'

'Now what?' she asks.

'Do you work tonight?'

She nods.

'I'm gonna come see you. If that's alright?'

'It'll be the best part of my night,' she says with a grin. 'Just like it always has.'

* * *

As much as I wanted to spend all damn day with Jade, I dropped her at her apartment so she could get ready for work. Now to work on my plan to ensure she dumps that weasel, Conner.

The door to Dax and Hollyn's flower shop dings open as I storm through. Compared to what this place was when they bought it, the building now stands out on the street, with flower boxes full of whatever is in season, and the windows are bordered with brightly colored painted flowers that match the ones on Dax's delivery truck. The shop looks even better than it did when Dax's father owned it.

One wall is made up of refrigeration for flowers arranged by color like a rainbow. Displays are sprinkled around the place, and I've never been here when there wasn't at least one other client.

'Dax!' I holler, startling a woman looking at a stand of houseplants, causing her to drop the one in her hand to the ground, breaking the pot it's in and spilling soil all over the floor.

As I round the counter to the back room where they prepare their orders, Dax and I smack right into one another as he makes his way towards the main shop to see what the commotion is.

'He scared me when he yelled,' the young woman explains, pointing at me as if I threatened to rob her.

'Not a problem. He's the most obnoxious guy I know, so I understand completely. Sometimes he even scares me,' he jokes as he picks up the mess and repots the plant so you'd never even know it happened.

'Ha-ha, funny boy,' I say.

Dax returns the plant to the woman, handing it to her. 'I hope this looks fantastic wherever you planned to put it.'

'I haven't bought it yet,' she reminds him.

'Consider it a gift from River.' He nods his head my way. 'Enjoy.' He ushers her out while she thanks him profusely, promising to recommend The Flower Boy to all her friends and family as I wait behind the counter for him.

'You owe me thirty bucks,' he says as soon as the door clicks shut behind her.

I yank my wallet from my back pocket, but I've only got twenties. 'Can ya break forty?' I ask, handing him two of the bills.

'Nope,' he says with a smirk, shoving the cash into his back pocket as he walks past me to the back room. I follow. 'Why are you here startling my customers in the middle of the day?'

'I need to make an order,' I say with a smirk.

He glances up at me suspiciously. 'You and Caite didn't make up, did you? After you disappeared upstairs, the "family dinner" was awkward, considering half the guests left without saying goodbye. I was a little worried you went home with her.'

'You were worried I went home with my ex and

her husband? Man, I thought you knew me better than that.' I scrunch my face. 'For the future, never let those words leave your lips again. Caitlin and I now have an agreement. I pretend she doesn't exist, and she does the same.'

'Alright, then why do you need flow—' He stops mid-sentence, a curious smile growing. 'Jade?'

I lift my shoulders to my ears guiltily. 'Maybe.'

'Maybe what?' My sister's voice echoes through the shop as she enters the back door. Instead of turning to face her, I pretend she doesn't exist until she pokes me in the spine.

'Ow!' I moan. 'Why do you resort to physical violence? Is it because you're the size of a garden gnome?'

She shoots me a glare. 'You once sat on me and farted,' she reminds me.

'I was *sixteen*. I haven't done it lately. Jesus, I think you poked a hole in my spine.' I wiggle around, trying to reach it, but everything feels intact.

'Riv is here to order some flowers...' Dax fills her in.

She sidles up to her giant of a fiancé and pecks a kiss on his lips, standing on her tiptoes to speak directly into his ear, but like the annoying sister she can be, she doesn't attempt to lower her voice. 'I'll do dirty things later if you tell me.'

'Good God, now you're trying to make my ears bleed?' I moan, making Dax laugh.

'Come on,' Hols says. 'Who are you buying flowers for? Could it be your new fiancée?' she laughs.

'Perhaps,' I say coyly.

Hollyn stops, turning to me, her hands on the tabletop and her jaw agape. 'Wait, what happened to her real boyfriend?'

'He's a douche, and she's finally starting to see that.'

'Really?' Dax asks with surprise.

'Yep. I think she's gonna dump him. For me.' I point both thumbs my way proudly.

'For *you*?' Hols asks like she can't believe it. 'Because you requested it, or to "do you" without shame?'

I shake my head, running my hand through my hair. 'I'm serious. There's something there. Even she's admitted it. Now I'm trying to find a way to make sure it goes perfectly. Obviously, I had to take advantage of my flower-loving buddy's services.'

'Oh my God,' Hollyn says with a grin. 'You truly like this woman.'

'I do. More than I thought possible.'

'Riv!' She swoons. The girl is lovesick. So much so that I almost can't wait for this wedding to be over. 'This is so exciting! What should we make for her?' she asks Dax.

24

JADE

'Finally,' Kai says excitedly after I announce that Conner and I are soon over. There's just no way I can continue with how things are going, not to mention the fact that I'm feeling something for someone else.

'She's found her worth and is dumping Mr wishy-washy wannabe ER doctor, for status. A boy who never put you above everyone else unless you were putting out. Gross.'

That is gross. I can't believe I was so blind to it. Love really does make you see things differently. If that's what this even was, love. But I doubt it. I suspect he caught me at a vulnerable time, just like River suggested not long ago. I probably would have said yes to anyone.

'Please, don't settle next time. Wait for Prince Charming. You deserve that.'

'In my defense, at the time, I thought Conner was that,' I say as I furiously wipe down the counter.

Now I have to figure out how to dump him. I wanted to do it via text, but Laney thinks that'll be too cowardly, considering we're engaged. So, I guess I've got a phone call to make. But not yet because I've no idea what words I'll use, and if I called him now, I'd probably stumble, he'd charm me, and I'd be in the same circle of dread I'm already in.

Adam rolls his eyes. 'He was never that, Jade. Prince Charming will bring you flowers, chocolates, and gifts while telling you how pretty you are.'

'Well, that guy has been proving difficult to find. I honestly don't understand how so many people are coupled up in the world. How in the hell did they find one another? And how did they just know they were the one?'

A rattle at the front windows startles us.

'We ain't open yet,' Adam yells from where he is, his back to the door.

'Oh my stars,' Kai says, looking towards the window.

I glance that way, and standing on the sidewalk out front is River, holding a giant bouquet while repeatedly knocking on the window with an adorable grin.

'Huh, say his name enough, and I guess he'll appear, like Beetlejuice, only less creepy. It would appear Prince Charming has arrived,' Adam says.

Roman unlocks the door to let him in while Kai and Adam do their best to pretend they're busy while hovering close enough to eavesdrop on every word. We're before opening, so the overhead lights are on. It's not nearly as magically tropical here as when we're open. Right now, it looks like a plain old bar that someone filled with relics of oceanside establishments taken from previous vacations.

'Mah lady,' River says dramatically, setting the flower arrangement on the bar before me. It's huge and filled with every tropical flower and greenery imaginable – palm leaves, Bird of Paradise, hibiscus, flowers I don't know the name of, even lilies. It must have cost him a fortune.

'I can't even see you around them,' I laugh. 'But they're beautiful.'

He sits on a stool where he can see me. 'I know a guy. He's pretty good with flowers.'

'They're amazing! I can't even remember the last time someone brought me flowers. Thank you.'

He nods. 'I've been doing some thinking. This

might sound completely whacked but hear me out, alright?'

'Alright,' I say nervously.

'Remember the seance we did recently?'

'How could I forget that? We caused the whole building to evacuate at four in the morning. I can never show my face there again.'

He laughs. 'Well, when you showed us your dream engagement ring, I almost shit my pants.'

I side-eye him. 'Wasn't that kind of the night's "theme" for you?' I joke.

His head drops, and he drags a hand down one side. 'I forgot you'd seen me at my worst.'

'*And* best, don't forget that,' I add. 'I mean, I definitely didn't complain about your underwear.'

'You saw his underwear?' Kai balks.

'Sshhhh, we're supposed to be secretly listening,' Adam reminds her.

'I don't suggest you two become private eyes,' River jokes.

'Why did my choice of ring surprise you? Was it bad?' I ask, wondering where he's going with all this.

'No,' he says. 'Not at all bad. It's gorgeous.' River reaches into his jacket, pulling something from the inside pocket. 'Oddly enough, we have similar tastes because it's the exact ring I bought for Caitlin when I proposed.' He sets an emerald-cut solitaire ring on the counter between us.

'*Shut. Up*,' I say in disbelief. I pick up the ring, and it sparkles under the bar lights, mesmerizing me immediately. 'Oh, it's even prettier in real life. Wow. *This* is the engagement ring, huh?' It truly is precisely the same one I wanted. How strange is that?

'Oh, Lord,' Kai says. 'He's proposing!'

He shakes his head. 'I'm not. What I am doing is loaning it to you.'

I look up at him from the ring. 'Why?'

'Before you dump Conner, I want you to wear this ring for the night and see what an engagement *should* feel like. Show it off, live it up, make up a story, and help me get my money out of that thing. Say whatever makes you smile.'

'River, if I wear this, people will think *we're* engaged.' I motion between us.

'Only these three. Everyone else already thinks you're engaged, and they ask to see the ring you don't have each time. How does that make you feel?'

I frown. 'Not great.'

'Perhaps you should experience what a big deal an engagement is?' he suggests, taking the ring from me and sliding it onto my left finger. 'After all, we are fake engaged.'

'I couldn't,' I say, staring at the most gorgeous ring I've ever seen, and I'm *wearing* it.

'Why not? It's just another science experiment. You like those, remember?'

I laugh, nodding my head.

'Plus, one day, this'll make an awesome story.'

'Awesome stories are kind of your thing.'

'Maybe they could be *our* thing?' he asks hesitantly.

I bite my lip, staring at the ring I now want to keep forever, even though I know it means bad things for him. 'Are you sure you want to leave this with me?'

'Positive. I thought about pawning it since it has zero sentimental value. But I think you'll get more out of it tonight. When you're done, bring it back to me, and I'll get rid of it, finally breaking the curse of what was never meant to be. I'll use the money from the sale to buy you all the Red Robin mudd pies to sink your feelings into after you dump that wad of a boyfriend. Hell, I'll even deliver. Deal?'

My eyes move back to the ring on my hand. This stupid thing makes me smile even though I know the truth. 'You've got yourself one weird deal.'

'Perfect,' he says, standing to leave. 'Let me know how it goes.'

'I promise.' I nod, shocked he's doing this.

'Follow your heart, Jade. I hear it's never supposed to be wrong.' With that, he exits the bar, shoving his hands into the pockets of his grass-green colored skinny jeans as he walks by the windows, glancing back at me with a smile before disappearing into the night.

'Uh, he's into you,' Adam says as if I don't already know.

'What gave it away?' Kai asks, grabbing my hand and admiring the ring. 'Perhaps the giant rock on her hand? Fuck-ing hell, Jade. I hardly know the guy, and I say marry him tonight.'

'He didn't propose,' I remind them. 'Besides, that's almost as ridiculous as saying yes to a man proposing after two months.'

'I know,' Kai says. 'But how romantic was this? He wants you to experience what you should have long ago.'

I won't lie; it is romantic in a very River way.

'Plus, he brought you flowers! For no reason. The last time I got flowers from a guy was because he'd slept with my roommate.' She rolls her eyes.

'You two really know how to pick 'em, don't you?' Adam says with a pathetic laugh before clapping his hands. 'Back to work, you lovesick hula girls. We've got five minutes to opening.'

'Holy Moses!' a woman exclaims as I deliver their drinks. She grabs my hand. 'Somebody loves you, girl. This is beautiful! When's the big day?'

These are my first customers of the night, and already someone is gushing over this ring.

'Uh, we haven't set a date yet, but we're thinking destination wedding somewhere tropical.' *This is just like making up how you got your tan, Jade. Dream a little; there's nothing wrong with that.*

'Oohhh, destination weddings are the best. My ex-husband proposed with a ring out of a vending machine, and we got hitched at the courthouse on a whim.'

'Hence the ex part,' her friend says with a laugh.

'Yeah, River, he's the perfect guy. He knows me well, I guess.' After the words leave my lips, I realize I didn't say Conner. I said River. I'm acting as if I'm engaged to *River*. Not Conner. And it feels... incredible? Anxiety fills my insides like a beehive when I think of marrying Conner. We'd probably have divorced within a year if it had happened at all.

Holy hell. *This* was the point of me wearing this thing. To prove who it is that has my heart, and somehow he knew it would be him.

'Did someone say ring?' another of their party asks as she walks from the bathroom. Her gaze follows her friends' and she beams a smile. 'Wowee! Have you gone dress shopping yet?'

I shake my head. 'No.'

'My advice is the perfect dress feels a little bit like the man who gave you this ring did. You'll just know, and you won't be able to imagine any other one being quite as perfect. Go with your gut, just like you did the man.'

I laugh nervously, realizing this feeling in my gut may be me 'just knowing'.

'She just got married,' one of her friends updates me.

'I did; if you need recommendations, I have loads. Hit me up,' she says, handing me the business card she's just pulled from her purse.

'Thank you,' I say, walking back to the bar, feeling like I'm floating on a cloud. I had no idea this was what this would feel like.

The rest of my night goes pretty much precisely like the way I bet River expected. Women ooh and aah over the ring and ask about the lucky guy who gave it to me. Men are buying me celebratory shots and asking if I have a sister. I handed out Laney's number twice; I know she'll approve of both. And Kai asks to see it whenever I'm back at the counter.

No one did this when I mentioned Conner and I were engaged. Everybody frowned like they didn't have hope he'd pull through, and they were exactly right. He didn't. He probably never would have, either.

'Another congrats drink,' Adam says, sitting a flaming shot before me.

'I'm starting to slur my words,' I say, unsure if another shot is a good idea. Yet I down it anyway, holding it up towards the guy who sent it while the table cheers after it's gone.

Usually, when people would question me on a story I was making up on the fly, I'd give a different answer, whatever came to mind. This time, my story never changed, and I've now got a list of islands for a destination wedding, along with recommendations on where to stay, what to do, dress shops, and photographers. If it has to do with a wedding, I've heard all about it tonight. I could sit down and plan this fake wedding in an hour with all the information I have.

Yet, with Conner, I didn't even know where to begin. I was afraid to even ask about wedding plans because he always shut me down with the stupid 'long engagement' thing. How is it so easy to make this big of a mistake with someone?

'Well, I think you got your results,' Kai says at the end of the night, referring to the science experiment remark. 'What are you going to do?'

'First, I'm going to need a ride home. Then to-morrow, I'm headed straight to my dad's to hear his thoughts, and I think this time, I may even listen,' I say with a giggle, my belly full of booze and my head full of wedding bells that don't really exist. Follow my heart, he'd said. For the first time ever, I think I know what it's telling me to do.

25

JADE

'Dad?' I call out as I open the door to my childhood home. A house we moved into when I was seven, so when I think of 'home', this is where my mind goes. Since Mom's been gone, it feels different. Heavier, yet I feel her here the most. It's not a huge house, just a three-bedroom, two-bath, ranch-style home in the burbs outside of Portland.

I follow the sounds of the TV, stopping at the top of the three steps leading into the sunken family room that was once our garage. After Laney and I became teenagers, Dad converted it into his 'man cave'. There was a time when he jokingly hung a sign at the entrance that said 'no girls allowed'. Too bad for him, we pretended it didn't exist, and he always welcomed us.

'Jadeybug.' He stands from his chair, happy to see me. The TV blasts some YouTube show about motorcycles.

All those tears I've held back over this Conner thing decide now's the time, and they fall freely, worrying my dad instantly.

'Is uh – is your sister alright?'

'Yeah,' I sniffle. 'I mean, I think she is, I don't know. Probably.' I fall onto the couch dramatically, dropping my purse to the floor.

'What's going on?' he asks, standing over me, clearly distressed at my current mood as he strokes his beard. 'You can't just cry and not talk. We're in it now; let's hear what happened.'

With a heavy sigh, I wipe away the tears and force myself to sit up. 'I don't want to marry Conner, Dad.'

He sits on the coffee table before me, resting a hand on my knee. 'Jade, sweetie, you don't have to do anything you don't want to...' His voice trails off as he grabs my left hand, lifting it closer to his face to inspect it. 'Wait a second. He finally bought you a ring, and now you don't want it?' His face screams that he didn't think Conner would pull through. And he's spot on.

'No.' I cry again.

'Jade, you're *wearing* an engagement ring.' He holds my hand in front of my face as though I don't know. 'If your fiancé didn't give this to you, who did?'

'River.'

'River?' He strokes his beard.

'We're just friends, remember? At least, I thought we were, but my heart is telling me something different.'

'Is it telling you to marry him?' he asks, his eyes wide as he awaits my answer.

'I don't know, but don't worry. He didn't give me this ring romantically or anything. It's more of a "borrow to prove a point" thing. I just wasn't prepared for what his "point" would do to me. When I put this thing on last night, people were so happy for me. The more I talked, the more I realized I wish River had given me this ring, for real.' My crying slows as I focus on the guy I *do* like as opposed to the one I'm about to dump. He just makes me happy in a way no one else ever has.

'Does he know you feel this way?'

'Not completely, but he knows I feel something. And I know he feels something for me. But I need advice. I don't know how to dump one man and tell the other I'm falling for him. Tell me how to do that,

Dad. I promise this time I'll listen to whatever you say.'

Dad chuckles. 'Sure ya will,' he moans playfully.

'I didn't mean to befriend River the way I did. How could I have ever known we had some kind of attraction to one another deep down? I thought it was just me, but he's been a better boyfriend than Conner without even trying.'

'I thought you said you *weren't* cheating on Conner the other night?' Dad seems surprised. 'I'd expected this of Laney but never you, Jade...' He says it so seriously.

'I'm not cheating,' I insist. 'At least not physically. It's more in my head, and possibly, here?' I point to my heart, sniffling away my earlier emotions. 'It's never been "romantic" with River. But I can't quit thinking about him. He's so handsome, he makes me laugh, he sang me a Neil Diamond song, he loves all of Mom's favorite eighties movies, his mother is mom's favorite singer, *and* he put up with Laney for an entire night. He's bought me flowers and is just the *perfect* guy.'

'His mother is who?'

'Penny Candy.'

Dad's jaw drops. 'We had our first dance to one of

her songs at our wedding. How old is this perfect guy?'

'Twenty-nine. Dad, you'd love him. He gives me advice I don't want to hear but need to – just like you would. He thinks I'm pretty and says sweet things when I least expect them. For a long time, I'd never seen him as anything more than a friend, and then when I was ready to tell him I was interested, things didn't go my way, and my world imploded not long after. I stayed the night taking care of him while he was sick recently—'

'Can we return to when this River gave you the engagement ring?'

I tell him all about my pretending to be River's fiancée. Then Penny finding out. I spill the story about the coronary burger poisoning, Laney's boyfriend burning bonfire, Conner's bullshit, the Office Max roller chair experience, and every embarrassing detail in between.

'He wanted to show me what getting engaged should've felt like before dumping Conner.'

Dad shakes his head. 'How would you wearing a random engagement ring show you what an engagement should feel like?'

I laugh. 'That's exactly what I thought.' I wipe

away tears that are finally under control. 'Dad, it was like magic. The second I put that ring on, people noticed. They oohed and awed and congratulated me like it was a big deal. I wish they'd reacted like that when I told them weeks before, but back then, their only response was checking for a ring and not seeing one.'

I hold my hand before me, admiring the diamond staring back at me.

'This is the exact one I wanted, and somehow River bought it for his ex years ago. We have so much in common, even this ring style. Of course, I have to return it soon because it's full of bad luck. His ex left him at the altar five years ago. Who does that? Anyway, I'm rambling. River plans to sell it when I'm done learning my lesson, but he was right. What I experienced last night was what I'd always dreamed of, and what I felt telling people about Conner's proposal wasn't the same. If someone truly loves you enough to propose, they *are* prepared. They *know* your full name.' I glance at Dad who grins slightly. 'Anyway, that's what wearing the ring taught me.'

He chuckles, moving to the couch beside me, throwing his arm around me, and hugging me against his side. 'Jade, sweets. I have another question. Have you ever spent all night nursing someone back to health who wasn't important to you?'

'Are you kidding? I stayed with Laney while she had chicken pox in college, which meant I got it too.'

'Funny, funny girl you are. But I'm serious,' he says with a severe stare to prove it.

I shrug. 'I mean Thomas, that one time. And Mom, I helped with her.'

'You did,' he confirms. 'Thomas, Laney, and your mom are important people in your life, right?'

'Yeah.'

'Hon, I think River has become important to you. How would you feel if he suddenly disappeared?'

'*What?*'

'Let that sink in while I grab some drinks, alright?'

I rub my temples while he's gone. Losing River, even though I don't actually 'have him' would make me feel horrible. Pieces of my heart would be all over the city and I'm sure I wouldn't smile as often because no one makes me smile like he does.

Oh.

My.

God.

I sit straight up when it hits me. Once again, I

hold my left hand in front of my face. There it is. A big, sparkling, cursed promise, sitting on the one finger that screams, 'Here's your sign.'

Dad walks back into the room, two bottles of his favorite 2 Brothers Brew in his hands, and it's not even noon.

'You think River is my "one"?'

He chuckles. 'Do you look at him the way you're looking at that ring?' he asks, handing me a bottle and sitting back in his chair.

Do I? I probably did the night he was in his underwear. 'Maybe?'

'As ridiculous as all this sounds, think about it. You two had an almost kiss before Conner even entered your life. And since then, he's always been there for you; happily, it seems.'

'He has. Truthfully, I'd like to spend every second with him,' I say confidently. I glance at Dad. 'Now what?'

'Now, breaking up with Conner would be your first step.'

Eh, the thought of it makes my insides swirl. I don't know why; he's made it so easy. At this point, it would take a two-minute conversation, and we'd be over – the engagement canceled. But something about doing it hurts my insides, and I think it's to do with having those expectations for the future crumble away when something big falls apart – but finding something bigger and better? That alone makes the pain worth it.

26

RIVER

It took me all night, but I have a plan. A plan to prove to Jade that I'm the guy for her. Is it too soon, considering she hasn't even dumped Corndog yet? Maybe. But I can't wait any longer because I can't risk missing my moment again.

I'm wearing her favorite cologne and my best Penny Candy vintage band tee. My hair is pulled up; I'm wearing my wedding suit jacket (Hollyn will be pissed if she knows; Mom told her I wore it before and I got the lecture of a lifetime. But she'll never find out) that brings out the blue in my eyes and my fave skinny jeans. I went a little less obnoxious than my usual rainbow of skinny jeans and just stuck with black. I decided to skip the long jacket as, while they may have been popular in the eighties, now they scream 'school shooter' ('Merica), and that's *not* the vibe I want here. I need to woo this girl hard because that's what she deserves.

The shop door dings open, and Mom doesn't even look up from the front counter, tapping away on her laptop. 'Welcome to Penny Candy Records,' she says robotically. It's her greeting for the shop. We all say it.

'Thank you, I need to borrow some shit.'

Her brows squish together as I round the front counter to the back room. She follows closely behind me. 'Borrow what? And why are you here?'

I open the stockroom door and flip on the light, standing in the center and looking around. Should I go completely old school or do an updated version of this? A giant boombox sitting atop one of the shelves, covered in dust, catches my attention. I pull it down, checking to see if it has batteries, and it works.

'*Hello?*' Mom says.

'I've got to do something for a girl. And I need some supplies. I'll bring everything back. Promise.'

'You need a 1989 tape player for a girl?' she questions. Right then, it hits her. 'Riv, are you talking about Jade?'

'That's none of your business.'

'You like her, don't you?'

I laugh. 'Understatement of the year. But yeah, I like the shit out of her.'

'And you need to do something for her...' she says, following me back into the shop and watching me dig through cassette tapes. Suddenly she gasps. 'Are you doing the John Cusack thing?'

'Perhaps,' I say, finally finding the tape I want and heading to the front door.

Of course I'm doing the Cusack thing. It's her favorite movie, and he's my favorite actor. How could I not? It's pretty much guaranteed to work. If she realized what I wanted her to last night and finally dumped Conner, this will work like a charm. My gut tells me she has, or is, or hell, I don't even care anymore. I'll dump him *for* her if I must. I just can't wait for one more second to tell this girl I'm falling for her. Hard.

'Good luck!' Mom yells from the front door as I speed to my next stop. Red Robin. Where I've ordered that pie I promised her, for pick up.

I've got no idea how I'll get into her courtyard, considering it takes a code I don't know. Could I have asked for it? Yes. But I didn't want to warn her I was coming because I wanted this to have the romantic punch I'm going for.

When I pull up to the curb in front of her building, I see Laney headed down the sidewalk. I duck, hoping she doesn't notice me, and blow this. I wait around ten minutes, psyching myself up that she will love this, and when I feel like the moment is right, I get out of my car, unload the boombox and take-out bag, and head to the gate. Here goes nothing.

27

JADE

I'm now back home, awaiting my sister, whose support I need to call Conner and tell him he's not the man for me. Love may have blinded me for a while, but more than likely, he's expecting this. He had to know I'd see my worth at some point.

'Cool down,' Spike says as I pace in front of his enclosure, which he's sitting on top of. 'You mad? You mad? Cool down.' His Ls aren't perfect, and it's as cute as him struggling with his Rs.

'I am mad, Spike; you're right. But I can't cool down because I'll lose my nerve.'

'She's mad. She's mad. She's mad. She's maaaad,' he sings, somehow lightening the mood. Like I've got a cheerleader to urge me onward.

'Do you remember how to say fuck off?'

'Fuck off!' he squeals, proving he does.

'I want you to say that as much as you can while I'm on the phone in a minute. Okay?'

'Okay!' he screams back. Who knows if he'll follow orders, but if he does, River will totally enjoy this story.

'Fuck off! Fuck off!' Spike screams, bobbing up and down as he walks around his cage top.

My front door suddenly opens, and Laney walks in. 'What's with all the fuck offs, Spike?'

'I'm dumping Conner.'

She breathes a sigh of relief as she drops her bag near the front door. 'Final-fucking-ly. Where is he?'

'Uh, Boston, remember.'

'Damn it! He deserves at least a bit of bodily harm for what he's done to you, but I can't do that from across the country now, can I?' she moans. Suddenly she throws a finger into the air. 'You got his address?'

'Yeah...'

'Good, we'll send him glitter and a bag of dicks. A dick for a dick.'

'Dick for dick!' Spike screams.

Laney laughs. 'I just love you, Spike.'

He giggles a proper giggle that makes me laugh whenever I hear it.

'Spike like pretty lady,' he says to Laney when she gets close. 'Woo-wooh,' he whistles, now reacting to her saying his name.

They bump nose to beak, their usual greeting before he squawks again. 'Pretty lady. Pretty lady!' He's dancing around the top of his cage, doing the weird feather ruffle when he sees 'pretty ladies'.

'I'm going to call him,' I say, lifting my phone.

When I pull up his contact, I hesitate. Damn it. He *is* cute, but no. What we have isn't love. It was just a fling. You don't marry flings. I jab the FaceTime button.

'Go over there!' I command, waving Laney to my kitchen. 'Spike.' I pat my shoulder, and he wastes no time hopping over. He bounces around as I wait for Conner to answer, and when he does, he smiles, but his eyes aren't on me.

'Spike!' he says, happy to greet my pet bird before the girl he supposedly loves.

'Fuck off!' Spike screams with perfect timing.

Conner's jaw drops, and the smirk on my face couldn't be more opposite of what I'm seeing in Conner. He looks offended that Spike just said what he said. Well, that's going to make the rest of this really hurt, then.

'Sorry,' I apologize, then notice Laney waving her hands like a maniac.

'You're sorry?' she whispers. '*Why?*'

Right. Why am I sorry? 'No, you know what, Conner, I'm not sorry. Spike took the words right out of my mouth.'

'What?'

'This call is not to chit-chat about our day. Truthfully, I don't want to know anything about your days ever again.'

Conner bites his lips together, dropping his head.

'Don't look away to hide the fact that this is what you hoped would happen. You're not walking away from this feeling good about leading me on. I've got some things to say, and you will listen.'

'Fuck off. Fuck off. Fuck offfffff!' Spike sings that last word.

'I will never beg any man to love me – whether we're engaged or not. For weeks that's what I've done with you and I'm over it.' For a second I stare at the screen, his serious face nearly making me crack and ask if he even cares. But does it even matter? He's proved he doesn't. Continue on, Jade.

'Consider our engagement officially over. I'll mail

back your ring.' I pause, watching him cock his head as though he's confused. 'Oh, that's right, *you never bought me one.*'

Laney claps her hands, proud of my sass.

'I should have known right then too. But I was willing to look past it. Anyway, you should know I'm moving on, and if you haven't already, which I suspect you have, you should too. Have a good life, and—'

'Fuck off!' Spike hollers again.

I momentarily stare at Conner's face, but I can't tell how he feels. He's emotionless, and that pisses me off. Am I not worth *one* emotion? Before he can speak, I jab the end call button, the screen going black. I feel slightly bad, but what did he expect after how he's treated me since he left?

'Woo!' Laney cheers, wiggling her fingers through the air. 'She did it! Fuck. Off. Conner!'

'Only one problem,' I say, lifting my left hand and flashing her the ring I'm still wearing for reasons I don't want to think too deeply on. 'I like this guy.'

'Who in the hell gave you that?' Laney grabs my hand, taking a good look. 'Do you have men lined up to marry you or what?'

'Not exactly...' I say, through a clenched-tooth grin.

'Where did you get this?' she asks again, impatiently waiting for my answer.

'River.'

'*River*?' Laney thinks about that for a moment, finally breaking into a smile. 'He *proposed*? Seriously?'

I shake my head. 'He didn't propose. It was more of a lesson in love.' It takes me a while to explain the situation, but she swoons the same way Kai did.

'No guy would do any of this for a woman he's not into. You need to call him over here on the ruse that you need to thank him, then do all the dirty things he'll let you because – as I've said before – he's hot as hell.'

'Intruder alert!' Spike yells, flying from my shoulder to the edge of his cage by the window. 'All intruders will be shot.' His squawk sounds mechanical.

He's staring out the window, pacing back and forth. 'Intruders will be shot! Intruder alert! Woo-woo-woo-woo.'

'His police siren is going off,' Laney says. 'It must be serious. Have 911 dialed, just in case.'

'I'm not going to call 911. It's probably just a squirrel or something.' I glance out the window he's staring out of, Laney joining me. But I can't believe what I'm seeing.

28

RIVER

Deep breaths, Riv. You're just wooing a girl, eighties style. The most amazing woman you've ever met, and if this goes wrong, you'll be heartbroken, but yeah, just relax.

I can't get in through the locked gate, so I've got no choice but to hold this beast of a boombox over my head, exactly like her favorite movie scene. Before I do, I turn the volume knob up, and hit play. Now we wait.

I spent all night learning a dance routine based solely on her love of British boy bands. The song I chose is 'Kiss You' by One Direction because if she goes for this, I'm kissing that girl like I've never kissed anyone before.

A chorus later, the front door of the building opens. Jade and Laney walk out, but I see only Jade's face. She's biting her lips together, holding back a smile. I set the boombox on one of the brick pillars near the gate, displaying my bomb dance moves without shame. After watching me make a complete fool of myself, she heads my way.

'What are you doing?' she asks with a laugh, typing the code into the gate keypad so I can get in.

'Come on,' I say as I walk through, extending my hand for her to join me.

She doesn't hesitate, and unsurprisingly (considering her love for boy bands of the past), she knows the moves and dances along, laughing with me.

'How are you *this* good?' she asks through a laugh.

'Did I never tell you my dad was a professional backup dancer for musicians of yesteryear? It's how he and my mom met.'

'Wow, you did not ever tell me that. It's kind of romantic.'

'It's totally romantic and sometimes a little embarrassing when a video pops up on my TV screen, and there's my father in all his eighties glory, white boy afro, and spandex pants, busting a move.'

She giggles at the thought of it. 'I might need to see those videos one day.'

'One day, you will. You'll see all the home videos too. And I'm sure he'll even dance for you in person 'cause it's what he does.'

We dance for a bit longer, enjoying every second. I even spin her around once successfully.

'So, do tell,' she says while dancing around her courtyard with me. 'What are we doing besides acting like lunatics in broad daylight?'

'You don't recognize this scene?'

'I do. It's my fave scene ever. I'm just not sure where it's going.'

'Well, you wanted an eighties movie-style romance, so I'm ending our film.'

The dancing stops. 'You're *ending* it?' she asks with worry.

'That depends on your answer to my next question.'

'Alright?'

'How was your night last night?'

She smiles, dropping her head shyly. 'Incredible. Everything you wanted me to realize, I did. And then some.'

I glance down at her hand, where my ring still sits. Eventually, I'll sell it, and in the future, we'll pick one out together if we get that far. And I plan on getting that far.

'Did you, maybe, dump that other guy?'

She beams. 'I did, just now, actually.'

She did it. My insides are exploding. 'Was I maybe a part of the reason that happened?'

'Oh, River. You were such a big, *big*, part.'

I can't hold back my grin. 'Jade Noelle Monroe,' I say through the grin, getting her name right and everything. 'You are the most incredible woman I've ever known. I adore everything about you. Never has someone "gotten" me like you have. I promise I'll never ghost you because you've officially become my favorite person on the planet, and even thinking of living without you hurts my heart. I may send emojis occasionally, but never to avoid talking to you, only to make you smile. What do you say we pass on the unromantic friend thing, and you be my girlfriend?'

While she's lost in the moment, I pull my phone from my pocket and text her least favorite things, emojis, in an attempt to prove she'll never regret getting emojis from me.

Fall leaf, the number four, and a hand pointing my way from her side.

Her phone dings in her hand, and she smiles as she sees my name. 'Fall, four...' She translates their meanings aloud, hesitating at the last one. Her gaze lifts to me.

'Me,' I finish her sentence. 'Fall for me? Because I'm already falling for you, gorgeous girl. Pretty please?'

The way she smiles fills me with so much joy. 'I'd be an absolute idiot not to now, wouldn't I?'

'The biggest,' I joke.

Her gaze never leaves mine. 'You are cute, and I'm not going to lie, my heart would hurt too if you weren't in my life. You're also shockingly sexy in your underwear *and* fully clothed.' She taps a finger to her bottom lip like she's thinking about it. 'This is a hard decision. I just got out of a relationship...'

I don't wait for her to talk it out because I know she's messing with me. Instead, I pull her to me and kiss her softly. Almost immediately, her arms are around my neck, pulling me closer. Her lips on mine are perfection. Soft, plump, and as sweet as she is. A tiny bit of tongue, just an introduction to what may come later, keeps things light and sends sparks through my entire body, head to toe.

After remembering we've got an audience, I break the kiss and hold her to me tightly.

'You are easily the most beautiful girl in the world, and I wish I'd kissed you before Conner came into your life to save you from the heartache he caused.'

'No need to wish it; you did.' The way she smiles could light up the dark. It's all I see. 'Want to know my answer?'

'I'm dying over here.'

'Yes, River Jonathon Matthews; my heart didn't hesitate at all when I saw you today, and you did exactly what I'd always hoped the man of my dreams would. Of course I'll be your girlfriend, but only if you'll be my boyfriend.'

I grin. 'Count me in. I can't believe you remembered my middle name after only reading it once on a now-deceased wedding invitation.'

'It's funny what you can remember when someone is important to you. Isn't it?'

Her lips meet mine again, reminding me for the second time that no one has ever felt this right. She fits me perfectly in every way. She's the girl I've been looking for, and finally, I've got her in my arms, and I won't ever let her go.

'Get a room! Gawd!' Laney yells after we don't come up for air with the second kiss quickly.

I grab my borrowed boombox and takeout bag. 'Send your sister home because I didn't bring enough to share...' That's a total lie; I could feed the whole complex with this pie. I just want to be alone with this woman. I pat the shopping bag over my shoulder. The one carrying the pie, wine, and non-poisonous take-out burgers from Jovi's, because why the hell not? I realized this woman might be something extraordinary at a burger truck, and as ridiculous as that may sound, it will make the best story one day.

'I'm out. Wear a raincoat, you weirdo!' Laney says in true Laney style as she exits the courtyard.

'Let's go have some pie, girlfriend. This time, I mean that in the most unplatonic way ever.'

EPILOGUE
JADE

'You want *me* to announce her? Live on air?'

'Is that a problem?' a blond man with the news station asks. 'Someone said you were her manager.' He glances at an iPad in his hand. 'River Matthews, right?'

'Yeah,' River says with a nod. His eyes dart to me, excitement dancing in them like confetti. 'Let's go over it over here,' he says, leading the man away from me with a coy smile.

This wasn't a part of the setup. River assumed his role would be getting his mother and her band here and ready to perform. Which, believe me, was a task. I know, as I've helped him a few times now and wowsers, Penny Candy is a very high-maintenance band. Now they want River to announce her big comeback, and they're doing a short interview with him and Penny after the show to discuss the upcoming documentary. He's nervous but excited. I've watched his documentary, and it is so *so* good. Anyone who enjoys Penny Candy will fall in love with it.

He may have thought he was a 'nobody' in the film business before, but he's finally getting the attention he deserves. I'm so proud of him.

We've been dating for a few months now, and I have to say, I've got no regrets. Not one. It's like we were made for one another. People tell me that's hard to find. He's my best friend.

'When's this gig starting?' Laney asks for the fifteenth time. This time she's got a bag of mint green cotton candy in her hand.

'It starts at eleven fifty-five. You know, close to midnight, when it will officially be the New Year.'

'Oh yeah,' she laughs. 'I almost forgot what day it is.' She pulls a cloud of cotton candy from the bag and stuffs it into her mouth.

'Where did you get that?' I ask, pulling a piece for myself. 'It's not mint flavored, is it?'

'Ew, no. Pretty sure any flavor besides pure sugar is against the law in cotton candy land. I got it outside. There's a vendor guy.'

She's right; it's sweet and makes me pucker a little.

River returns, smiling as he pecks a kiss on my puckered lips, smacking me on the ass as he walks by, busy as a bee directing both this shoot and his mom's live performance.

'You two are so stinking cute,' Hollyn says.

'We are cute, aren't we?'

We're all crammed into the Crystal Ballroom. River's friends and family got to be VIPs, so we feel important. Laney forced her way into the VIP section by threatening to cut off River's hair in his sleep. How could he say no to something as charming as that? I don't think she'd ever do it, but that's their relationship.

'I've never seen River so smitten with anyone. How are things going?' Hollyn asks.

'Absolutely perfect. I've never been so...' I hesitate with my words, only because River and I haven't even said them to one another yet. After my disaster of a relationship before, we decided slow and steady wins the race.

'So *what*?' Laney pries.

But I can see Hollyn has already figured it out with her wide-eyed grin. 'Oh my God, you love him! Do you love him? Please tell me you love him.'

I laugh to myself. 'Ssshhhh, I plan to say it for the first time at midnight. *If* he's not too busy, that is, then I'll do it later.'

River walks by us again. 'Hey!' Laney yells, causing him to stop in his tracks.

'What?' he snaps.

'Did you find him?' she asks, glancing around the room. 'I just want to touch him. I promise I'll go easy even though he seems like the dirty type.'

He rolls his eyes. 'You can't meet *or* touch Eminem because he's not here, and I don't know him.'

'But your mom is a pop star. Whatever happened to the six degrees of separation thing? Someone you know *has* to know him.'

River looks at me with wide eyes, shaking his head. 'Ten minutes!' he yells, ignoring Laney completely.

He stops by my side, leaning into me. 'Holy fuck, ten minutes,' he repeats in my ear. 'I can't do this. I can barely think, and now they want me to get up there and introduce her and the tour. What if I swear? What if I freak out? I'm going to be on the freaking news, babe.'

I grab his hands, squeezing them tight and planting a soft kiss on his lips. 'In ten minutes, you'll be able to breathe a sigh of relief because this will all be over. Enjoy it. This is what you've worked so hard for. Alright? You did it. You completed your first documentary and somehow got your mother onto the national New Year's Eve coverage. I am so proud of you, and at midnight, I will be kissing the hell out of you.'

River smiles, his hands now on either side of my neck. 'I like that. You are amazing. Pay attention while I'm up there, alright? I'll never remember what I said.'

'I'm recording the whole thing,' I remind him, flashing my phone.

This is the second time today he's told me to pay attention while he's up there. I'm dying inside. There is zero way he's doing something crazy like proposing because we both agree that a proposal before you've been together at least a year is a mistake. We're happy where we are and not looking to rush through every phase. That said, I'm nervous as hell.

Penny is the last performance before the ball

drops, so the national news station airing this decided to give her a big chunk of time. Apparently, half the news staff were Penny Candy fans in their younger years, and they're excited to have her second-chance debut on the show.

We are all wearing Penny Candy merch to make things more fun, and the band will count down to the ball drop within seconds of her performance.

'What do you think he's going to say?' Laney asks.

'Maybe he'll ask you to move in with him?' Hollyn suggests. 'That's what Brooks did with Mercy, and look at them. Happy as clams those two.'

Mercy and Brooks couldn't be here tonight because she's performing with Dylan somewhere else, and he's at work. New Year's is wild, so all cops were called on duty.

'Nah. He hasn't quite charmed Spike yet, so we want to wait until I can uncage the sweary bird and not risk him biting off one of River's fingers or something.'

Laney laughs. 'I think Spike thinks you're *his* girlfriend. Maybe Riv is popping the question?'

'Nope. I can't be the girl who's had that question asked twice in one year, and he agrees with me.'

'Oh, I hope it's something good,' Hollyn says. 'I'm

going to go find Dax. I must kiss my man at midnight so our wedding isn't jinxed.'

Hollyn and I have become pretty good friends. She's sweet, shares many traits that River does, and she's so in love with Dax, a real sweetheart. They get married this upcoming Valentine's Day, and I've been asked to be a bridesmaid along with Mercy, the maid of honor. I'm so excited. This will be my first time as a bridesmaid! I feel like a part of the family even though River and I have only been together a few months.

And... my dad *loves* River. He's questioned his outfits more than once, but all he ever wanted was for someone to look at me the same way he looked at my mom, and River does that.

'I'm going to find Dad and Thomas,' Laney says. 'I'll cross my fingers that whatever River wants you to pay attention to is good and not him strutting the stage in a new pair of obnoxious underwear or something.'

I laugh. I wouldn't be opposed to that, but I don't want to share my man with the world in that way. Oh, there he is. I pull my phone up and hit record.

'Hello, PDX!' River says into the mic, looking more nervous than ever. 'You guys begged and pleaded, and so here she is, Penny Candy, back for a brand-new tour starting next year. Tonight they'll release their new single, and tomorrow it'll be available wherever you buy your music. But before they get started, I did want to say one thing. In the crowd is a woman so beautiful I can't look away. Jade, this has been the best time in my life with you by my side, and I just want you to know I love you so freaking much.'

The crowd around us awes, looking for wherever this Jade girl is. Luckily he didn't request a spotlight to reveal me. I giggle, watching him say the exact thing I was going to say to him tonight.

'Now put your hands together for a brand-new Penny Candy!' he yells into the mic, clapping his hands above his head and jogging off the stage towards the VIP section where I am.

When the band starts to play, he approaches me, stopping before me.

'Please tell me you got that?' he says, pointing to my camera.

I nod. 'I did, and yet again, you read my mind because I planned to say the exact same thing at the stroke of midnight.'

'That I'm the most beautiful boy in the world?' he jokes.

'No, well, *yes*, but I wanted to tell you that I've

fallen and never want to get up.'

He looks deliriously happy right now. 'So have I. In fact, I've fallen so hard it's a little scary.'

'Me too. But I'm not scared.'

'No?'

I shake my head. 'How could I ever be scared of someone I love so much?'

'I do love you,' he says to my face, kissing my forehead sweetly.

I squeeze his hand in mine. 'I totally love you.'

We watch the rest of Penny's performance in silence, his arms around me and my head on his chest. You'd never know it's been nearly twenty years since they did this; they're that good. The local crowd is also going nuts, which is an excellent sign that the music world will receive them well.

'You all are amazing!' Penny says into the mic as they wind down. 'Who's ready for the ball drop? It looks like we've got twelve seconds to go. Countdown with me! Ten, nine, eight...'

The crowd echoes around her, counting down the seconds until we travel in time to the next year of our lives.

'Three, two, one,' River says, kissing me at the stroke of midnight like he means it.

This is the best night of my life so far. Especially

considering just three months ago, I was begging a man to love me. Now one a hundred times better just volunteered the words and even looks happy that he said them.

'This is our year, baby.'

'It's our year,' I repeat, kissing him hard while the crowd screams in response to the ball dropping. But in true River style, he slows things down, sending butterflies through every part of me with his lips on mine and his fingers in my hair. He says he likes to remember every second of the important moments, so he does this often. 'You never know what might become a core memory,' he once said. I really hope this becomes one. He is the best kisser, and I wish I never needed to breathe, but as I pull away to take a breath, I can't help but smile.

'You are perfect,' I say, causing him to tighten his grip on me as he lifts me off the ground.

'Really?'

'Totally,' I say, laughing through him kissing me repeatedly. 'I love you so much.'

'You'd have to be an idiot not to,' he says, repeating my words from the night he asked me to be his girlfriend.

'But I'm not,' I say. 'You're my favorite man in all

the world, and I promise, you're the last man I'm ever saying that to.'

'I'd love to be the last boyfriend you ever have.'

'It's a deal,' I say, leaning into him while he kisses my forehead before we head to the stage to congratulate Penny Candy. Let the New Year begin.

ACKNOWLEDGMENTS

Five years ago, I'd never expected to fall in love with a publisher. Publishing is a hard industry and I've had hills to climb and ditches to fall into but my amazing team at Boldwood have made things fun and easy. We're three books in and I'm still so excited to be a Boldwood author! My books are better because of all of you. Thank you for taking the chance on me and my daydreams.

To the women who consistently talk me up and find ways to laugh at shit reviews, imposter syndrome, writer's block, and everything else that comes with this career. I could be lonely, only spending time with my imaginary friends, but y'all keep me sane. Thank you.

Last but not least, to all the #bookstagrammers who've recently fallen in love with the words I write. Anytime I log on to see a tag from one of you, my soul smiles. For real. I don't know if I could keep going without you. So, keep on reading, continue to fall in love, and shout about the books you love to others. I so appreciate you all. A reader lives a thousand lives and I'm so honored to have my books be a part of that.

A NOTE FROM THE AUTHOR

Thank you so much for reading *Stuck With You*. I hope you loved this group of friends and their wacky families as much as I loved creating their stories because there's one more chapter to this trio. Dax and Hollyn's wedding!!! Keep an eye on my socials for info, as it will be a novella told by all six leads POV.

As always, if you loved the book (or even if you didn't – honest reviews welcome) I'd like to ask you to please leave your review on Amazon (or GoodReads, Bookbub, Barnes & Noble, wherever you buy books). It doesn't have to be much, just a line or two. Thank you in advance. Reviews help authors so so much more than I can explain.

Want to say hello? I'd love that! I'm all over social

media (my phone and I are in an intimate relationship at this point...) and I would love to hear from you. Follow, friend, email or subscribe to my newsletter to keep in touch and never miss an update. Stop by my website https://aimeebwrites.com for info on how to keep in touch.

PLAYLIST

'Crazy Little Thing Called Love', Queen
'I Hate Her Boyfriend's Face', PmBata
'Dancing on My Own', The Regrettes
'Boy Problems', Carly Rae Jepsen
'Looking for Love', The Strike
'Heartbreaker', Tayo Sound
'It's Raining, It's Pouring', Anson Seabra
'Stunnin'' (feat. Harm Franklin), Curtis Waters
'Material Girl' (feat. Taylor Hanson of Hanson),
AWOLNATION & Hanson
'Who's In Your Head', Jonas Brothers
'Hello Again', The Cars
'Love On the Rocks', Neil Diamond
'You Spin Me Round (Like a Record)', Dead or Alive

'On Read', Austin Millz & Pell

'Sad in Hawaii', Claire Rosinkranz

'is your bedroom ceiling bored?', Sody & Cavetown

'Death of a Bachelor', Panic! At the Disco

'Twilight Zone', Golden Earring

'Bad Idea', Dove Cameron

'Vertigo', Alice Merton

'Dirty Thoughts', Chloe Adams

'Hell Yeah', corook

'Stay', The Kid LAROI & Justin Bieber

'Feeling For You', Milky Chance

'Beat It', Michael Jackson

'You Shouldn't Have Said That', ella jane

'In Your Eyes', Peter Gabriel

'You Give Love a Bad Name', Bon Jovi

'Rock DJ', Robbie Williams

'To Be a Lover', Billie Idol

'I Fall Hard', The Strike

'Love of Your Life', RAYE

'Enchanted', Taylor Swift

'Woman', Harry Styles

'F**k You', Lily Allen

'Kiss You', One Direction

'I Love You Baby', Emilee

MORE FROM AIMEE BROWN

We hope you enjoyed reading *Stuck With You*. If you did, please leave a review.

If you'd like to gift a copy, this book is also available as an ebook, paperback, hardback, digital audio download and audiobook CD.

Sign up to Aimee Brown's mailing list for news, competitions and updates on future books.

https://bit.ly/AimeeBrownNews

ABOUT THE AUTHOR

Aimee Brown is the bestselling romantic comedy author of several books including *The Lucky Dress*. She's an Oregon native, now living in a tiny town in cold Montana and sets her books in Portland. Previously published by Aria, her new series for Boldwood is full of love and laughter and real-life issues. *Love Notes* is Aimee's second book with Boldwood.

Visit Aimee Brown's website: https://aimeebwrites.com

Follow Aimee Brown on social media:

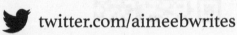

twitter.com/aimeebwrites

facebook.com/authoraimeebrown

instagram.com/authoraimeeb

bookbub.com/authors/aimee-brown

Boldwood

Boldwood Books is an award-winning fiction publishing company seeking out the best stories from around the world.

Find out more at www.boldwoodbooks.com

Join our reader community for brilliant books, competitions and offers!

Follow us
@BoldwoodBooks
@BookandTonic

Sign up to our weekly deals newsletter

https://bit.ly/BoldwoodBNewsletter